# The Cowboy's Claim

# The Cowboy's Claim

## A Coyote Cowboys of Montana Romance

Sinclair Jayne

The Cowboy's Claim

Tule Publishing First Printing, June 2024

The Tule Publishing, Inc.



First Publication by Tule Publishing 2024

Cover design by Lee Hyat Designs



ISBN: 978-1-962707-10-7

# Dedication

I want to thank author and friend Rusty Keller, who listened to me grapple with the pieces of this series and each story at a writer's retreat on the Oregon coast days before the Pandemic shut down the world. I felt read to pitch it to Tule, but the team initially passed and chose my second idea, the Misguided Masala Matchmaker, instead. But I couldn't let my five heroes go so the brilliant Jane Porter, brimming with so much creativity, commercial spark and tough love I sometimes think I'm bruised (I am not), sat down with me a year and a half later and helped me lasso these Special Forces cowboys into the romance heroes of my dreams. And always, my editor, Kelly Hunter, who jumped in mid-series with an enthusiasm and story genius that inspires me always to dig deeper to find the sparkle. Thanks, y'all.

# Dear Reader

*The Cowboy's Claim* is book five in my series, the Coyote Cowboys of Montana. I have loved writing this series so much. It's already hard to say goodbye to this former Special Forces Group of loyal friends and strong, fiercely determined men. I hope you have fallen in love with my heroes as much as I have. Happily, it's not a total shut door as the new, temporary Coyote Cowboy team leader, Wolf Conte, vows to honor his friend Jace McBride by fulfilling his promise to return to Last Stand, Texas. It's the last place on earth this prodigal son and brother wants to go, yet go he does in *Christmas with the Texas Cowboy*, releasing October 16, 2024.

# Chapter One

THE SIROCCO TORE at the corners of the airplane hangar screaming vengeance. The howls matched the way Otis Calhoun Lael-Miller V's soul shrieked as he watched his best friend's bloody helmet make the rounds through the large, capable hands of his Coyote Cowboy brothers. Like most of his team, his head was bowed as if in silent prayer, although he knew none. It was far too late anyway.

Using peripheral vision, he watched the helmet's progress as each of his teammates drew a slip of paper out of the helmet. Jace's amends. Or vows. Plans that he'd never get the chance to complete.

Calhoun's throat squeezed, and his chest felt crushed. His eyes burned.

Sand.

Yeah.

Not tears. Millers didn't cry. They tamed land. Ran cattle. Built towns and then cities. Racked up architecture awards. Had Emmy-award-winning shows based on their lives. The Lael side of his family crafted award-winning wines in several different states and two countries. They launched fashion houses and brands that were global and every celebrity It Girl's wet dream.

If either side of his ambitious, famous, and extravagantly wealthy family was asked—and he doubted they had thought about him in years—he would be the underachiever.

By design. He'd walked away at eighteen, dumping Otis and Lael and the Roman numeral and any stake in the empire.

His family wouldn't consider that not dying in the desert or jungle or mountain pass in a country few Americans could find on a map counted as an achievement. Ditto for saving the lives of people who weren't and never would be shareholders.

Calhoun had built his own ladder of success until it had crashed down on him because he'd gone with instinct, not training. When his team had received faulty intel or had been compromised, and the mission had spun south, he'd run to protect his military dog instead of his team leader.

Seeing Duke take two hits, he'd slithered into his lizard brain, sprayed the field with returning fire and launched himself into Duke's position, slapped two pressure field bandages on him, picked him up and called for an emergency extraction before he realized Jace and Huck had been hit. Pinned down because he'd given their enemy a clear shot at their position with his Spider-Man leap, Calhoun—whispering reassurances to Duke—had dug in and kept returning fire while Huck worked on Jace, and Rohan crept to higher ground to pick off the two nests of snipers so Huck could retreat with Jace.

They'd had to shoot their way out to the extraction point. Duke had made it. Jace hadn't. And Huck never said a word about it to command.

Another team had completed their mission, a first for the Coyote Cowboys unit.

And Calhoun would have to exit his prestigious service career with that stain on his soul, if not his record.

He'd planned to muster out along with Jace McBride, one of the best friends a man could have. But Jace was gone, and Duke's career was over—though he'd survived the two surgeries that might save his life.

It was touch and go, and despite the gravity of this morning's situation, Calhoun kept looking at his phone for updates from the vet's team.

He dragged in a ragged breath and out of the corner of his eye saw Wolf Conte, the new temporary team leader, focus on him. Damn. He angled his shoulders back, spine rigid. He was a sequoia standing vigil for centuries, unbowed by fire, earthquakes, storms or anything else God or fate wanted to toss at him.

Wolf didn't speak. He rarely did. Only when necessary. Calhoun waited, pretending to be at ease.

Wolf inclined his head, pivoted and walked outside the hangar while the other Coyote Cowboys finished their beers and waited for the plane carrying Jace to finish preparations for takeoff.

Calhoun followed.

DR. JORY QUINN stripped off her scrubs, peeled off her cotton body suit, balled it up into a small, webbed bag that she tucked into her gym bag to hand-wash when she got home and then slid her feet into her Oka-B silver flip-flops with the frivolous flowers—one of her few financial splurges in life—and stepped under a cool shower.

She closed her eyes and pictured herself at the Four Seasons Resort Hualalai at night in the open-air shower by the pool. She imagined she could hear the rhythmic roar of the ocean and the soft calls of the birds settling in for the evening. The soft, cool pulse of the water flowing over her head and down her goose-bumped skin washed away the smells, pain and demands of work that puddled at her feet and swirled down the drain. She sighed and visualized the last warm kiss of the sun as it tucked behind the horizon of pinks, oranges and purples.

She held tree pose for thirty seconds with her left foot and then thirty seconds with her right. Jory then stretched her arms over her head, palms together and back arched, counting down from thirty. Then she did warrior II pose on both sides for thirty seconds each before bending forward and placing her palms flat on her feet. She kept her eyes closed, feeling her body in the space of the hospital locker room shower. She still held the image of the velvet sky, tiki torches glowing, the long lap pool, crisp water gleaming and beckoning her to swim the length, surrounded by swaying palms to the end, and contemplate the mercurial Pacific.

Jory quickly used her L'Occitane lemon verbena body wash, shampoo and conditioner, rinsed and turned off the water. She was shivering by the time she scrunched excess water from her curly bob and quickly blotted water from her skin with a towel before smoothing lemon verbena body oil over her taut olive skin.

"*Mahalo*," she murmured as she reluctantly opened her eyes.

Jory Quinn had never been to Hawaii. And as for the Four Seasons Resort in Hualalai where basic rooms started at thirteen hundred a night on the website, that wouldn't be in her budget for years—probably never.

*No.*

She was sick of Montana winters. They were marrow-sucking cold, and the snow wasn't done with the fools who lived here well into April, sometimes beyond. She'd looked at the temperature and knew, just knew, she'd be scraping ice off the windshield of her ancient but reliable Subaru.

"Like always," she muttered resentfully, thinking of the one inch she'd had to scrape off yesterday morning after the end of her shift, but she loved working nights because she hated being home alone at night.

It was April and her need for sun and warmth was primal, and working nights allowed her mornings, and a stolen late-afternoon hour or two to absorb what little sun the universe would gift her. Walking into the day—work complete—had become her routine since finishing residency, and the mostly rural hospitals in Montana needing locums hospitalists always jumped to sign her up because she took night and weekend shifts without complaint.

Because she was meeting briefly with the chief of the medical staff this morning, she added a soft pink lip gloss and swipe of mascara. She didn't need foundation or blush or contouring for her clear, olive skin, thick dark brows, large dark eyes and ethnically ambiguous high cheekbones and strong nose.

"Where are you from? What are you?" had been nosily asked as long as she could remember.

"I'm me," usually shut them up.

In a professional setting and at college and medical school she'd learned to soften the shut-down a little with a smile and shrug and say her family had deep roots in Montana's Paradise Valley.

Not that Paradise Valley and the small town of Marietta were eager to claim any Quinns, nor did Jory particularly like Montana. And as soon as her commitment to the state was complete, she was driving southwest and never looking back. Yes, she'd still have her medical school loans, but working in rural hospitals for a four-year commitment had halved her loans, and frugal living had allowed her to pay down her debt ruthlessly while still helping her mom and her oma finally sell off the last little bit of the Quinn land and start over outside Lodi, California.

No more Quinns in Montana. No more dark family secrets. No more poor Jory Quinn whose daddy was in and out of jail before finally taking his son and leaving his mom, wife and daughter behind for good.

No one had been surprised. The sheriff hadn't even sent a deputy to take a statement because her father and brother didn't matter. Her family had been considered lowlifes. Losers. Although only highly civically engaged Carol Bingley had been willing to say the quiet part out loud: 'Good riddance.'

The Quinns, landowners for well over a century, had never fit in with the good churchgoing people of Marietta. And Jory, despite her stellar grades and long hours working at Monroe's Grocery Store, had still been side-eyed with suspicion like she was a shiny apple hiding a rotten core.

Jory stuck her tongue out in the mirror at her past and turned away to catch up with Akil Chopra, the head of medical staff at the hospital in Helena. Tonight was her last shift as a locums hospitalist, and she was planning to take a week or two break to visit her mom and grandma and see how they were settling in before the next contract with her locums company.

She'd used up most of her savings for the hefty down payment for the few acres and small ranch house for her family. The low-rate doctor loan made it feasible that she could still pay the small mortgage for her mom, along with her medical school loans. And in another month, escrow would close on the final parcel of Quinn land, along with the tired-looking farmhouse, and for the first time in their lives, her mom and oma would have financial security when that money was banked.

She zipped her gym bag shut after rolling her damp towel in a waterproof bag and went to find Dr. Chopra to say thank you and goodbye and probably get a job offer she wouldn't take. And then she'd head home to her suite at the Comfort Inn and call her mom and then the locums agency to book her next Montana placement. At least the late spring and summer wouldn't involve any snow, but with Montana, she crossed her fingers. You never knew.

CALHOUN KICKED AT the slick snow on the sidewalk outside Grey's Saloon where he was supposed to meet his Coyote Cowboy brothers for a welcome-home beer. Not that Marietta, Montana, was home. Nor did it appeal, particularly. It looked unbearably cute—western-movie-set vibe. He didn't do cute. And he was sick of snow. In April. No, this town was no longer his final destination without Jace, and he was shocked that his brothers were still here. And ashamed to face them. He should have helped with Jace, even though Huck had grimly shrugged off his apology months ago with a growled "no one could save him."

But maybe if the two of them… He broke off from his dark, unprofitable thoughts. Time to focus on his last mission. He was here hopefully for a day or two tops to discover if Jace had or hadn't seen a murder or accidental death when he'd been a kid. At least that was Calhoun's takeaway from Jace's cryptic scrawl on the to-do task he'd drawn from Jace's helmet. He wondered what his brothers' marching orders had been and if they'd succeeded yet.

He felt keyed up. Ryder had collected a now healthy Duke, who, at the advice of the Last Stand–based former soldier, Chance Rafferty, who rehabbed and retrained military working dogs on his family's ranch, had been renamed Kai. Calhoun couldn't wait to be reunited with his buddy. Tonight, he'd do some research after the reunion, and then tomorrow he and Kai would take a drive and hike along some access roads over Rohan's family ranch and play Sherlock Holmes. But maybe—he regarded the double saloon-style doors with wry amusement—he should consider himself Walt Longmire. No, those books were based in Wyoming, another snow-littered landscape he hoped to avoid.

But he couldn't return to California like his ultimate betrayal of his family had never happened. Burning those bridges had been a conflagration likely visible from space.

Where did he want to settle? After Jace had died, Calhoun hadn't thought about the void of his future beyond adopting Kai and giving him the best life he could. He'd never intended to leave the army until his friend and team leader Jace had asked him to.

He ran a hand through his sandy-colored hair that he intended to grow long now that he was stateside and checked that his dark Wranglers and dark blue T hadn't rumpled from the long drive from the base in Washington. He laughed at himself. Kai wouldn't care how he looked.

*But will he remember me?*

Calhoun hadn't seen Kai since July when he'd been sent for life-saving surgery. His recovery had been several months, and then Calhoun had paid a hefty donation to the nonprofit in Last Stand for Kai to stay and recover from any emotional wounds and retrain to enter civilian life. Calhoun had also asked for Kai to have the opportunity to train for search and rescue because even though his future was uncertain, he knew he and Kai would need a purpose.

No office for him.

No big city.

Again he looked at the double doors of Grey's Saloon. All he had to do was open them.

But all the Coyote Cowboys would be in there waiting. Did they know what he'd done? Had Huck finally told them?

Would he face welcome or judgment?

Judgment had loomed and shouted his entire life because he hadn't lived up to the Lael or Miller names in any way. After fifteen years away from his home, a prestigious military academy, years serving his country, he shouldn't care what anyone thought.

*Except my brothers.*

But Kai was inside. And this was the first step into his future.

Calhoun grabbed both doors and swung them wide.

MARIETTA. MONTANA. SNOW.

Jory glared at her reflection in the elegant bathroom mirror with the vintage sconces on either side of the vanity. Dark eyes, olive skin, poofy lips that had been an object of rabid teasing when she'd been a kid and now looked like she'd had one too many squirts of filler. Dark, arched brows that were also natural and a thick, curly bob. Her hair and her brain were the two things she liked best about herself.

But she knew being self-critical was a spiral into a deep hole she'd spent much of her life crawling out of. She'd hated her family's reputation growing up. She'd hated being poor. She'd hated how everyone had felt free to comment on her 'exotic' looks and lack of height like she was a piece of furniture they'd decided not to buy.

She smiled at herself in the mirror. "Be kind."

It was something that she'd often said to herself—self-care even before self-care had become a bragged-about movement.

She was lucky. She was smart. Hardworking. Healthy. Her body was strong, petite at five two and one-hundred and five pounds. And so what if she looked like a 'doll' with her small size and wide-spaced dark eyes. She was achieving her goals—except she was back in Marietta—temporarily.

Jory turned off the lights and sat in the dark on the edge of the bed in the beautiful hotel room at the Graff Hotel, still stunned that she'd been assigned to the hospital in Marietta. Her mother and aunt had said a visit now wasn't convenient and that they didn't need help settling in. With nowhere else in mind to go, and not wanting to spend the money for a real vacation, Jory had contacted her locums company and been stunned to silence when they'd assigned her to Marietta. Her inability to speak had unleashed a torrent of pleas as the hospital was desperate, and then a rather large bonus was tacked on for taking the two-month position and starting immediately.

Jory never had turned down work or money so here she was.

Back where it all started only in much swankier digs. But she didn't want to spend her bonus on the Graff. She'd have to find something cheaper and very temporary.

Tired of her thoughts and her own company, Jory stood up.

This was it. A chance to take charge of her life in a different way. She had the education. The career. She was close to the financial security. Now she had to pursue…happiness?

That sounded like something stuffed in a fortune cookie or on a fridge magnet.

"Be the change you want to be," Jory mocked the turn of her thoughts. Still. She didn't intend to hide in her room for two months, only coming out at night to work. She wasn't a vampire.

"New rules to a new attitude." She bounced up off the bed. She'd go for a walk. No. She'd go for a drink at Grey's Saloon. Her daddy had often disappeared in there for hours, drinking and swapping stories with friends. She'd always been curious, but since she'd left town at barely seventeen for college, she'd never been inside.

She'd give herself a makeover, the same as the town seemed to have had since she'd left for college. Take the Graff. When she'd been a kid, it had been a derelict building, empty, falling apart and inspiring stories about ghosts. Now it had been restored by another long-time local family, the Sheenans who'd managed to hang on to their land, family and money.

According to the glossy brochure in her room, Marietta was now a travel destination boasting of restaurants, a chocolate shop, a brewery with music, dude ranches, adventure companies, seasonal outdoor activities and more. Tourists visited the town year-round now, not just for a brief photo stop on the way to Yellowstone.

Maybe if she thought of herself as a tourist—not Jory Quinn the forgotten daughter, the one who never fit in, the problem—she could have her own personal renaissance.

She kicked her feet into her plum leather ankle boots—the one western-style thing in her entire wardrobe. And slid her arms into a pink cardigan, leaving it unbuttoned over her white tank top.

She paused. Should she wear a bra? Not that she needed it, and she didn't imagine the cowboys who'd steered well clear of her in high school would swivel around on their barstools now for more than a cursory look.

Still, her first college roommate had insisted that ninety percent of success was attitude. Jory thought it was more determination, goal setting and hard work, but Lisa had had confidence and charisma that wafted around her like a cloud of perfume, and while it hadn't rubbed off on Jory, she had observed Lisa's bouts with destiny.

Marietta had changed, and she could too. Tonight she'd channel a little of long-ago Lisa's swagger and bubbly personality and walk into Grey's and order a drink. She was no longer the socially awkward woman who'd finally had sex in medical school when she'd been twenty-three, not because she wanted to, but because she'd been embarrassed by her virginity.

The sex had been a disappointment, and an experiment she hadn't put much effort into since, but that could change.

Tonight.

"Yeah, you go, Cowgirl," she mocked herself and scrunched some product on her curls to tame the frizz.

She looked at the results of her primping.

She was a long way from the sad, hungry, anxious but determined teen she'd last been in Marietta. That had taken will, not luck. And she had will in abundance.

"I will have fun tonight," she told her reflection.

Jory squared her shoulders and firmed her glossy lips. She was walking into Grey's Saloon and drinking a cocktail and dancing if they had dancing. She vowed she'd strike up at least one conversation and not with the bartender. She'd be fun, flirty, and maybe even seduce a cowboy, which had been a secret fantasy in high school and college.

Why not? She was an adult. Successful. A doctor. She'd never see the cowboy again. Besides it was a waste to enjoy the Graff's thread count alone and unconscious.

Was it safe?

Probably. This was Marietta. Besides, she knew how to wield a syringe. She made a gunslinger move in the antique mirror near the cherry mission-style wardrobe and swiped her hotel key and purse off the quilt folded at the foot of her bed and then she hurried out of the room before she could change her mind.

The door clicked shut behind her.

# Chapter Two

"WHERE'S DUKE?" CALHOUN stared at Cross, Rohan and Huck, who'd all stood up from their table and quickly crossed the room to greet him.

"Kai?" Rohan broke the rhythm of the handshake to push back so he could look him in the face.

Calhoun knew he'd been unbearably rude—not greeting them, just asking about Kai, but seeing Duke go down, get back up and take out his target, even as blood soaked his fur…

"He's fine." Rohan gripped his shoulder. "He's good. Better than good. Adjusting. Healthy."

"Why isn't he here?" Calhoun hadn't wanted to meet the Coyotes at a bar. He'd wanted to go to Rohan's family's ranch where Ryder worked and pick up Kai.

"Kai's with Ryder."

"Yeah, I know," Calhoun snapped then sucked in a breath.

He'd asked Ry to pick up Kai from the rehab facility if he was ready before Calhoun had mustered out, and the mission with Wolf had dragged on longer and become far more complicated than either of them had imagined.

The three men—his brothers; they'd been called the Coyote Cowboys—just stared at him. They probably looked ridiculous, facing off in a cowboy bar like Wild West gunslingers.

"Ryder's had Kai a little under a month," Rohan said like he was trying to defuse a situation, which he most definitely wasn't going to have to do.

And that burned.

"Yeah." Calhoun's tension rose. He'd counted on seeing Kai, checking him out, reintroducing himself, starting their new life together.

"Ryder's in full swing of rodeo season," Rohan offered, his green gaze piercing. "Kai travels with him on the road."

"What?" Calhoun demanded.

He'd imagined Kai running free on the ranch, tagging after Ryder while he worked there—herding cattle, checking fences, laying pipes for irrigation. Calhoun knew how to do it all—his family made sure of that even as they had hundreds of employees working long hours to make the Lael-Miller ranch and vineyards operate smoothly and at a staggering profit.

"Thought *you* were going to give the rodeo cowboy gig a spin." Calhoun looked at Huck.

"I did. For a summer," Huck said. "Only wanted a taste—something to do with Jim, the man who fostered me in my teens. I had to wait until September to honor my commitment to Jace so Jim and I hit the road and I competed last summer."

That was something else they had to talk about. Jace. His gut felt like a stone, and his chest felt compressed like he'd just taken a round that his vest had barely stopped.

"Did you honor Jace? Did you finish the task for him?" Calhoun asked, feeling edgy.

What were they all doing now other than staring at him like an alien specimen dropped on the saloon's wide-planked floor? It felt weird standing in a cluster in the middle of a bar. He felt utterly exposed. Couldn't relax.

His nerves screamed with tension.

"Hell yeah." Huck held up his left hand and Calhoun stared at him.

"What the…" He broke off seeing a band of gold around Huck's deeply tanned finger.

"Got a baby too. Little girl. Born late March—Jacie."

He heard the words but couldn't process them. A kid. A wife and a kid? Huck had nearly died trying to save Jace last July. Ten months later he had a wife and a baby and had honored their brother by naming his kid after him?

Huck could have said he'd been elected to the US Senate, and Calhoun would have believed it more.

"You?" He choked out the word, rudely.

"I ain't that ugly." Huck rocked back on his heels, his eyes glinting with amusement and challenge.

"Me too." Rohan held up his left hand, and Calhoun was dazzled by the sheen of gold around Rohan's third finger.

"Wanted to wait for you, but after your second delay, we went ahead with the wedding over spring break so Ginny and I could take a trip together. Adopting her son. Lucas. I'm a dad."

Calhoun couldn't even form the words. Helpless he looked at Cross. The one man he could count on to be as immovable and removed from drama as a mountain range, but he too had his hand up, only his band was more of a gunmetal gray that matched his narrowed gaze.

"Married in September," he said, "'bout five weeks from the night I first laid eyes on her."

Calhoun's vision tunneled, and his ears rang, and everything seemed muffled like after a blast.

But Cross wasn't done talking. "Got a teenage daughter too, and it's all due to Jace so you'd better sit your ass down, Cowboy. Time for a beer and to catch up and wait for destiny to saunter through the door and take a chunk outta your ass."

IT FELT WEIRD crossing over the railroad tracks to head into town. At first Jory held her breath, expecting to be recognized, but maybe she was being too paranoid. She'd been gone fifteen years. She'd grown up, cut her long, curly hair, paid for her own braces in college. She was an adult. Successful. Who cared what people thought? She'd put herself through college, medical school and the grueling years of residency, paid her bills and had even helped her mom and oma start a new chapter in their lives.

She turned on to Main Street and stopped, mouth dropping open in wonder. The town looked so charming in the evening. Couples strolling, shops lit up, though closed on a Sunday night. Crawford Park still had fairy lights in the trees, and the flag flew proudly over the stately courthouse.

For a moment, her nerve failed her. Maybe this would be enough. She didn't ever walk into restaurants alone—not the type that you sat down at a table and ordered off a menu from a server. Coffee shops yes. To pick up takeout, definitely.

And now she was going to walk into Grey's Saloon, the oldest building in town that used to be a bar and brothel? Alone?

In Marietta, Montana?

"Yes." Again she squared her shoulders and balled her fists.

Lisa had always waxed confidently about 'manifesting.' Jory thought it was easy for Lisa to manifest as she'd been born wealthy, adored, blonde, tall and beautiful. Still Lisa had been kind to the dazzled, so far out of her comfort zone Jory.

"Picture what you want," Lisa had told her one evening as she'd demonstrated how to apply lip liner or eyeliner, or contour her sparkling eye shadow under her perfect winged brows. "But always figure out the steps you need to get there. Picture, plan, execute."

So there in the middle of the sidewalk Jory Quinn pictured herself striding through the double doors of Grey's, sauntering up to the bar and ordering a drink and then she'd catch the eye of a man and say something.

*Like what?*

No ideas formed so Jory decided this night too would be the debut of her spontaneous side. Besides, she could always sip her whiskey, smile enigmatically—another Lisaism—and raise one eyebrow inviting the hot cowboy—in her manifesting fantasy—to say something first.

Hopefully nothing too cheesy as that would spoil the fantasy.

"Showtime." She marched down the rest of the block, eyes on the double doors so she saw the man come out. Dang he was tall. Broad shoulders. Brown Stetson angled on his head just so. T-shirt so in love with his body it clung. No belt buckle. Two full sleeves of tattoos.

Her stomach bottomed out.

Ink had not been part of her fantasy, but it should have been. She was finding it a little difficult to suck in a breath. So much for all the times she'd hit the hotel gyms.

He was gorgeous. Hotter than the sun. But he was also totally blocking her path, and her confidence was bleeding out like air on a busted tire.

"Excuse me?"

Ugh, her voice sounded like she was a little girl. Too tentative.

"Um…" Did you call unknown cowboys sir? Dude? Mister? Jerk?

"I'd like to…can you move just a little? You're a man, not a mountain." She shifted one foot to the other, but then her training kicked in.

He was utterly still. The expression in his eyes blank. And his skin had a pale grayish tinge, sweating a little, and the evening was not warm.

"Sir, are you okay?" Jory placed one hand gently on his forearm, and nearly gasped at the strength and tension running through it.

*Like a coiled snake.*

"Excuse me, sir." Jory used her doctor voice, the deep one that someone in residency had told her was so soothing that it reminded them of a pond in the mountains surrounded by fir and hemlock. "Do you know where you are?" she asked. "Do you know what day it is?"

She released his arm, only keeping the tips of her thumb glancing on his wrist while her index finger took his pulse. Damn. Fifty. He could be suffering from bradycardia. Low $O_2$ saturation or low blood pressure could make him lightheaded.

*Or he could be an elite athlete.*

He sure looked like one. She placed a hand on his back to measure his breath, but he spun around and grabbed her wrist. His eyes blazed brown gold, but the pupils weren't dilated or contracted. Good news. A million things she should have said burbled up in her mind, but they danced just out of reach of her tongue. Instead, her brain went lizard.

"You are gorgeous," she breathed.

He looked like he'd been carved out of Copper Mountain. His forehead was wide and flat, and he had a widow's peak, and his sandy hair fell a bit disheveled around his eyes, but it was shaved short on the sides.

His cheekbones were high, sharp slicing hollows below. His nose was long, too bony to give him a polished look, but definitely ethnic, distinctive, lending him an old European royal air. And his mouth. Wow. His mouth was so sensual and sexy and stern, and she wondered what he'd look like smiling or what his lips would feel like on her skin.

*Like that would ever happen.*

His shoulders were broad and developed. She could see the twist of each muscle that her brain started to name like she was studying for a muscular system final in undergrad again. His khaki cotton, green T could barely contain that much muscle. His waist tapered, and his legs were long and muscular, and she bet he was rocking a six—maybe an eight-pack under his shirt, and she'd sure like to look to see if he had an Adonis belt.

She'd seen thousands of bodies in her practice, but nothing close to his, dang it.

His fingers easily wrapped around her wrist. She looked into his blazing eyes. She should feel trapped. Nervous maybe. Instead she felt thrilled. She stared at the tendons and veining in his hands, the length of his fingers, the tight trim of his nails, and all she could think of was 'yes, please.'

"You should be in an anatomy class," she said stupidly. "But that would be bad because you'd be dead, and that would devastate women everywhere."

She clapped her free hand over her mouth.

"Shutting up now."

"Why? It's just getting good."

Good? Jory felt like she'd blasted by that boring adjective the second she'd spotted him.

Was he flirting with her? She moistened her lower lip. He dried all the spit in her mouth and shorted her neurons so all she could do was stare at him.

"If there's a woman alive who could think of a snappy retort while looking at you, I definitely don't want to meet her. No. Wait. Maybe I do. I need tips. Desperately."

*Still should be shutting up.*

This was why she didn't go to bars.

He blinked. She could see the moment he came back into himself. The awareness felt like a blast of heat, and then humor lit those beautiful dark-honey-colored eyes, and his sensuous but hard lips twitched into a hint of a smile.

He still shackled her wrist.

"Ummmm, sir..." She looked down at his hand still

wrapped around her arm.

"Sir?" Now he definitely smiled. "That takes me back when I've barely left."

She stared into his warm gaze. Genetics definitely favored the few. He was damn near perfect.

"You are the total golden ratio," she breathed, her mind calculating his features, his shoulders, his arms, torso, legs. Her gaze felt hungry, greedy, and she'd never see him again, and she wanted to remember everything.

"I was thinking maybe I'd feel a man's touch tonight," she said, her mouth jumping in even as her brain sputtered. "But not exactly like this."

He released her, and she felt bereft. The quiet breathed between them.

"How did you imagine being touched?" He formed each word carefully, his gold gaze lasered into her eyes, and she felt like his eyes were a spotlight reading every lost, rejected, loner moment of her life when she wanted him to see the intelligent, determined, successful, confident woman she'd become. She straightened, chin up and out, shoulders back under his scrutiny.

"To be determined," she said.

"Fair enough."

He felt like a soldier on review, and while he wasn't relaxed, he felt easy, like he'd made a decision. What had thrown this beautiful man off his stride earlier? The thought of him vulnerable filled her with cognitive dissonance.

He hesitated a moment and then his mouth twitched into a crooked smile. He raised his eyebrows.

"You going in or out?"

"I thought I'd go in, but if you're leaving, what's the point?"

This time his smile hit his eyes. "The night suddenly has possibilities."

"Are you leaving?" She pressed her advantage.

"I don't really have any place I want to go," he said softly, and there was something in his voice that caught at Jory. His comment sounded more than literal. More than situational, and she could relate to that.

"I'm only in town for a short time," she said, wanting to be upfront, and she couldn't be any less cool than she already had been. "I don't want to be in Marietta, but I am, and rather than hiding in my room, I thought I'd slay a few demons from my past. Have a drink. Play darts. Pool. Dance. See what happens."

She issued it like a challenge.

"I have a few demons who need their asses kicked," he mused, his eyes lighter than they'd been before—no shadows. "And I too am passing through Marietta. I'm doing a favor for a friend."

"I've always wanted to try a whiskey," Jory said. "I could buy the first round, and we could toast demon slaying."

She forced her words to be a statement, not a question. Why wait a moment longer to take charge of her life? She needed to seize her confidence cape, fling it around her shoulders and let it ripple out behind her.

"I'll drink to that."

# Chapter Three

HER HAND FELT small in his. Delicate. Elegant. Everything he was not. And what the hell was he doing here with her? Yeah, a one-night stand would blow the lid off some of the tension clawing through him, but was it fair to her?

Slaying demons was not the same thing as slaking lust. But her bold gaze—black as an oil slick—was determined and gleamed with the promise of fun. Still, Calhoun held back. She didn't even whisper hookup vibe.

And he wasn't himself.

He wasn't even sure who he was anymore. He'd been counting on Kai and duty and his brothers to ground him.

He didn't want to hurt her with what might feel like a broken promise tomorrow.

He'd been born into that life, had bathed, breathed, and eaten bait and switch his entire childhood. He'd deliberately left that life and his family behind to live a life of honor.

He was thirty-three now. Had he succeeded?

"My friends call me Big O," he said as they walked back through the double swinging doors of Grey's Saloon that made it feel like they'd both been sucked back in time, and yet Rohan had assured him that a high-priced decorator hadn't created the look. Time had. The building was the oldest one in town and the longest-run establishment.

She laughed. "I can just imagine how you got that nickname. Big O. Then I guess for tonight I'm Little J."

Her laugh was addictive. It was big. Loud. Unexpected for such a small woman, not at all flirty, but her laugh spoke more of being surprised and amused than trying to entice.

He nearly explained why he hated his given name Otis. He was the fifth, and none of them had lived lives of honor in his opinion. They'd only wanted money and power. They'd wanted to be envied and feared and courted, yet never liked, not even by their wives or children. Growing up had been more like being held hostage instead of belonging to a family.

But why did this woman so easily encourage him to snap open the lid on his past? Suspicion stirred.

"Let's do this. Shoot a whiskey." She angled for the bar, shoulders back like there was a test waiting. "Wow," she faltered, and he felt the small press of her body briefly against his. "How can there be so many?"

She turned to him, her eyes wide with wonder and full of stars, like it was his fault. "What do you want?" she asked. "I should have known a cowboy bar would have a Selection with a capital S. I'm open to suggestions. Should we splurge—isn't there a brand called Top Shelf?" She looked up at him so trustingly that his heart skipped a beat.

Damn, but she was sweet. How could she be so innocent and sexy at the same time?

"Darling," he drawled. Yeah, he could get into the cowboy spirit again. Cross, Huck and Rohan made it look effortless, and they all had jobs at ranches already and had assumed he was looking to do the same.

What did he want?

No idea. Cross had been out since last August. Huck a bit before that. And they were both married. Fathers. Family men. Ranch hands.

Their happiness shouldn't feel like a body blow or a slapped-shut door.

He smiled to shake off his creeping dark doubts and laid his finger under her sharp chin that had the sexiest dent. Startled, her eyes skewed to him, and he tilted her chin up.

"The best whiskey is literally kept on the top shelf."

She turned back around, scanned the top shelf behind the bar and laughed. "Outted for being a Grey's Saloon virgin." She pressed up against the bar and held up a small hand like she was hailing a cab.

"What's it gonna be?" asked the handsome bartender, who Rohan had earlier greeted as Reese.

Jory looked at him, then the top shelf and then back at the bartender.

"I'm a neophyte. I want a whiskey," she said. "A really good one."

Reese's attention shifted to him, his expression professionally polite, but silently asking him price range. Calhoun had already scanned the labels. Nothing his father had taught him how to drink and savor over a business deal would be small-town Montana, but he'd left California a long time ago.

"Two fingers of Blanton's Gold for both of us," he ordered. He handed over his credit card. "Open tab."

"I was buying first round," she objected, and he nearly said she could buy him breakfast. "I can pay for my drink, Big O," she objected, and his mind shot to having her up against a wall, legs around his waist, with how dirty she made his teasing nickname sound.

"I know, J." Again he touched the dent in her chin because he wanted to. "But not tonight and not with me."

The bartender poured the drinks and slid them toward them.

"I should pay," she said, expression serious. "I don't want you to expect..."

He handed her the whiskey and brushed his lips over her full mouth because it had been tempting him since she'd first gaped at him, and it was public enough and light enough that she'd feel safe.

"Don't worry about me, J. I am the king of no expectations." He remembered to smile to soften the bitterness the words evoked. He clinked his glass with hers.

The bartender snorted softly and left to serve someone else.

“Do we shoot it?” she asked looking at the amber liquid doubtfully.

“Your choice. You can shoot or sip and savor.”

“Really? Huh. Do you know about wine too?”

What he didn’t know about wine despite his best intentions would fit in this tumbler.

“Yeah. Cheers.”

She sipped. He smiled at how her eyes widened, and the tip of her tongue moistened her upper lip as if chasing a drop.

“It’s good, but it burns.” She smiled up at him, and the memories of his father’s anger and bitterness, settled. He’d tightly leashed thoughts about his past and his family when he’d been serving, but his grip seemed to have loosened over the past couple of days after musting out.

“Kinda like life,” he threw out, taking another sip.

“It should be. I want it to be. No more hiding.” She held up her glass, holding his gaze. “Cheers.” She took another sip. “You don’t have to keep an open tab. I won’t drink another. I like to be in control.”

He could take that a lot of ways, and he liked each one.

“Oh. But you might. Or we might want food.”

“Let’s keep our options open,” he suggested.

“I like that, Big O.” She tested his name. “It sounds so sexual, but I suppose that’s the point.” She laughed again. “I’m glad I braved it, put on clothes and left my hotel room.”

There were dozens of one-liners that streamed through his head, but he was probably pretty feral by now, and Little J seemed naïve. Innocent. Everything he hadn't been for as long as he could remember.

"Me too. You had a list for tonight. I believe whiskey was first and darts was somewhere on it." He looked across the bar to a large alcove that held two pool tables and beyond that several dart boards safely spaced apart.

Her smile lit her eyes, and he found himself also glad that he hadn't left with his buddies when each of them had offered him a place to bunk for the night.

"WE WON! WE won!" Jory pumped her arms high in the air and did a little dance. She'd never played darts before, and it was fun. She'd been surprisingly good at it too—usually books, tests, grades and medical diagnoses had provided her only victories in life.

"You have deadly aim." Big O gave her a look that curled her toes.

He held his palms out, elbows a little higher than ninety degrees, almost like he was surrendering to cops. What? Oh. High five.

She double high-fived him, and he held his hands down low and then twisted in a half circle one way and then another, and she chased his palms, loving the slap and the feel of his calloused skin against hers.

"Thanks, man. Gracias." Big O high-fived and shook hands with the two ranch workers they'd played against.

His Spanish had been flawless as he'd spoken to their two opponents, and he'd asked a lot of questions about the town, the ranches, and the work that proved Jory's suspicion that he wasn't local. She hadn't let on that she too was fluent, and she wasn't sure why.

Was she really brave enough to toss caution and inhibitions to the wind and bring him back to her room? Could she have a one-night stand with a gorgeous, sexy stranger? Did he want to?

She watched him talk to the two men. With his wide shoulders; deep voice; powerful torso that narrowed at his waist and hips; his long, muscular tatted arms with such a visual flex of muscle and tendon, ending in large hands, Jory had a feeling she'd regret it for a very long time if she didn't try. Even clad in denim, his legs hinted at strength.

And he was friendly, fun. She'd felt for the first time in her life she'd been on a team.

Big O was unlike any man she'd ever met.

"Pool?" His thick brows, dramatically darker than his sun-tousled hair, rose in inquiry. "I believe that was on the list."

"I've never actually played," Jory said, but she wasn't going to let that stop her. "But I was really good at geometry."

Her answer threw him for a moment, and then his spectacular eyes lightened in amusement. "Let's see how theory and practice collide."

Pool was fun. Jory loved the way Big O racked up the balls. The way his hands deftly touched the balls was sexy, and when he showed her how to hold the pool cue, she almost grabbed his shirt and propositioned him to go back to her room right then. The effect he had on her was visceral.

Exciting.

But she was happy they'd stayed, because pool was amazing foreplay. Once, Big O helped her to line up a shot, his body so tantalizingly close, that she could feel his heat and smell a hint of something citrusy and green and earthy that made her hungry. She could listen to his voice, deep and warm, forever, even if he was reading instructions to construct IKEA furniture.

She had a feeling he was going easy on her and that sparked her competitive personality. She walked around the table, looking for a shot, aware of the way he watched her, and even the fact that she didn't know his real name—Omar, Orlando, Oliver; she didn't know—was hot.

*Olive would be a cute name for a girl.*

What was happening?

She'd never thought about having a kid in her life. No. She'd avoided the possibility of it by hermitting and focusing solely on her studies and training and work.

She drew in a deep breath.

No. No babies. And her biological clock was not allowed

to start tick-tocking. Ever. Kids were expensive. And being a kid was lonely.

She bent over the table, eyes on the spot where she wanted to hit the red ball.

"Nice ass." A man she hadn't noticed sidled up to her, his hand already cupping her and pressing her against the pool table. "Tight. Buy you a drink?"

Jory, who'd never been felt up by a stranger in her life because she was rarely anywhere but at work, squeaked in shock and froze. Before she could accept that this was really happening and process—stunned embarrassment and fear—Big O had caught the man's hand, jerked it around his back high and pressed him face down into the pool table.

"Never. Ever." His voice steeled. "Ever touch a woman like that who's not yours and hasn't indicated she wants your hand anywhere near her body. Clear?"

Jory didn't know what to do. The area around them had quieted. She felt like she stood in a spotlight. Had she enticed the man with her determination to make the shot? She didn't want Big O to hurt him, but an unexpected warmth filtered through her at his reaction and casual show of strength. Never once had anyone defended her or stood up for her.

She almost said, 'it's okay,' but O's glittering eyes sparked fire and his hero's jaw was so sharply defined she wanted to lick it. The warmth that had been burbling in her belly all night and making her limbs feel fluid heated and burned, and her panties felt beyond damp for this man.

"We got a problem?" The bartender, Reese, had left his post and stood between the bar and the entertainment alcove.

"None because he's leaving," Big O said, not loosening his grip, but not appearing to strain.

"You got a ride home, Ross?" the bartender asked.

"My brother," the man mumbled, and another man approached the table.

"I got him, Reese. Sorry, ma'am." The man looked at her and tipped his hat, and Jory felt like she was in a movie.

No one had ever called her ma'am, and if anyone in the bar knew who she was—and she was a bit weirded out but relieved no one had recognized her although she'd seen a few familiar faces—they wouldn't be ma'aming her.

Would they?

She'd changed. She was no longer the girl with the free school breakfast, lunch and afternoon snack. She didn't get a backpack of food for the weekend or Mrs. Monroe at the grocery store encouraging her to take the misshapen fruit and vegetables and expired pasta home. She was successful. Financially solvent. Employed. She'd taken care of her family—what was left of it.

Maybe her former tormenting classmates had changed too. It wasn't like everyone had been awful, but she'd only focused on the negative comments, the shunners.

O released the man, and stepped back, his body loose-limbed yet ready, but nothing more happened. Ross left with his brother, and the moment of tension popped like it hadn't been.

"Hungry?" He turned toward her, blocking her from the view of the remaining patrons in Grey's that had been slowly emptying on the Sunday evening. His hand lifted and she thought maybe he'd touch her. She wanted him to, so badly. She closed her eyes and leaned in hoping to feel the brush of his fingers against her cheek.

She drew in a shaky breath. How did women do it? How did a woman show a man she wanted him? She wanted Big O to make a move but was excited about trying to find some of her own sexual power—okay, probably not power, but maybe a spark?

She was nervous and yet excited to take the next step.

"I feel a little like Cinderella at the ball," she said, "only I have no intention of running out or leaving a shoe behind. These were expensive." She stuck out one ankle boot.

"A ball?" he echoed. "Being homecoming king at my prom was as close as I ever got to a ball."

"Of course you were the king. I never even went to a dance in high school." What a social disaster that would have been, although Mr. Lane—the guidance counselor—had told her the school had a scholarship fund for activities and one of the moms, who made the costumes for the plays, Mary Krummel, had offered to make Jory a dress. She'd shown Jory the material, and it had been a beautiful maroon and plum ombré, and she'd talked of making it an empire-waist style with tiny silver stars beading the belt, and Jory had been so stunned by the beauty of the fabric, touched, surprised and embarrassed by the offer, she'd whispered 'no' and then had run away to hide in the bathroom and cry.

Or course she'd been discovered and mocked.

But now was not the time to remember past social disasters. Now was the time to create a new Jory Quinn, although looking down at her suede boots that she'd purchased as an impulse before heading to Marietta, she wondered if she'd chosen them because of the color and how it had reminded her of the dress that never was.

"We can rectify that," Big O said, smiling down at her, and Jory had a feeling he was far more perceptive than she wanted him to be, and yet, in a way, she longed for someone to see her—really see her. And like her anyway.

"Would you like to dance, or we could eat something first?"

He stared into her eyes, and Jory felt like she stood on the ledge of something that had nothing to do with food or dancing. She wanted to step off and fly, but what if she crashed?

*I'll get up again.*

"Yes." She covered his hand with hers. "Dancing then eating sounds good to me."

"Me too." He pulled her into his arms, his hold light, but she felt the stamp of him on her bones, and she wondered if he was talking about food or, like her, sex. "This isn't a high school gym with a bunch of balloons or a fancy hotel ballroom, but—" he held out his hand "—I would enjoy dancing with you, J."

They still hadn't exchanged names, and the secrecy was exciting and added to the fantasy element of the night. She tentatively clasped his fingers, and he led her to the small, cleared-out area of the dance floor, just as Blake Shelton's 'Home' started to play.

Not a message appropriate to her or her life, and yet what if she had a place she wanted to be, a person she wanted to be with?

Pushing away the ping of sadness, Jory focused on making another fun memory, losing herself in the music and the man. Jory had no idea how to dance, but when he pulled her into his body, and she felt his hard, warm strength meld with her smaller, physically unremarkable frame, she didn't care. She closed her eyes. Tonight she was outside of herself. Outside of her life. And she was just going to let go and live.

They danced to two slower songs, his body guiding hers around the small, makeshift dance floor, and she didn't care that no one else was dancing. O really knew how to move, and she wanted to savor every second, every nuance, and when someone put on a faster song that she was totally unfamiliar with as she'd avoided country music because it always reminded her of Marietta, Big O taught her how to two-step.

When the song ended, she held on to his hands. 'Now,' everything inside her whispered, and she thought of the song from *Hamilton* that she'd never had the chance or the money to see on the stage. But it was time to take her shot.

"Want to get something to eat, J?" he asked, but his expression asked something different.

"I have a room at the Graff," she said, hoping she sounded coolly sophisticated instead of nervous and wildly inexperienced. O likely had women hitting on him when he walked down the street. She hadn't missed the greedy and appraising looks aimed at him all night. And she'd been stunned his eyes hadn't once appreciatively appraised any other women.

"They have room service if you're *hungry* hungry."

*Oh. My. God. I sound like a dork.*

"I'm not as interested in food, at the moment, J, and I want us to be clear."

He was going to leave. She'd blown it. But she'd gone further tonight than she'd imagined she could.

"Let's walk," he said.

Of course. Cowboy code. He'd walk her back to the hotel and since there were still a few single woman chatting in groups, he'd probably return for a better offer.

She tried not to feel deflated when he paid the tab and, arm around her waist, he led her outside.

"I'm just looking for tonight, J."

"Me too." She was so relieved she almost jumped on

him. "Just tonight and then poof."

He smiled. "Another fairy-tale reference? I'm no prince, J."

"And I'm no princess in need of a rescue," she replied and really did feel like Cinderella—shoe returned—when he smiled.

HAND IN HAND they walked the few blocks to the hotel.

"Cute town," he commented. "Couldn't believe what I was seeing when I first drove in." He couldn't believe what he was doing—holding J's hand. He'd had too many one-night stands to count, but he'd never left holding any woman's hand like they were sweethearts and walked down a western-tricked-out downtown.

"Yeah, me too." She sounded rueful. There was a story there, and Calhoun had an urge to ask, though sharing more than their bodies was not on the manifest tonight.

*Manifest.*

Not in the military anymore. Calhoun hadn't felt in charge of his life or his choices until he'd seized the prestigious West Point scholarship offer to play lacrosse at eighteen in an adolescent, testosterone-filled surge of righteous fury. It had been a blatant middle finger to his father, and a permanent rent from his family. His father had chased him out of the house, fists flying, and Calhoun had for the first time stood his ground.

And no family members had stepped forward to intervene. Calhoun had held his pose like he was in the ring, ready to block this time. Ready to let rip. Usually his father yelled, but that day his father's voice had been ice.

"Never come back."

And he hadn't. And he wouldn't. And before he could pack anything, his father had started seizing everything in his room and hurling it out the window where he'd lit it on a 'funeral pyre.'

He'd managed to grab a few things—his lacrosse gear, laptop, a few clothes and his truck keys—and as he drove out of the old olive-tree-lined lane and through the massive metal gates to the family's legacy ranch the final time, he'd seen the smoke rising up.

He wasn't sure he'd made the right decision for years, not until he joined the Special Force team of the Coyote Cowboys. He'd finally felt valuable. And when he'd switched career tracks to be a working military dog handler, he'd finally felt a bond he'd been missing all his life.

"You've gone quiet," J said. She paused as they turned the corner and he saw a beautiful hotel a block away, luminous and welcoming in the dark. She tugged on his hand, and he tore his gaze away from the hotel that looked like something his family would have purchased and gutted and renovated until the charm, history and context were dust.

"It's okay to change your mind."

He stared down into her midnight eyes. She meant it. Kindness and understanding radiated from her, and something pinged in his chest—what? Conscience? A reminder of how he'd once been, 'sweet'? Vulnerable? 'A pussy' was what his father had often called him, which hadn't made sense since his sisters and aunts had been strong women and his grandmother definitely went toe-to-toe with her husband and sons.

"That's my line." He had to dig for his usual 'just one of the guys' persona.

"Since I am in full possession of my agency, not visually impaired, and the one whiskey metabolized after the first hour, my mind is made up, unless yours isn't."

She had an unusual, quirky, sort of formal, overeducated way of speaking sometimes that should have been weird, but he found it charming.

He brought her knuckles to his mouth and kissed each one, his gaze searching hers. She wasn't his type, not at all. And he had a feeling he was only seeing about twenty percent of her picture, if that. J was more of a deep plunge into a glacier-fed alpine lake than a quick swim across a gym pool. And that was troubling. But she had expressive eyes that grounded him, a mouth made for kissing, and a cute, compact body. And she was smart—just the way she'd discussed the angles and trajectory for the games and added up everyone's dart scores without writing anything down showed she was a math whiz.

Intelligence was a huge turn-on for him.

*Which is why I don't look for it in one-night stands.*

He was getting smart with her tonight. Maybe even smarter than him. But instead of turning away, he was rooted. Intrigued and man enough to not turn down what she was offering. His first night of freedom, and this was where he was headed.

He dug up a smile and volleyed her words back to her.

"Since I am in full possession of my agency and not visually impaired, I have not changed my mind. I had an unexpectedly good time tonight, J."

Her head tilted and surprise gleamed in her midnight eyes at the word 'unexpectedly' and he liked that too—that she caught nuance.

"You are fun and just what the doctor ordered on my first night in town."

Her brow crinkled. "How did you—" She broke off. "I don't think anyone has ever called me fun," she said. "I'm usually seen as too serious and studious."

"Maybe you were hanging with the wrong people."

"Solid conclusion." She smiled. "I'll keep that in mind the next time I walk on the wild side."

"Wild?"

"You look like you can offer wild, Big O."

That dumb nickname. She deserved better, and yet he liked being anonymous. He felt unmoored being alone and out of the service. He'd counted on Kai anchoring him, and yet Ryder wouldn't arrive with Kai until tomorrow morning.

"Can you?"

"As wild as your historic yet elegant-looking hotel can allow."

"It was called the Wild West for a reason."

He liked her quick rapport. He'd never had that with another woman.

*Because you weren't looking for that.*

He'd just wanted to get laid to shake off some tension. Tonight he was acting out of character.

*Unmoored.*

Maybe he should have gone navy, he mocked his thoughts.

"Shall we?" He looked up at the hotel with the wide sweep of a circular drive and stairs that matched. The doors, even from this distance, looked massive and custom.

The lobby was just as beautiful as the outside of the hotel, and when he saw the Irish-themed pub, he paused, inspiration hitting.

"Just a sec, I want to look at their wine list."

"You don't need to try to get me tipsy." She followed him.

He scowled. "If you were tipsy, I'd be helping you to your room and leaving."

"I'd be doing the same for you."

"Who said chivalry was dead?"

He asked for the drink list, flipped to dessert wines and

ordered a glass of port.

"Port?" Her dark brows furrowed. "That's a new one. I don't even think I know what that is. It sounds like something they'd drink in an Agatha Christie book before someone keeled over and Miss Marple starts dithering during her devastating detecting."

"Nicely alliterative. Characters often drank sherry in Christie mysteries, and you're going to like the plans I have for the port."

Fire flared in her eyes along with curiosity, and he was happy he'd followed his impulse. Her voice had been so analytic, tinged with a little sadness when she said that she'd never been considered fun.

He'd had a lot of fun over the years. He'd made the fun happen as if he was still pushing against his old man.

No reason not to make his first night in a new town memorable. Tomorrow he'd meet up with Kai and fulfill his vow to Jace. After that, his future was a blank slate.

# Chapter Four

HER HEART POUNDED, and not from walking up three flights of stairs to her room. She wished now she'd splurged on the suite, but she hadn't known how long she'd be at the hotel—it depended on how quickly she found a short-term rental. But as soon as she opened the door, the elegant king-size bed dominated.

How did women do this so casually? There was nothing casual about the way her body was acting. She felt hot, achy, and uncomfortable in her too-small skin. She also felt hungry but not for food.

O put the glass of port on one of the nightstands and untied the laces of his thick-soled boots. She'd not noticed them before. They looked like the real deal, like he was going to command troops into battle, and that should not make her hot, should it?

*Maybe I'm a closet pervert?*

"You're going to need to get some cowboy boots if you stay in Marietta," she noted, nervously, and immediately wished she'd kept her big mouth shut because he paused in the act of placing his boots carefully by the door.

"I have cowboy boots," he said, peeling off his socks and

placing them by his boots. "A friend bought them for all of us, but I'm not staying in Marietta."

She could barely swallow. "Me neither."

He looked at her, his gaze heated honey, and she would have never guessed 'brown' eyes could have so many colors and expressions or be so fascinating.

"Your turn," he said, stalking across the room and guiding her to a wingback chair. Knees weak she sat.

"To do what?" She could barely breathe.

He sat back on his haunches, and carefully slipped off her ankle boots and tucked them under the chair. He eased off her socks, his hands cupping her feet, warming them, and then he began a slow massage.

"Oh, my God," Jory moaned low in her throat as pleasurable sensations rolled up her leg to her core, sparking fire. Even her tummy flipped and heated like he'd started an engine.

The man was magic. He continued to massage, his thumbs pressing on pressure points that shot sensations through her body like a pinball ricocheting and lighting her up. If she hadn't been seated, she would have fallen.

The whole time he touched her, his gaze remained on her face as if reading each nuance, and helpless to look away, she stared back, even though she'd never experienced anything so intense with anyone in her life. She felt like she needed to hold on to something and that he needed to stop before she burned up, but she didn't want to miss anything.

He paused and reached for the glass of port, and she moistened her dry lips wondering what would happen next. Nerves danced. Would he have her sip the port? She had no idea what to expect, yet didn't want to be impaired by alcohol so she couldn't remember every second with this spectacular masculine specimen.

He dipped his finger in the port and smoothed it over her lips.

"Taste it," he breathed.

Jory licked her lips and chased his finger, sucking it into her mouth. His breathing changed and his eyes briefly closed before they snapped open. A flush skirted the sharp angle of his cheekbones, and she stared fascinated.

She'd had sex before. Twice, but it had never been sexy or playful. He kissed her fingertip and took a sip of wine. He raised one brow as he leaned forward.

Oh. He was asking to kiss her. With the taste of port on his tongue. He was taking charge, inviting her into an intimate moment, which was shocking and thrilling because Jory usually gave the orders in her professional life.

She was not in charge, and she didn't want to be because she had no idea what to do, but she felt safe. Hesitantly, she leaned forward close enough to kiss him, but she paused, scared to ruin the moment. She'd never liked kissing. She wasn't sure what she should do. And her body always felt in the way. Clumsy. She was so short, and yet seated with O crouching, they fit.

The minute his lips touched hers, his tongue slid teasingly along the seam of her lips, which parted. The port tasted like liquid gold, burst of honey, fruit and sin. Jory deepened their connection so she could finally sink her fingers in his thick hair that had teased her all night as she'd wondered at its texture and marveled at the lighter colors and sun streaks when compared to her dark messy waves and curls she was never quite sure what to do with.

His hands smoothed down her back to her butt, and he lifted her and switched their positions so that he was seated, and she straddled him, all without breaking contact with her mouth.

"Mad skills," she complimented lightly, biting down on his lower lip that had fascinated her all night.

"Just getting started," he murmured against her mouth, and then their lips met again, and again, and Jory realized that she had never, ever been kissed before. Not really.

Straddling him was unbearably hot, and before she could think too much about it, she shed her cardigan, and then her shirt.

"Whoa." O's face lit in appreciation as if she had breasts that men would ogle, though she definitely didn't.

He smiled, his palms cupping her small offerings while his thumbs teased her dark nipples into stiff peaks that sent shivers coursing through her body.

"You're exquisite, J," he murmured, eyes glittering.

He lifted her a little, angling her back, and his mouth

explored her breasts, and Jory's rare, late-night self-explorations had never come close to what O made her feel. He was magic. And for the first time in her life, she felt beautiful and cherished.

So pathetic that a man who didn't even know her first name had the power to show her the world.

Jory shoved aside the self-reflection. This was her shot, and she was taking it. Total hot man who knew what he was doing, and she wasn't going to miss out by being shy or insecure. Shedding her past and her doubts, she bunched his T-shirt in her hand.

"Yes?" She asked for his consent.

"Affirmative." He ducked his head so she could whisk it over his head.

"Wow," she breathed, stunned. She'd seen a lot of male bodies in her residency and career, but nothing, not anything like O's.

"Who's the real exquisite one?" she asked rhetorically.

Her appreciative gaze feasted on his golden skin, the hard flex of muscle, the tats that covered one shoulder and pec and scrawled down both arms.

She caught her breath. He looked like a sculpture. He could be in a museum—the perfect male. As a model, he could sell anything, and she'd buy it.

"You don't even look real." She hesitated, nervous to touch all that fabulousness. She'd never be the same.

"I'm very real. And I'm right here."

And she could feel the most real, pushy part of him large and hard against her core as she straddled this Nirvana of a man.

She'd never been with a man with tats. But looking at O, she'd never really been with a man.

"I hope you're not sleepy," she said. "This is one night and I want every minute."

His smile was a little lopsided, but it was the biggest one she'd seen from him yet, and her heart warmed.

"Greedy," he said. "But so am I. Definitely don't intend to waste what remains of the night with sleep," he said. "All yours to command."

Jory had had no idea what to do with this much man, but her life had been one of loneliness, hardship and sorrow. Hard work and determination had saved her. This was her one stroke of luck, and she was seizing it.

Feeling inspired she picked up the glass of port. "I'll drink to that," she said softly, tipping a little of the amber liquid in the hollow of his throat and licking him clean as droplets raced down his muscularly defined chest. He took the glass as she explored his body—licking, kissing, stroking, nipping—until he groaned and strained as she rode his denim-clad erection.

His hands gripped her body with thrilling purpose, and their breath tangled. Jory felt like she was in a movie, and she wanted more. She reached for the button on his jeans, but hesitated.

"Yes," he gutted out, his hands there first tugging down her jeans and panties with nimble fingers. She was clumsier, her hands shaking, and it was he who unbuttoned his jeans and carefully worked the zipper. His glory sprang free.

"Is that commando?" She gasped, the slang term finding purchase in her brain. She'd never once imagined saying or seeing anything so sexy.

His laugh slicked more heat between her thighs, and fascinated, she tried to slide off of him so she could taste what he was offering. She'd never gone down on a man, hadn't once been tempted, but now her mouth watered, and she stared fascinated that a part of a stranger's anatomy could tempt and captivate her attention so fully.

Instead, his hands were on her hips, and he pushed her to standing, her feet on either side of his thighs on the chair.

"Damn you're strong."

"Couldn't resist this view."

Before Jory could begin to feel embarrassed, he breathed against her shivering core.

She moaned. "What…?"

"Hold on."

To what? She was standing in a hotel room on an antique chair, facing a circular guilt mirror with a patina of age that just may or may not be real, and then O licked along the seam of her vaginal lips, and she squawked in surprise, and her body danced, shocked by the intense sensations his exploratory lick unleashed.

And then his mouth got serious. He held her in place, and Jory gripped the curved cherry sides of the chair while O's tongue, lips and teeth utterly ravaged her, and all she could do was shake and make animal sounds, and she didn't care because never, ever, ever had she felt so good.

"I…" She bucked against him. He should stop. She was going to come, and no orgasm had ever built to this level. She might truly detonate and injure him. It was frightening. "I don't know what to do," she gasped out, wanting him to stop but not wanting him to stop with even more ferocity.

"Let go, J. I got you."

His hands played with her breasts, while his skilled mouth brought her to a sensuous crest. She stared at herself in the mirror. Her face was flushed, expression carnal, and her eyes glittered like they'd been sprinkled with stars.

"I want to watch you come," he demanded looking up, and his fingers replaced his tongue, and Jory, who hadn't thought there could possibly be more, learned how wrong she was.

She white-knuckled the chair with one hand and pressed her forearm against her mouth to hold back the scream that ripped out of her throat. Her vision fuzzed, and her knees gave out, but O caught her, eased her back on his lap, and she melted against him, breathed in his slightly earthy, masculine scent that held a hint of something citrusy and spice—orange, cinnamon, bergamot? She didn't know, but his scent careened through her, making her dizzy and drunk with longing.

His heart slammed against hers, and it astonished her that he seemed as aroused as she was.

"I…" She kissed his neck. "Give me a sec and I can return the favor."

She felt him smile against her cheek.

"It's not quid pro quo," he murmured licking along her ear, and she shivered in pleasure.

"I want to taste you," she said. "I want you to feel as good as I do right now."

"Who's to say I don't?"

Jory, who had so little experience with men, but who had heard plenty of women in classrooms, breakrooms, locker rooms and at nursing stations over the years, discuss their bed partners' sexual appetites, prowess and most often, lack of skills, wondered.

"I think I've been missing out," she confessed, starting to get her second wind.

"We've got a lot to make up for tonight then." He kissed his way along her jaw, and Jory tilted to give him better access.

Naked, she slid herself along the length of him once or twice and then with more intent. His groan was earthy, and she cranked up from a post-orgasm buzz of three to a needy eleven-plus instantly.

"You feel huge and amazing," she said happily. "Condom."

"Already on," he said. She looked down. Dang, he was smooth and prepared. Of course he was.

"That's my job." She wanted to touch him. Feel his power.

"You can ask nicely again next time."

And even though there wasn't going to be a next time, the words thrilled her, and for a second she allowed herself to imagine her world with this man in it. His size. His presence. The way he moved. The way he looked at her and listened when she spoke. His hint of a smile that lit his golden eyes.

She angled up and over him, and even though his tongue and fingers had already been inside of her, this felt magically intimate. A connection she hadn't realized she'd even wanted.

Gazes fused, she lowered herself, reveling in the way he stretched and filled her. She wanted to hold on to this moment, even though the need to move, and feel all that pressure and friction pushing authoritatively into her body, stretched her nerves to snapping.

"This is perfect," she breathed. "You feel perfect. Perfection."

Something skittered across his expression, and he closed his eyes, and then hands on her hips, he angled her slightly back and began to thrust into her, and Jory let go, put her brain on pause and instead savored the hunger and sensation that clawed through her.

CALHOUN SPRAWLED ON his stomach, completely sated and relaxed for the first time he could remember. They'd had sex twice, ordered room service, and he'd eaten a burger and felt his strength rushing back. J's sweet, small, perfect breasts brushed along his spine as she leaned over him, her finger tracing a pattern on his skin.

He smiled into the sheets. The woman was obsessed with his body. Yeah, he was jacked from years of sports and keeping his body machine-ready for every mission, but she hummed when she touched him, and her fingers and lips felt reverent. Calhoun had never felt particularly special, even though he'd been a standout athlete in high school and college. And as a soldier, he'd been promoted quickly until he took a different track to become a K9 handler and part of Special Forces.

"You are so beautifully made," she whispered. "I can almost believe in God again."

He rolled over and pulled her on top of him. Even though she was so much smaller, she fit. He was becoming rather obsessed with her compact body and cute, pert breasts that didn't need a bra. He imagined taking her out to dinner and her wearing a silky button-up blouse that she'd leave mostly unbuttoned. They would chat in a public place, and he could watch all the tantalizing expressions play in her eyes and across her expressive face, and all the time he'd wonder if he could catch a glimpse of her nipples, and answer his question—would they harden into tight buds he'd be able to see through the fabric when she'd feel his hot gaze?

He'd always thought women wearing low-cut blouses were sexy AF.

But he and J had only agreed on a night. He couldn't change the rules. He had nothing to offer her. No date. No dinner.

*But we could.*

The thought punched through his sexual haze. He didn't have to head back to base. He didn't have to head anywhere. Other than his obligation to Jace, he was free. For the first time in his life, he was free. He'd ripped off the chains of family expectations and been cut off as much as his father could legally cut him off. The son. Finally after four daughters. Premature due to his mother falling off a horse. Colicky. 'The runt,' his dad had called him as he'd pushed harder for his son to achieve and to toughen up.

He was probably lucky his father hadn't drowned him in one of the cattle-watering stations or a vat of pesticide sprays stored for the hundreds of acres of vineyard.

He'd probably thought about it.

And all the anger and bitterness he'd shoved aside for the past fifteen years reared up like a kraken.

But then J was there, taming the beast.

"Do you have more stamina than the average man?" she asked him so earnestly, already palming his erection that preened at her praise.

He laughed. This woman had made him laugh more in one night than he had during college and his service.

"I'm not sure how to answer that."

"And that's another beautiful thing about you," she said quietly. "You don't puff out your chest and boast. If I looked like you in female form, I'd be strutting down Main Street naked."

"You would not." He laughed again, and then fell back on the bed as she sucked his length into her mouth.

Her mouth was heated heaven and felt incredible. Her uninhibited pleasure blowing him was another fascination because at times she seemed shy and inexperienced, and yet she was earthy, curious, and savored his body.

"Oh God." He breathed through his nose, and tried to hold on to his thread of control. It was past two in the morning, and he didn't want any hotel guests complaining.

"You're having a religious experience too." She looked up at him cheekily, over his throbbing tip. She looked beautiful—eyes shining, lips plumply glistening, and her a beautiful bronze in the filtered moonlight. She held his gaze and licked a circle around his tip.

"I love the way you taste," she said. "I'd wondered."

"What?"

Before he could begin to process her comment, she'd engulfed him again, and his brain short-circuited as she brought him to the brink again and again until he was begging—yeah him, Otis Calhoun Lael-Miller V, begging for a woman's touch.

"I need to be inside you," he bit out, reaching for the last condom.

He'd have to buy some in the morning.

No. Tonight was it.

He paused then reached for the square package. He'd make this last time with J count. "I got it."

Calhoun always gloved himself up. Always. Never trusted a woman to do it. He placed the condom over his tip, and then J was there, rolling it down with her mouth. She checked the fit, and he stared at her, stunned by her dexterity. He still couldn't get a read on her—shy and inexperienced or a femme fatale? His body no longer felt like it belonged to him, but more of an extension of J's as she hummed and, straddling him, lowered herself with exquisite control.

And then he began to move, deeper, harder, faster, feeling more desperate than he could remember feeling, but convinced that if he just kept reaching, striving, he could arrive at the place he wanted, no needed to go.

JORY SIGHED. THIS had been the best night of her life. Now she understood why there was such a fuss about sex. But she'd never thought that she would share in the experience.

She'd imagined emotions would be involved. Trust. Years together. But somehow O had broken through all the barriers she hadn't ever realized she'd erected.

She'd wanted to make some changes in her life. Tonight had definitely been a sprint toward a new beginning, but she wasn't so naïve that she thought she could pop on over to Grey's Saloon anytime she was in the mood and replicate what she'd experienced with Big O.

"Let me get rid of the condom," O murmured near her ear as she sprawled on his chest.

"I'm not sure I can move," she said. "And I'm certain I'm not the first woman to be paralyzed by your skills. Your fabulousness should be patented. No, bronzed."

"I think that's you."

The hint of laughter in his voice warmed her. No one thought she was sexy.

"Mmmmmmm." She kissed his salty neck that tasted like him and her and sex.

"You are unique, J."

"That's the nicest thing anyone has ever said to me." She had to blink back tears.

*Don't be stupid.*

To stave off the rush of emotion—she wouldn't be that woman, the clingy one always wanting more—she slid off of his wilting erection.

"Ummmmm..." She stared at his naked penis.

"What?" He jack-knifed to sitting and swore. "Where is

it?"

Jory rolled left then right. They'd been even more vigorous than the first two times, but it wasn't like she was a cast member of Cirque du Soleil or anything.

"Oh. Ummmmm…" she repeated herself as a horrible thought hit.

He swore again and reached for her.

"I got it." She swatted his hand away, ironic because bits of him had been inside of her all night and she hadn't objected once.

She rolled off the bed and wondered if she could make it to the bathroom with any sort of dignity and privacy.

"Excuse me," she said coldly when he followed. She'd had to fish tampons out of her vagina over the years when the strings had gotten tucked up or tangled, and she didn't need his help on this expedition.

"What the hell?"

Even as she made it to the bathroom, he was behind her.

"Tell me the condom is not inside you." His large hand was on her shoulder.

"I'm going to check." Jory pushed at his chest, waiting for something to splat out on the bathroom floor and a little relieved but freaked out when it didn't.

She closed the door in his face and locked it.

"Did you find it?"

"Calm down," she muttered. She could feel him hovering almost like his energy was trying to bleed through the door. Jeez, did he think she'd planned this awkward moment? Or that she was so desperate for a man that she'd execute a condom mishap with a stranger?

Yeah, he was hot, but she didn't even know his first name, and she definitely didn't want to now.

Jory sat on the toilet, legs spread wide and heard the soft plop. Then she peed.

"Got it," she said.

"Let me see."

Seriously?

"Was the ejaculation mostly still inside the condom or…?" He sounded like he was leaning against the door now.

"It's not show and tell," she said, his tension amping up hers. "And there are millions of sperm. This is why condoms are only ninety-eight percent effective."

She clearly heard him swear.

Damn. She closed her eyes. Of course she couldn't hold on to anything wonderful and beautiful for even five minutes before it turned and bit her on her ass.

"And even if a women is optimally fertile, there's still only a thirty percent chance of conception."

"That high?" He swore again.

Jory flushed the toilet, washed her hands and then turned on the shower. It would be fine. He could grab his clothes and leave and she'd…she'd…she racked her brain from where she was in her cycle. Day eleven.

Of course she was.

That didn't mean one of those little suckers would get lucky. But she was young and healthy.

"And only a thirty percent chance of making it to eight weeks in the first trimester," she raised her voice over the water to reassure him. After eight weeks, the chances of miscarriage plummeted, but she didn't share that.

She stepped under the hot shower.

Damn. She could practically feel a sperm soldier racing toward its destiny. She never should have said that thing about believing or not believing in God. It was like her deeply Catholic mother and grandmother were admonishing her from over a thousand miles away. And probably her ancestors were shaking their fists from their graves.

Jory hated that she was going to wash away his scent, but she didn't want to be reminded of the awkward way her night of stepping out of her lonely, yet safe comfort zone had ended with him acting like she'd done something wrong.

A baby? She'd never imagined having one or even having the opportunity. And she shouldn't entertain the idea now. She didn't even know his name. She'd never see him again. He definitely didn't want a kid. He was pissed. And she wasn't where she wanted to be financially, yet.

It was okay. She was a doctor. She could get Plan B. Stop ovulation. Or...she didn't want to think about the other options.

She squirted some of the high-end body wash on her hands and closed her eyes as a sob ripped out of her chest.

She wouldn't cry. She wouldn't. Besides O was gone. Why would he stick around when her father, who'd had a loving wife and daughter—desperate for the attention he lavished on her brother—had left her behind years ago?

She didn't hear either door open, but then O was there in the shower, lathering her up with scented body wash, his hands gentle.

"Sorry for the freak-out," he said after a long while, his chin on her head while the water rained down and steamed around them. "I lost my cool. Not acceptable. I'm really sorry, J. That's never happened before so I was caught off guard. It's not your fault. Protection is my responsibility, and I take it really seriously."

*Can the speech.*

Of course he sounded like the perfect male now. Too late.

"So do I," she said. "I'm responsible for myself." She turned around and looked up at him. "How did you get in here? I locked the door."

"I have skills." His smile ghosted, but didn't reach his eyes. "Sorry I was such a jerk, J." He cupped her jaw and with his thumb traced the cleft in her chin. "My reactions are a little off. I just left the service. Still pretty feral."

He was a soldier?

Her tummy flipped. The body made sense now. The boots. The tats. And his whole enigmatic, ready-for-anything vibe. He served people, as did she.

"I'm not in town for long, J. I'm catching up with some friends, and I need to do a favor for..." He sighed, and pulled her tightly against his body.

"I'm not a good bet. I don't have a job right now. Don't have a place to live or a plan. But I got money saved. I don't know how long I'll be in town. A few days maybe more if I'm dumber than Jace thought, but we need to stay in touch even if it's against the rules we set, J. I won't leave you hanging if..."

He sounded so determined. She could picture him stoic, going off to war, willing to step up and sacrifice. Be the martyr. She wouldn't do that to him or to the remote possibility of a child.

"Where are you in your cycle?" He kissed the top of her head.

She could imagine the words he wasn't saying, although men were surprisingly ignorant about women's reproductive systems and cycles. Ironic since they spent so much time and energy trying to get inside women's bodies.

"Pretty safe," she lied. "But I can take Plan B. It delays ovulation."

He didn't respond. She felt the distance like ice down her back. She squirted body wash on her hands and stroked down his body to touch him one last time and delay the inevitable loneliness and isolation.

# Chapter Five

CALHOUN WOKE ALONE. Sun streamed through the window, and he stared in disbelief. Checked his watch. Nine. He hadn't slept more than a handful of hours at a time in years. And couldn't remember when he'd slept so late. And J wasn't here so he'd slept through her not only getting out of bed but also leaving, which was weird because it was her room.

He jumped up, his body limber and relaxed even after the marathon sex. He prowled the room in growing disbelief. She'd made coffee in the Keurig and had taken a shower again.

Was she coming back?

Did she expect him to be gone?

Yeah. That had been the original agreement. He picked his phone off the nightstand just as a text flooped in. His heart and cock jumped, but that was stupid. He and J hadn't shared numbers. They hadn't shared names.

Ryder. Picture of Kai riding shotgun, morning breeze ruffling his fur.

*Bucking Bulls back home. Leaving ranch. Meet in fifteen Java Café.*

Calhoun's knees gave out and he sat on the bed.

Kai looked happy. Healthy. He'd been smart to arrange for Ryder to pick up the pup after he'd been rehabilitated in Texas. Kai had had nearly four weeks living and traveling with Ryder. This hadn't been the first picture or update Ryder had sent from the road.

Calhoun had craved every picture and update and now he was only fifteen minutes out. He jumped in the shower. He'd deliberately walked away from this type of luxury, but shame rushed forward because the double-headed shower, high water pressure and vast space—he didn't have to duck to get under the showerhead—could become addictive. The tiled, deep-seated shower bench reminded him of how conducive the shower was to sex, and he fully perked up at the memory. He tried to ignore biology but failed and rubbed one out, picturing J's hot midnight gaze sparkling when he drove her over the edge.

Her amazed surprise at each orgasm stuck with him. Made him feel like he'd done one thing right, when the rest of him felt so wrong.

He hadn't even told her his name. Last night that had seemed sexy, like he was still on a covert op, but this morning as he was about to head out to meet Ry and Kai, he felt like a fraud. And a douche since the condom fiasco.

Well, he'd leave his number, but he still felt like a jerk. Even his brothers didn't know about his family.

"I wish I didn't know about my family," he murmured, turning off the water even though he could have stood there another ten minutes.

He grabbed a fluffy towel, one more reminder of the luxury he'd turned his back on.

The price had been too high.

But he had money. His father had ruthlessly and furiously carved him out of the family trust, company and his will. But both his grandmothers had put money in trust for all their grandchildren, defying his father's directives.

Not that he intended to use the money. He had no claim on it. He'd made his decision to live free. Now he just had to figure out what that looked like.

He dressed quickly, his eyes scanning the room one last time, as he inhaled the lingering scent of Jory and sex. Last night had been spectacular, until the end. Never before had a condom slipped off during sex, and he'd had some pretty raunchy hot sex over the years.

He'd dismissed Cross's warning that destiny was going to march in and hand him his ass last night as he tried to complete Jace's last wish, but now his brother's teasing reared up, mocking.

No. He was in charge of his destiny. But for the first time in a long while, it hit him that he might intend to live free of family obligation, but he might not be able to.

When he'd entered the army, he'd had to make a will and have a beneficiary. He'd chosen several animal rescue organizations, and then later after he became Kai's handler, he'd added the foundation in Last Stand, Texas, that took on the 'impossible' cases of injured and traumatized military dogs.

"Damn."

He had to get a move on. He didn't want to be late to meet Ryder and Kai. He was the last man who should play family man, but he'd never shirk responsibility to his kid and the kid's mom. J had said she'd take Plan B. He wasn't sure exactly what that did, but he didn't want to assume anything, and face a furious teenager looking for closure or connection eighteen years later. No way was he going to ignorantly play the role of deadbeat catalyst for another Lael-Miller disaster generation.

He peeled off a piece of hotel stationery. Wrote his name—OC Miller. And his cell. But was that breaking the rules? Too bad.

In case you need to get in touch with me.

And he left the room, closing the door firmly behind him.

He took the stairs, and left the hotel, crossing quickly to Main Street. He'd left his truck near Grey's last night and figured he'd retrieve it after he met up with Ryder. The morning was crisp. Clear. Gorgeous, and he tilted his head back as he walked, breathing in the fresh mountain air that was scented with pine, grass, dirt, animal and snow.

Maybe Montana really was heaven. From what he'd garnered last night, Cross, Huck, Rohan and Ryder were all staying put. They had jobs. Women. Purpose.

*Family.*

He stumbled a little. That damn slippery condom.

He didn't believe in coincidence, but what else could it be? Cross had come to Montana for Jace to fulfill a vow and had ended up adopting a teen girl and marrying. Huck had come to walk Jace's sister down the aisle and instead had become the groom to a pregnant bride, and he was in the process of adopting Willow's infant. Then Rohan had peeled off at Christmas to deliver a letter for Jace and had met up instead with his high school sweetheart who had a son and now they were an instant family. He hadn't heard Ryder's story yet.

Then there was him, hooking up anonymously in a saloon and having his first ever condom mishap.

"Flippin' classy," he berated himself, ashamed.

But that had had nothing to do with Jace, he reassured himself. J had nothing to do with his vow to Jace.

"Big O!"

Calhoun shot to instant awareness. Ryder drove in the opposite direction, window down, Kai lunging toward the window, yipping, wiggling and squealing.

Calhoun's joy was just as intense—internally, if not externally. He heard Ryder's full-bodied laugh, and then Kai hurtled out of the open window, and Calhoun jogged across the street, already slapping his chest for Kai to jump. And then even with his lightning reflexes, he was too slow. He heard the rev of an engine, squeal of brakes, flash of black and blue in his periphery.

He reached for Kai and lifted and hurled him back toward Ryder, barely registering Ry's look of shock and horror before he was hit hard from behind and also from the side. His vision grayed then blacked out. He couldn't breathe. He couldn't feel his body, and his last thoughts tumbled through his brain. Irony was a bigger bitch than even he'd imagined, and he'd failed Jace.

"MY FATHER'S OFFER stands," Rohan Telford said as Jory stood outside on the mowed grass and stared at the rebuilt farmhouse that looked like it should be in a Montana tourist brochure, instead of the dilapidated eyesore that was too hot in the summer and freezing in the winter.

She'd met Rohan here at his texted request. She'd not wanted to visit her own home even though her mother and grandmother had asked her to clear out the last of their things they'd left behind—donate, keep or dump—but she had because she hadn't wanted to return to her room secretly hoping O would still be there.

She was an adult. She knew the rules. Last night had been a one-off.

"You can stay here rent-free while you're working at the hospital, and my brother or I will help you if you need anything hauled away. We packed up everything in the old barn, which we are going to turn into an equipment shed and office, once it's emptied out."

"But you fixed up the house," she objected, stunned by the generous offer. "Your family must have plans for it."

"My dad wanted the land. He wanted the access to summer pastures and also to keep the land from being developed. My buddies and I…" Rohan broke off. A shadow skittered across his face and then was gone like a passing cloud on this glorious morning that kept unfortunately reminding Jory how beautiful Marietta could be.

"My dad wants a caretaker up here as this part of the ranch is isolated and having someone living up here will discourage more wildlife incursions on the cattle in the summer," Rohan said. "But if you end up taking the job at the hospital…"

"I won't," she said decisively and then winced at her rude interruption. "Sorry, Rohan. I just can't see myself staying in Marietta. I didn't even want to come here."

"Why not?"

She shot him a look. Dang he was handsome—even more so now that he was a man, but nothing compared to O last night.

*And you need to stop thinking about him now.*

She wasn't going to fall in love with a man who could break her by pulling a disappearing act.

"Growing up in Marietta was different for me," she admitted. "My family…my dad, his dad before him and his dad before him had been…" how to describe them "…not model citizens," she settled on. "Cattle rustlers, gamblers, fighters, schemers. Heck, one of my ancestors was supposedly dragged behind a horse to encourage him to leave town for good," she added wondering if Rohan had heard that story. "Definitely not good ranchers or honest men and not a one of them stuck around."

Her voice cracked.

*Get a grip.*

Her father had left them years ago, and Rohan didn't need her to toss her family's dirty laundry on his freshly mowed grass.

"I wanted a fresh start," she said.

She'd chosen books over people.

"Coming back here—" she waved her hand toward the house "—feels like a step back."

Rohan nodded. And for a moment, neither of them spoke. It was quiet. No traffic. Just the slight chill of the breeze tumbling down Copper Mountain.

"I'm the first to admit it can be tough coming home again," Rohan said after a long while as she stared at the mountain, which she'd always felt was judging her, or poised to devour her as a snack.

Her curious gaze skewed toward his. "You? You were golden. Popular. You fit. You and your family were…are what Marietta is all about. Good people. Community service. Success."

"We've had our struggles," Rohan said. "And making a mistake always felt bigger than it actually was at the time," he said soberly. "So, if you want to stay here instead of at the Graff for the few months you're here, the house is yours. You can cull through your family's things we stored in the barn and maybe slay a few ghosts while you're here."

She squared her shoulders. He made it sound easy, but maybe she was the one who was making it hard. She still felt like that eight-year-old girl left behind.

Living here alone also sounded lonely.

But her frugal self rose to the surface. She'd pay rent of course, but this could be ideal. Short term. Clear out whatever her mom and oma had left behind. Bury her ghosts and painful memories and finally move on. Last night had been the first step. Staying here could be the second.

"I'd need to pay something," she said.

And Rohan smiled as if he knew he had her where his family wanted. Although why?

"Can you show me what you've done to the house because on the outside it looks totally different? Even the window to my room looks different."

Her childhood bedroom hadn't even really been a bedroom, more like an attic nook. "The house no longer looks like it's about to crumble in on itself."

"Sure." Rohan bounded up the stairs to the wide, wraparound porch that no longer had any broken or cracked planks. He unlocked the door, and Jory looked at the key he'd placed in her hand earlier.

She climbed each stair with deliberation compared to Rohan's imitation of a border collie coming home for supper after a long day herding on the range.

She stopped in the doorway.

"Whoa." That was all she could say for a moment. "You've been busy."

"Friend of mine is a contractor and has a crew. They've been out here shoring up the supports, refurbishing the floors, new windows, new kitchen—bit more of an open concept, and we punched out the upstairs area as well, added another bathroom and partial loft. The three bedrooms are still down here, and we added another bathroom as well.

"But why go through so much trouble if your dad doesn't want the house or won't accept rent for it?" She was mystified. She didn't know much about construction, but it wasn't cheap.

"My dad has some thoughts," Rohan said slowly. "And so do I. We've had discussions." His green gaze lasered back on her now. "Nothing firmed up, yet, so you staying here for your contract at the hospital actually buys us—me and my other Coyote Cowboys—some time that we need."

The hair rose on the back of her neck. "Coyote Cowboys?" Rohan had been in the service for a few years. What if he and Big O knew each other. Instinctively she pressed her legs together and then nearly laughed at her ridiculousness.

That horse was long out of the barn.

"We're in the process of drawing up a business plan, and this house and the outbuildings feature into it, but we need to make the numbers work."

Jory nodded, slowly. She knew all about trying to balance the numbers.

"But would my being here during the day mess up your plans? I'm working night shift four nights a week for the next two months. I'd be sleeping during the day."

*Like a vampire.*

"No," Rohan said decisively. "Like I said, you'd be buying us time. My dad likes the idea of having someone up here to watch the property. If you stay here…"

"I could drive the access roads," she said. "After shift and before I go in. My car's four-wheel drive."

Rohan smiled. "I'm working on a plan. I'd probably bring an ATV over, and a couple of horses."

Jory's heart leapt. She'd always wanted a horse, but they'd been too expensive growing up, and wildly impractical now as she traveled around and often stayed in long-stay hotel suites for business professionals.

"It's been a hot minute since I rode," she said, not able to shake off the image like she should. "And I don't think I would scare anyone." She waved her hand down her body. She knew how to shoot. Her daddy had taught her, but she hadn't picked up a gun since he'd left. "And I couldn't shoot anyone if you're worried about cattle rustlers. And I'd have a hard time shooting a coyote or wolf unless it was attacking."

"I like that about you," Rohan said softly.

Was he making a joke?

He smiled, and Jory felt less defensive. Rohan had always been swoony in high school. So many girls had dreamed about dating him because not only had he been handsome, smart and athletic, he'd also been so kind—always helping others and standing up for the awkward kids who didn't have poise or connections.

"Stay here if you want, Jory. I'll have someone from the ranch making regular patrols. The cattle will be up here on the hills soon so you won't be alone, but no one will come to the house, except perhaps to the equipment barn. They'll be quiet. Keep to themselves. You should consider getting a dog."

"I'd love one," she answered quickly. "But I move too much."

"Why?"

She didn't know how to answer that, so she shrugged her shoulders and looked around the house that no longer felt familiar. And with the sun pouring through the double-paned windows and the fresh mountain breeze teasing through the open door, it hit her then, that she did want to stay at her own house. The well of longing that poured through her shocked her. She felt closer to her brother here, her father. It was like she could allow herself to remember them again.

The house was even fully furnished.

"Boone and I packed up what your mom left in closets in totes and put them in the barn—that's refurbished too. We kept your rope swing and even added a little more fun."

She stared at him, curious. She could almost feel her brother Josiah's arms around her as they swung drunkenly in circles, looking up at the bats roosting in the barn's eves.

"I'll leave you to look around, tell my dad it's a go. You got my number. Let me know if you need anything."

Then Rohan, light on his feet, was gone. She waited until his truck started and crunched away down the long gravel drive. He was taking the shortcut off the small ranch—there was still a rough, barely there road that led down to Peavine and then to the highway. The few locals had used it at one time, but now no one lived up here or down on what had been the backside of the Quinn property.

She walked slowly through the house, admiring the changes. The house was still farmhouse style. Rustic. Spare lines. But she liked the building materials and the pine flooring shone, and the spots where it had been replaced blended in. Did she really want to revisit the past just to save some money?

Maybe she should simply pay someone to haul away the last of the Quinn junk and make a fresh start herself—like her mom and oma finally had.

It would be dark here. Lonely.

But she'd be working nights.

She walked up the narrow stairs to her childhood bedroom and stared in awe at the changes. She'd always loved her room, the smallness, the window that looked out on the lone oak tree where she could spy on squirrels and birds. She felt like she was in a tree house, part of nature, not stuck inside.

The room was bigger now—eaves pushed out and painted a soft green, but the ceiling still sloped, and the small window was now a bay style with a comfortable seating nook and a view that went for miles. Jory lifted the lid, marveled at the craftsmanship and closed it again. Storage, a place to sit, and a view with a morning and afternoon breeze. She cranked the window open and thought about a book she'd read in a humanities class—Virginia Woolf's *A Room of One's Own*.

This room looked like a room where she could imagine a future, write a poem.

Smiling at her unexpected imagination, she leaned out the window to see if the nesting box she'd made with her high school woodworking teacher, Mr. Lane, was still there. It was.

She smiled, and then pulled her head back in the window. Something brushed through her hair, and she flipped her hand at it thinking spider, but no, something metallic flashed in her vision.

Jory's fingers caught at the chain. And her breath fractured, everything in her going still even as her heart galloped. She'd forgotten all about her necklace from her great-granddad. She untangled the chain with the small medallion from the bare curtain rod and sat down. With her thumb she traced the tarnished image on the Buffalo coin.

A strangled laugh along with a cry tore out of her.

So stupid. Pretentious and tragic.

Her great-grandfather had wanted to create a family crest for his disdained family so he'd taken antique Buffalo nickels and ruined whatever value they might have accrued, by adding a fractured piece of turquoise found by some relative, along with copper to represent the vein of copper another broken ancestor had found and lost during the short-lived copper boom in the mid eighteen-seventies. The Quinn family's luck always drained through their fingers, and this medallion was another reminder.

The intention was to create a family heirloom—passed father to son. Her father had given his to Josiah on his tenth birthday, and her grandfather, out of prison for the longest time she could remember, had made another medallion for her, not caring that she was a girl. He'd added a Montana sapphire that family lore said he'd stolen, to the medallion, before gifting it to her the same Christmas when she'd been eight.

It had been their last Christmas together as a family.

She held the necklace up to the light streaming in through the window and watched it twist. She'd been proud to wear it when her grandfather had put it around her neck.

"A lucky nickel," her granddad had said. "It will always

give you something of value and remind you where you came from."

The medallions hadn't been lucky. Before half the year had passed, her grandfather had died in a holdup gone wrong in a gas station outside Billings, and her father—always wandering off to participate in some sketchy scheme that would finally make them all rich—had taken her brother and left for good. Her mom had withdrawn and Jory's already precarious childhood was shoved that much further out onto the ledge.

Still, she'd risen to the challenge.

At age eleven, she'd accepted that her father and brother were never coming home, but just in case, she'd hung her precious medallion on the curtain rod to guide them home if they ever chose that path, and then she'd lived for herself, determined to leave the Quinn legacy of poverty, pain and abandonment behind her as soon as she left.

"And now I'm back." She palmed the necklace, and then after hesitating a moment, she slipped the chain over her neck. When she'd been a child, the nickel had been more like a pendant. Now it sat a little higher, but she could still tuck it under her T-shirt as a reminder not only of where she'd come from, but how far she'd traveled.

Maybe coming home wasn't the step backwards she'd imagined.

# Chapter Six

JORY WATCHED DR. Lacy Cooper cheerfully wave and make a heart shape on her chest. "Have fun tonight. Welcome aboard."

Jory had been a traveling hospitalist for almost four years now, and she was used to being thrown into new situations and mostly abandoned, but Dr. Cooper—the day shift hospitalist—had given her a quick, speed-walking tour around the surgical unit, recovery room, ICU and main floor.

Marietta General, like many rural hospitals Jory had worked at, was small, but fairly well equipped. Bozeman had a higher-level trauma facility, but since Marietta had a large ranching population and major highway running through the mountains, it had its fair share of traffic, farming, ranching and rodeo accidents. The staff was highly trained and could handle many cases locally, except—like many hospitals, nationally—they were chronically understaffed.

"I'm heading home." Dr. Witt Telford, an orthopedic surgeon, stopped by the nursing station where Jory had headed before starting her rounds. She needed a coffee before her shift, and hoped the staff lounge had a Keurig or at least a coffeepot. Even better, one of those automatic espresso machines would be heaven right now.

He introduced himself.

"I'm on call tonight and have two patients on the floor. My patient Mr. Miller in room three-ten didn't have the orthopedic injuries we anticipated with his accident, but he was pinned between two trucks, so compartment syndrome is a concern. So far he's not presenting, but I want a lower extremity exam for mottling and pulse and reflexes and vitals on him every hour. He's young. Fit. I think he's clear. He's also sustained cracked ribs, and a bruised and punctured lung. Dr. Samantha Gallagher ended up doing a splenectomy so check the patient's incision site and possible fever." Dr. Telford paused, and he replaced his last patient chart at the nursing station and turned to leave. Then he paused, drew a deep breath and turned around.

"Need anything?"

"Tell me there's coffee."

"Coffee and pretty decent snacks," he said. "I'll show you the doctor break room and the call rooms if you ever need one."

Jory worked shifts, not call, so resting in a call room was not an option. Coffee couldn't get in her fast enough. She nearly yipped with pleasure to see the automatic espresso machine.

"The high life," she said, happily making herself a latte and adding sugar-free caramel flavoring.

"I hit this up at least a couple times when I'm here instead of my clinic," Dr. Telford said. "The nursing staff is great. Probably could run the place and do most of our jobs, so you're in good hands. Welcome back to Marietta."

"Thank you." She followed him out, not surprised that he knew she'd grown up local. He had too, although he hadn't moved in with his birth father and family until he'd been in middle school from the rumors she'd heard as a kid. Witt, like his younger half-brother Rohan, had been an outstanding athlete.

He too had left Marietta after high school graduation, and she hadn't seen him again, but he was back as well.

"Like a contagion," she murmured, sipping her latte and then heading off to see her first patient.

She left her latte tucked in a safe place at the nursing station, introduced herself and then grabbed the first chart.

"Hottie alert," one young nurse murmured.

Jory wished she hadn't heard that. It wasn't professional.

"Good luck keeping him in bed. He woke up in recovery, nearly tore the curtain off and reinjured his drain so the ER doctor had to restitch and resedate using different meds and call security."

Jory's expression automatically schooled to bland, professional interest. All the information would be in the chart, but she was a little daunted that security had been called.

"Has he been difficult since?" she asked, wondering if she should summon security.

"No. Some patients don't handle anesthesia well. He's one and built like a buckin' bronc so things might get interesting tonight. He's got a friend with him now, who looks like he can handle anything. I'm Davina. I'm lead nurse tonight and the next three nights so let me know if you need anything, Dr. Jory."

"It's Dr. Quinn," she said.

"I know. That used to be my gran's favorite show. *Dr. Quinn, Medicine Woman.* She just loved Jane Seymour. Just sounds weird to hear it in real life. Dr. Quinn," she said.

Jory wished she had more time to take a few more sips of her latte and find something to eat. She'd spent most of the day at her old house, shocked by the number of things her mom and oma had left behind. She'd hired a moving company for them to help pack and reassemble in Lodi so she wasn't sure why they'd left so much. Had they wanted to escape the same way she had?

She scanned the chart of Otis Calhoun Lael-Miller V. Wow, that was a mouthful.

Jory pushed open the door and blinked a couple of times, not sure how to process what she was seeing. A giant dog—maybe a German shepherd that looked like it could bite off her head and still be hungry—sprawled next to the patient, blocking her view, but the dog alerted when she walked in and targeted her.

"Wha…?" Jory took a step back.

"Kai, down."

Jory looked at the man who spoke. He was young, incredibly handsome with streaked chestnut hair that grew back from features that looked honed from Copper Mountain's peak.

"Good evening, Doc," he said, expression friendly, open and with a smile that could sell toothpaste and probably everything else. She noted he had a cowboy hat resting on the other chair for visitors. A second cowboy hat was on the small table in between.

*Dear, God, save me from Montana cowboys.*

There was another one of them roaming around the hospital.

"I'll just pick up Kai so you can examine Calhoun. He finally stirred a while ago, sort of. I heard he caused a ruckus in recovery and had to be darted back to dreamland." The man sounded proud and amused.

"Ahhh." She wasn't really sure how to respond to his apparent good cheer. She was used to family members of patients being somber, worried, sometimes angry, and always scared, but the dog was blocking any view she had of the patient, so if the cowboy was willing to take charge of the dog, hopefully for the duration of the patient's stay, she would be grateful. "We don't dart patients, exactly."

But they did use needles and strong sedatives in the IV so technically it was a bit like darting.

The man rose. Dang he was tall and built like O.

*Don't think about him. Working.*

"I'll take Kai for a walk. Might need to wrestle him out of here. He's not wanted to leave Calhoun's side. He saw the accident and is feeling guilty."

The man's voice was pitched low, and he spoke softly.

"The dog really shouldn't be here," she said firmly.

"Kai's a service dog, Doctor. He's well trained and a former soldier."

Kai was also staring at her with a focused look that chilled her blood. But hadn't she just been thinking she'd like a dog, especially if she stayed out on her old homestead? Seeing this massive beast was making her rethink. She'd been picturing soft and cuddly, but maybe deadly was the way to go.

"Excuse me, ma'am. Doctor." The man scooped the dog up in his arms like it couldn't bite his face off, with a softly murmured command, and then he walked out, leaving Jory staring into the pale face of O. Make that Otis Calhoun Lael-Miller V.

HE WAS FLAT on his back.

What the hell?

Had he taken fire?

Kai.

Calhoun jerked to consciousness and tried to sit up, but something pulled in his gut, and his ribs ached like the devil had stomped on him.

"Kai's fine. He's safe. He's with your friend. You're in the hospital, Mr. Miller."

When was the last time he was called Mr. Miller? Where the hell was he? Why was a woman here?

Even more disoriented, Calhoun struggled out of the wet, clinging gray of his half-consciousness, and reached out for Kai, but instead encountered two, soft, warm hands on his chest. He gripped one, hoping it was a lifeline he could use to pull himself into full consciousness. But the woman firmly pressed down on his shoulder, with more strength than seemed possible. Or was he weak?

"You're in the hospital, Mr. Miller," she said. She'd already said that, right?

"You've been injured, but you will make a full recovery."

Hospital.

Injured.

How?

With an embarrassingly large amount of effort, he opened his eyes and saw her. The woman he'd dreamed about. So, he was still asleep. Large black eyes full of sympathy and stars. Long lashes that curled, and dark hair that waved and curled in a sassy bob. Olive skin that looked like sun-kissed silk.

"I dreamed about you."

"Mr. Miller." She moistened her sexily plump top lip, and he had a sudden vision of that mouth going down on him. His dick stirred so at least he hadn't been injured too badly.

Another dream. Or had it been real?

"Do I…? Are we…?" He felt a wave of nausea that he battled back, and cold sweat rushed over his body, and the horrible itching was back.

"I want to sit up."

"You just had surgery."

Nothing was making sense. "My teammates? Did we take fire? Was anyone else hit?" He grabbed her hand again, willing her to give him the right answer this time.

"No one else was injured."

Relief rushed through him, making him feel even woozier. "I need to sit up." With all his will, he strained, but she held him down with just one hand.

"Let me."

Hell no, a woman wasn't going to help him to sit, but then the bed began to move, and his stomach lurched.

A plastic bowl was there, and Calhoun miserably choked, and spit and heaved, even though there was so little in his stomach to evacuate. Just looking at it and smelling it made him go through the whole process again.

And then the bowl was gone and a cool, damp cloth was on his face, wiping away his sweat and mess around his mouth, and he leaned back.

"I'm going to start you on Zofran in your IV."

"No drugs." He could barely open his eyes. "Pain meds

all make me sick."

"Zofran is anti-nausea." She left the side of his bed, and he heard her typing something. "Your body is reacting to the anesthesia. It's not uncommon, but I don't want you to reopen your wound again."

Wound. He'd been wounded. He plucked at the stiff cotton covering him. What the hell was he wearing? He tugged harder, heard a small pop and the scratchy material was gone, only now his ribs screamed in protest, and he could hardly catch his breath.

"Mr. Miller." She was back in his face again. "You cannot be naked in the hospital." She marched to a tall cabinet, opened it and pulled out another torture garment.

His life was coming back to him now. He did know her. Her scent was familiar—lemon and something, and he knew that small, firm touch of her hand.

"Let's put this on."

"Fine you put it on."

Her expression was so shocked and outraged, and everything slowly clicked into place.

"You weren't so determined to clothe me last night."

"Oh." She sat down on the chair beside his bed looking quickly at the partially closed door.

"I'm sorry about that." Her skin had a dusky rose undertone.

"I'm not." He poked at the small incision. His ribs were black and blue. "But what happened? Why am I here? Why are you here?" She was wearing a white coat or blazer like an office drone.

"I'm sorry," she said stiffly, again looking at the door like somebody was going to bust it open and arrest them.

"Stop saying that. Tell me what happened. Where the hell is Kai?"

"Ah…Mr. Miller."

"Calhoun," he snapped.

She was looking more distressed, and the accident was coming back in pieces, but he remembered Kai was in his arms.

He tried to swing his legs off the bed, but everything hurt.

"Stop, you'll reinjure yourself. Stay."

Jory covered him quickly with the blankets and tried to work his arms through the holes in the hospital gown, but he was having none of that.

"Don't give me one-word commands. I'm not a dog. I want out of here."

"You were hit by a truck and pinned between two trucks. Luckily, the trucks weren't speeding, but you are not being released tonight, and you are getting dressed because there's no one else here to help you."

"I don't need help. Who made you boss?" He was shocked at this side of her. "You playing nurse, J?"

"Doctor."

That was his J. Quick comeback.

*Not yours.*

"Even better," he murmured. "But the game's gone on too long. I hate hospitals. I want out."

"You're injured, O…I mean Calhoun." She flushed a prettier pink under her olive skin that distracted him enough that she got the hated gown tied in the back. "And I'm going to get a nurse so that everything is done with proper procedure because I am your doctor, which is inappropriate considering but there is not another hospitalist on shift, but I assure you I will not take advantage of you."

He stopped trying to get out of bed and pulling off the blankets, even though he still itched like fire ants were crawling all over him.

Was she for real?

"*Now* you're worried about my virtue, J?" He stared at her. "Bit late."

She puffed her cheeks out. "I'm sorry." She squirmed a little on the chair. "I had no idea that you would become a patient."

What a crime. She wasn't psychic.

"That makes two of us. It's not a big deal. Doctor, huh?" He looked at her. He'd known she was smart last night. Definitely upping his game. "That's a first."

And hopefully a last.

"I feel in very good hands with you, J—examine away."

"This is not funny," she hissed. "It's unethical. I'm your doctor."

"You weren't last night," he reasoned, surprised he could find humor when he felt like crap and was totally humiliated that the woman from the hot-sex one-night stand was now witnessing him after he'd been knocked on his ass by a truck on cutesy Main Street, Montana.

His father would snort with contempt.

How had he been so stupid? His Coyote Cowboys were never going to let him live this down.

"You've seen it all," he said. "Though in a bit better condition last night."

"I could be brought up before the medical board for this." She stood up and started to pace. "I should call Dr. Gallagher, your surgeon. Maybe she can…"

"You're overreacting," he said. "It's not like I'm going to announce that we bounced last night."

"It's the principle," she hissed.

Now that his brain was functioning, even though his body still felt battered and humiliatingly nauseous, he could track the conversation.

"We were strangers. We were consenting. It was fun. It's over." He hoped he sounded firmer than he felt, and with how much he was scratching, he probably looked like a monkey.

"But now you're here in my hospital." She sounded horrified and was wringing her hands. "Stop itching. You'll hurt yourself."

She might as well ask him to stop breathing. His skin

screamed fire, but her hands gripped his. "Bring me my clothes. I need my phone to call Ryder for a pickup. You're sure Kai is okay?" He couldn't focus his train of thought.

"He's fine. Huge and protective and going for a walk with your bodyguard." She seemed to relax. "That will help—if your friend stays in the room with you."

"The day I need protection from a hookup who could practically fit in my palm is the day I'm calling it over." Irritated, embarrassed, and feeling like he'd been put in a garbage compressor, he tossed off the covers, threw the hospital gown across the room—though it only landed on his feet—and pulled himself to standing.

"Eeek." Jory's squeak of alarm would have been funny if it hadn't been directed at him, and if the world hadn't spun. His knees buckled.

She rounded the bed like she could catch him.

"Hey." The door opened. "Done with the exam, Doc? Whoa."

Then Ry was at his side along with J, and they helped him back in the bed. Stupid anesthesia.

"The patient is noncompliant," J said, her voice stiff with annoyance.

"Part of him is very compliant," Ry joked.

"Shut up," he said, but Kai was there, pushing his nose in his hand and Calhoun closed his eyes so the world would stop spinning.

"I have the Zofran from the pharmacy," he heard a new

voice say and then a 'wow' was tagged on.

"The nurse is impressed, but the doctor's pissed," Ry whispered in his ear, his voice heavily laced with amusement. "I'd say behave, but that's not how you roll, and who knows, being flat on your back for a few days could be a prime hunting opportunity. You do need to play catch-up on the family man score, bro."

"I assure you we are very professional here." J sounded like her voice had been iced, and he wanted to smile, but the room was still spinning even though his eyes were closed.

"That's too bad," Ryder said.

"He needs to wear the hospital gown," J said. "Perhaps you can help the patient, Nurse?"

"No thank you." Calhoun was riled. This was his childhood all over again—pain, discomfort, powerlessness, his wants ignored.

"His skin's very delicate, ma'am. Doctor," Ryder said, and Calhoun opened his eyes to try to glare at him, but there were three Rys—two too many.

J was up by his head now. He could smell her subtle lemon, herb scent. She fiddled with his IV. Kai moaned low in his throat, and Calhoun reached out for the dog to comfort him, but instead got Jory's leg.

She squeaked and jumped away from him, and something clattered.

"Dude, you need to work on your game," Ryder said, lifting Kai to the bed where the dog stretched out beside him.

"Apologies," Calhoun said, watching J. Despite her discomfort, her moves were smooth, graceful, sure.

She changed out the empty saline bag, replaced it and then injected something into one of the ports. The change was almost instantaneous. The world stopped spinning and his stomach stopped heaving like he was on the high seas.

"God, that drug is magic." And one of the few his body seemed to tolerate.

"I'm adding in a fast-working antihistamine. It will make you thirsty."

"He's definitely thirsty," Ry joked, and Calhoun contemplated if it would be worth it to punch Ry in the face.

"If you feel better, perhaps your mood will improve, inspiring you to be more compliant so you can get out of the hospital faster," J said, ignoring Ry's sexual inuendo.

"My mood?"

"Calhoun recently exited army Special Forces, Doctor," Ry said helpfully. "He's accustomed to the finer things in life—silk dressing gowns, caviar and room service."

Calhoun snorted his disagreement. It hit too close to home. That crap was more his dad's taste than it had ever been his.

"Marriage hasn't improved your humor," Calhoun said, running his hands through Kai's fur to comfort and check for injury.

It seemed he'd been quick enough to get his bestie out of

harm's way. How the hell had he been so stupid? He'd still been on a sexual high from J, and then he'd seen Kai and Ry, and he'd hurried out into Main Street, Montana, like it was a one-horse town and bam, flat on his ass.

"J, what's your name?"

"Dr. Quinn," she said in an affronted teacher style that was cute as hell.

"There's my boy." Ryder fist-bumped him, and J all but rolled her eyes. If Ryder only knew, but Calhoun didn't want his brother to know.

"Dr. Quinn," Ryder said like a star pupil. "I have Calhoun's duffel. I can get him in some sweats if you'd like, Doctor."

"The gown works better for our needs," J said. "I am going to need to monitor his legs closely this evening for potential compartment syndrome."

She sounded calm as if whatever that was, was no big deal. He needed his phone to google.

"Is that what they call it?" Ryder murmured, and Calhoun's weakness was starting to freak him out. He needed to get out of here. Hole up for a couple of days. He didn't want Ryder or his buddies to know how badly he'd been injured.

"The nurse will put your gown on now, Mr. Miller. You will not fight us on this." J's voice was steel and the expression on her delicate features were still determined. He had an immature impulse to kiss that professional mask off her face forever.

Kai alerted as J and the blonde nurse approached. Both he and Ry had their hands on Kai and spoke in unison. "At ease," they both said.

Ryder lifted Kai off the bed, and took him across the room and sat in a chair, his hand fully on the harness.

J examined Calhoun, her expression relaxed, professional, and her hands had a deft, impersonal touch that irritated him. She was nothing like the wild woman from last night. Nothing—because he was the patient. Not a man.

Demoralized Calhoun stared at the ceiling, and for the first time, he began to worry that he'd been badly hurt.

"I can stitch this closed for you tonight on my next round," J said. "Or I can put a call into Dr. Gallagher, and she can do it tomorrow morning. She left the drain in out of an abundance of caution."

J peeled off her gloves, and Calhoun wished he didn't find that hot. What was wrong with him? She was worried about crossing the line and being unprofessional, but he was the one behaving like a creeper.

"I saw no sign of compartment syndrome," she said, meeting his eyes, and her remote expression was that of a stranger and he felt dismissed, old, irritated.

"Dr. Telford wants you assessed every hour, and the nurse and I will follow his instructions. How is your pain level?"

"No pain meds."

"Pain level?"

He liked this J who took none of his crap and insisted on having her professional way. She was two sides of the same coin. Two sides, he mused, watching her and speculating what it would take to get her to see him as a man again.

He'd always had a bit too much ego.

But thinking of coins made him remember the medallion that he'd given to Ryder for safekeeping.

How was he going to honor Jace if he was injured?

*I'm not that injured.*

"If you had pain meds on board, it would help me to monitor for signs of compartment syndrome."

There was that ominous word again.

"Compartment syndrome?" Calhoun didn't like the sound of that, and his pain level sucked—everything hurt, legs, ribs torso—but he wasn't about to tell her that. "What's that?"

"I'll get you some literature," J said. "And keep your clothes on."

"Said no woman ever, bro," Ryder said.

The light in J's eyes shut off, and her professional mask tightened. "I'll leave you gentlemen to visit."

She made the word 'gentlemen' sound like a curse.

"Ouch." Ryder grinned as the door closed.

"She does need to work on her bedside manner," Calhoun observed trying not to take J's coolness personally, though he was, and it kicked up his competitive edge.

She'd rocked his world last night. Tonight, he was her patient.

Ryder pulled out his phone. He texted someone and then was scrolling.

"What are you doing?" Calhoun's skin was still crawling from whatever pain meds they'd last tried. Apparently the antihistamine didn't kick in as fast as the anti-nausea drug.

He reached for the cup of water with a straw, but it was too far, and his core screamed when he tried to move, like he was an out-of-shape ninety. Great. Ryder handed him the cup.

"Researching compartment syndrome. Not good. But since you're not showing signs of trauma twelve hours after impact, that's good. Usually shows up soon after the trauma."

Ryder sounded perky, the bastard. "Trauma," Calhoun muttered. "All over the world in dozens of hot spots, and I get frickin' felled on Main Street, Montana."

"Cross is on his way. We'll take shifts just in case the doctors and nurses are too busy to check on you tonight."

"I'm fine. I'll be better when you get me out of here." He tried again to sit up but winced and Rydwe's glare had him settling back down again.

"At least get the tube out of your chest first before you go Supermanning out any windows. Geeze, I practically vouched for you. Oh. Here." Ryder handed him the charm he'd been keeping safe. "This can keep your mind occupied while you're waiting for Dr. Not Amused or Impressed to return and stick you with more needles."

# Chapter Seven

PULL IT TOGETHER. *You are a professional.*

She might not have much, but she had her career.

Jory checked in on the next two patients on the floor, introduced herself, and logged on to the computer. This she could do. Review charts. Check on progress. Confer with patients, nurses, discuss the treatments with family and verify that all was well.

She headed to the next patient's room, her fingers idly fiddling with the medallion through the fabric of her scrubs and the soft, thin body suit she always wore underneath for warmth and comfort. She'd put the chain on as an impulse, and now she wasn't sure how she felt about it—holding her back or pushing her forward? As a kid she'd worn it proudly, but under her clothing so no one would tease her or ask about it. Then she'd worn it as a talisman to lead her brother and father home.

She swallowed a rueful smile. She'd lost hope a long time ago, but still, she always thought Josiah would find her. She'd looked for him, online, but nothing. Perhaps her father had changed their names. Now she felt that by wearing the necklace she was once again calling out to her brother, soul-to-soul.

She reached for it, thinking she should take it off but hesitated. The medallion was all she had from her past, and she needed to own it so she could move on.

"Excuse me, Dr. Quinn." A nurse hovered at the door as she made a note in the computer.

"Yes." She looked up. Tall, blonde, sparkling blue eyes, bright pink lips and a dazzling smile.

"The patient in room 310 has asked for you about the drain. You'd mentioned you could take it out?" The nurse looked friendly, expectant, and Jory wondered if she should recognize her from high school. There had been a lot of tall, blonde cowgirl and rodeo queen beauties, and she had tried to fly under all of their radars.

She checked her phone. Dr. Sam Gallagher had texted back a thumbs-up.

"Yes, I can." She steeled herself. He was a patient like any other. Professionally she couldn't ignore him. "Are you free to assist?"

Puzzlement flashed over the nurse's features and then enthusiasm.

"Certainly, Doctor. You might not remember me. We were in chemistry together. I was a sophomore. You were a freshman and got the highest score on every project and test that Mr. Lynch had ever had in twenty years of teaching. Rhianna Masters—MacIntyre now. Are you home in Marietta to stay?"

The nurse had a little hop in her step like that would be a good thing. Why would she care? And yes, she remembered her now. She'd been a highly ranked barrel racer and had worn rhinestones on everything and sparkling eye shadow, lip gloss and cheek bronzer. She'd glittered like Christmas every day.

"I'm a traveling hospitalist," Jory said. "Marietta was the only opening in Montana, and they had a high need, but it's only for two months."

"Oh." Rhianna's wattage dimmed a little. "I was hoping you were home for good. It would be nice to have a hospitalist who understands the community and is invested."

Jory nearly tripped over her Dansko clogs—and that had nothing, absolutely nothing to do with the fact that they stood together outside room 310.

The usual excuses burbled up—she liked to travel and wasn't ready to settled in one place, but Rhianna looked so sincere that Jory couldn't mouth the lie.

And it was a lie.

She'd been running.

"I make more money doing locums." Jory surprised herself with the truth. "I'm still paying down my school loans, and I help out my mom and grandma. They sold up and moved to California."

What was she doing—bonding?

Rhianna nodded like she seemed to do everything—brightly.

"I still have college loans too. My husband Dillon—you probably remember him—he was a rodeo cowboy and buckled a lot. He and Rohan Telford were always neck and neck in the stats. He joined the army and did two tours so he could get most of his college paid for. We lived with my folks so we could save enough to buy a place. I have a daughter and a son. My mom was helping with childcare, which is why I work the evening shifts, but now that Dillon has finished his degree, and is working regular hours, he'll cover the evenings I'm working."

It was a lot of unasked for information, and Jory wasn't sure how to respond.

"Sounds like you've got it all worked out," she finally said as Rhianna seemed to expect something.

Rhianna nodded. "We have a house in town, and my folks still have their twenty acres, so I keep my horses there and still ride. Dillon and I are hoping to buy them out when they're ready to retire. Keep the land—small as it is—in the family. Dillon's family sold their land, and some influencer bought it and created some monolithic horror and gated it all up like they're some A-lister. Sad."

Jory nodded. Her family land was gone too. She'd thought good riddance. But then she wasn't planning on having a family.

She steeled her shoulders. She'd stalled long enough. Usually she didn't engage in small talk with staff, but it had actually felt natural.

"Sure you want me in there?" Rhianna whispered. "It's pretty crowded with all that ex-military testosterone surging." She winked at Jory like she hadn't been the town outcast and object of pity, "but I'll protect you." Rhianna winked.

*Like we are friends and colleagues.*

Something hot gushed in her, and for a moment she was panicked that she would start crying right there outside of a patient's door.

"Definitely I want you in there with me."

Rhianna grinned. "I'll play bodyguard and deflect the man eye candy."

"I'm more worried about the dog."

Rhianna evidently found that hilarious. "Kai is a sweety." She laughed. "Military dogs are highly trained as long as you don't pose a threat, but even then, Kai's handler would have to give the attack command."

"That's supposed to be reassuring?"

"At least Mr. Miller doesn't have a catheter in. That makes men cranky."

And as a professional, Jory should not be feeling so flushed.

She rapped on the door and eased it open. There were now three large men in the room, along with her patient, who was sitting up in bed, looking mildly pissed.

"Huck could sew me up. You should have brought him and sprung me."

"Not until you're healed, and Huck has baby duty," a large man with witch-black hair to his shoulders said, leaning against the closed bathroom door.

The room pulsed with masculine energy. Rohan smiled at her.

"Hey, Jory, good to see you again. Rhianna." He dipped his head like he was still wearing his hat.

Rhianna grinned and waved. "See you brought backup. Y'all could be a cowboy boy band, Rohan."

Rohan snorted. "How'd it go at the house, Jory? Did you exorcise any ghosts?"

"I think your reconstruction and remodeling booted any spirits," she said softly and immediately wished she'd spoken with more power because Mr. Otis Calhoun Lael-Miller was watching her like she was a target. "You'll need to clear the room. Kai, too. Nurse McIntyre and I will take out the drain since it's no longer needed. Less risk of infection."

Rhianna shooed the men out, but Kai remained at attention at the patient's side. Yes, she would just think of O as the patient. That would help. What would help more would be if he'd look more like an invalid, but no, Calhoun had arms like cinder blocks and highly defined abs—no mere six-pack for this man, but an eight.

"How are you feeling?" She nervously fiddled with her medallion, but quickly crossed her arms.

"Like an idiot."

Jory didn't know much about the accident, but looking

at his chart, he must have been hit soon after leaving the Graff Hotel. Guilt niggled. He wouldn't have been at the Graff if she'd behaved herself like she always did.

Rhianna bustled around the room, getting the materials that Jory would need.

"I need to grab some lidocaine, Doctor."

Damn.

"Leave the door open, please, Nurse MacIntyre." She sounded like a pompous ass.

Rhianna shot her a surprised look but pulled the privacy curtain and swung the door wide.

O's grin was feral. "Maybe it's a good thing Kai stayed? Worried you'll jump me? Do I need protection from the randy doctor?"

"No. Certainly not, and this is not funny, Mr. Miller."

"Please. I've been inside you."

"Shshshsh," she hissed at him. "Not one word more. You aren't funny. This is…" How could he not see how wrong the situation was? "You are in a vulnerable state, and I am in a position of authority, and…" She broke off as he groaned and pinched his nose.

"What's wrong?" She quickly approached him, hands out ready to assess his ribs, his incision, his pulse points in his feet. "Are you in pain?"

"Psychological pain for being such a dumb-ass that I didn't look before I ran into a street and got caught between the grille of a teenager late to high school English and texting, and another construction worker doing a bakery run for his colleagues and trying to get there before the coffee cooled. Do you know how stupid that sounds?"

"That's why it's called an accident."

"The sooner I get out of here, the sooner I can put the whole moment of stupid behind me."

He didn't say it, but she had a feeling that he wanted to put last night in his rearview as well.

*Which is what I want too.*

But looking at him sitting up, bare-chested, slash of color across his cheeks, and his eyes glittering almost bronze with temper, he was utterly tempting.

*Patient, pervert.*

"I can't release you tonight, Mr. Miller."

"Stop with that mister crap, Jory."

"You are my patient. Patient. I could lose my license."

"Why?"

Her mouth dropped open but no words emerged.

"Will you medically treat me if I say I won't sleep with you again?"

Jory strode to the door and closed it firmly.

"You can't say things like that, Mr. Miller."

"Calhoun. Say it."

"Why?"

"You never said it last night. Say it now."

"You didn't tell me your name. I didn't tell you mine. It was deliberate. We had a deal."

"And now?"

"There is no now?" she whispered, her anger fizzling to terror. "I could lose everything, Calhoun. Everything I've worked for. My license. I'd have nothing. No way to pay my loans. Help my family."

He said nothing for a long moment, and Jory felt that she was the one stripped naked.

"You are a patient," she whispered.

"Don't sell me so short. I would never hurt you. Never."

His voice rang with honesty, anger. But so much was at stake.

Rhianna knocked and opened the door, lidocaine in her hand, she looked at the door and then at Jory, a little quizzical. Relieved, Jory approached Calhoun—no, the patient.

"I won't be a patient for long, Dr. Quinn," he said quietly.

Jory deftly removed the drain, and quickly stitched the small wound closed. She could have let Rhianna take over, but Jory knew Calhoun was going to push his limits and perhaps impede his recovery. She checked his incision site, put the back of her hand on his forehead and back of his neck even as Rhianna took out the thermometer.

"I'm going to run a quick diagnostic to check for signs of compartment syndrome. What's your pain level?" she asked as she examined his lower legs. Wow they were powerful.

"Depends on the type of pain." He grinned and tried to catch her gaze, and it took more effort this time to not respond.

"Physical."

"I'm used to pain, working through it. My insides feel like they were put in a blender, and my ribs are screaming at an eight, but I'll deal. I heal fast and I don't want any pain meds. I need a clear head. I got a little job to do—a problem to solve so Kai and I can be on our way. Not getting bit by whatever magical love juice my brothers swallowed at the town watering hole."

"Good luck with that, Mr. Miller," Rhianna chimed in. "This town is full of cowboys and single women looking to lasso one."

"Hard pass."

"Famous last words," Rhianna said, her wedding ring sparking in the fluorescent lighting. "All cowboys get roped. You know why?"

"Nurse, I have other patients to see," Jory said, starting to feel claustrophobic. If Calhoun didn't stop looking at her like he was mentally taking her clothes off, she was going to melt.

"Why do they get roped?" Calhoun asked like it mattered.

Rhianna winked. "Because they want to."

"All of them?"

Jory peeled off her gloves, determined to ignore the flirty teasing or whatever it was. She was so bad at the social stuff.

"All of them."

Rhianna opened the door, and with raised eyebrows at Jory, who nodded, Rhianna left the door open as she returned to the nursing station.

"I was a cowboy once."

This had to stop.

"Mr. Miller." She marched to his bed as she spoke, keeping her voice low.

"Calhoun."

"You have to stop flirting, or whatever you're doing. I told you I'm not good with social things and too much is at stake."

"What the hell is that?" O reached for her necklace that had fallen out of her shirt. "Where'd you get this?"

He sounded like a cop.

She tried to pull her medallion back to tuck it back into her shirt, but it was between his fingers. "Where'd you get it, Jory?"

"It's mine. It's a family…" How to describe it. "A gift. A family crest of sorts although my family wasn't a family that had crests. Delusions of grandeur or wishful thinking on my great-grandfather's part."

She pulled the medallion back with more force, suddenly frightened. She tucked it deep into her shirt, but she wanted to pull it off, tuck it in her pocket and run.

Her pulse pounded and she flushed as if with fever.

"I don't believe you're at risk to develop compartment syndrome, but I'm still keeping you under ob…" she stumbled over the very familiar word as in this setting it suddenly sounded pervey "…servation for twenty-four hours, and… Stop."

Calhoun was trying to sit up again, and his grimace of pain felt like a flaming dart shooting through her.

This man. Didn't he know how to not push it?

Jory held him in place and pushed the button on the remote to raise the bed.

"Follow the rules," she said. "You're going to reinjure yourself and have to stay longer."

"No. I have to get out of here. I have things to do."

"What things?"

His face twisting in pain, he reached for his dog's harness. He dangled something between his fingers and Jory felt the blood drain from her face. Her lips felt numb, frozen, and her ears buzzed, and she could hear and feel her heart thump.

"Where'd you get that?" she whispered, swaying on her feet.

She felt the intensity of his stare blaze over her like a torch, but she still felt as if she'd been struck by an arctic blast, but before Calhoun said anything, she heard the alarm for a code blue. Her training kicked in and she pivoted and ran out the door.

# Chapter Eight

WHAT THE HELL was wrong with him? Had he hit his head in the accident?

Why had he insisted Jory say his name?

They weren't dating. He got it that she was playing it cool for her job, but he'd wanted her to acknowledge him as more than a patient, as more than the generic Mr. Miller, on a visceral level that still had him shaken.

And what was up with the medallion?

How could she possibly have a duplicate and not be involved in his vow for Jace—like his brothers' now wives?

Calhoun felt like he was going to throw up again, and it had nothing to do with the pain meds that were finally working their way out of his system.

"The doctor went flying out of here." Ryder breezed back in without knocking. "Something you said?"

Cross and Rohan were on his six. Seemed like some things were easier to change than others.

"You're going need to up your woman-winning skills now that you're out. You can't just look silent and tough at the off-base bar," Ryder advised, helping Kai back up on the bed so he didn't jump and hurt Calhoun.

Even with his brothers back, he felt like Jory had taken all the warmth and life energy with her.

"What scared her off?" Ryder teased. "You practicing your moves now that you're embarking on a business venture with us?" Ryder's tone was teasing, but Calhoun heard the question behind it.

Calhoun didn't know much about a potential business. Jace had mentioned pooling their resources, but he didn't know what he wanted to do. The future looked gray—fuzzy around the edges. But helping his brothers launch a business would be a good use of his money. He needed to play it cool. Find out what they needed before he staked his claim, but he didn't want to personally commit.

*Story of my life.*

"What's up with that?" Cross, arms crossed, leaning against the wall, jerked his head at the medallion he still held wrapped in his hand.

"I don't know. Yet." Already his instincts hummed.

"I saw her touching something that looked similar when she blew outta here." Cross wouldn't let it go, and damn the man for never missing anything.

"You knew her name." Calhoun stared down Rohan, ignoring Cross's question.

"Huck should be here. Wolf too if we're going to break the rules," Rohan said, unyielding.

"What rule?" Calhoun demanded, irritated. He hurt like hell, and he hated that he wasn't just soldiering through it like Jace would have. Jace had been hit, badly, and he knew his time was running out, yet he'd still barked orders into his com even as he choked on his blood. Huck had desperately tried to stop Jace's bleeding even as Jace had slapped a pressure bandage on Huck's gaping neck wound instead of one on his own.

And Calhoun had scooped up Kai. Stopped his bleeding and returned fire, leaving Huck alone with Jace.

He dragged his attention back to now, not wanting to remember his animalistic retreat as he fought through the enemy lines to retreat to the extraction point with his team. It was one of the few failures to complete their mission.

"Who is she?" He stared down Rohan.

So much for their agreement to remain strangers. Calhoun knew her name and job and that she hummed when she went down on him but little else.

"Jory Quinn," Rohan said after a long beat of silence.

"And?"

Rohan shrugged and didn't meet his gaze, whereas he and Cross faced off across the small hospital room like rival sentries.

"What's so top secret about who she is?" And how the hell did he hook up with the one woman who held a key to the mystery he was supposed to solve? The statistical probability of that was laughable, and spooky.

He looked at his three Coyote brothers. They'd come here for Jace. They'd stayed. Made lives.

*Maybe…*

No. He shut himself down. He was not going to continue the Lael-Miller DNA strands. The toxicity and greed and narcissistic selfishness wouldn't die with him unfortunately—he had four sisters, and his parents had siblings, but he wasn't going to contribute.

"We took a vow," Cross's voice rumbled like it had been released from a cage. "No shirking. No sharing deets until the task is complete."

Pain screamed through him, fingernailing down his patience.

"You all had a specific, knowable task from Jace," he accused.

"And you just got a shiny medal?" Cross said softly.

Calhoun wanted to flip him off, but he was too tired. Bone-deep.

"I could use some help." The minute the word was out, he regretted it. Three pair of eyes drilled into him.

"We're always here for you," Cross said. "You know that but looks like you got a lead for your task with the petite doctor who has eyes full of stars."

Calhoun felt helpless in the bed, at a total disadvantage, like his entire childhood and anger stirred in his gut. He grit his teeth so he wouldn't answer. This was how Cross got others—officers, soldiers, rebels, civvies, hostiles to spill their guts. He found their weak spot and poked until he got the information he needed.

"Throw me a bone about Jory," he said to Rohan. He needed a starting point.

To his surprise, Rohan looked uncomfortable. Then he looked at Cross, who nailed the Easter Island statue vibe. Primitive and aloof.

"Her story is her story to tell," Rohan finally said, his voice firm, but there was a hint of sadness in it that hit Calhoun dead center in his chest.

"Since you're not getting sprung tonight, one of us will be back for your sorry carcass tomorrow," Cross said. "We'll get you and Kai set up so you can heal and start your hunt."

Calhoun would make his own plans. He wasn't ever going to be under anyone else's control again.

"I'll walk Kai again before I leave and feed him, and I'll be back O five hundred to walk him and feed him again," Ryder said. "I'm heading out on the road again Thursday morning. I can take Kai with me."

"I'll be mobile," Calhoun said, not letting doubt in.

"I know," Ryder said. "But…" He trailed off. Took a treat from his pocket and fed it to Kai without him having to do anything. "The first few weeks out are tough," he said. "Tougher than I thought. Keeping busy helped, but I googled a splenectomy. Hard on the body. You're going to need to take it easy for a while, and that gives you time to think and…"

"I'll be fine, Mom," Calhoun said, and even as he spoke he wished he'd been kinder, remembering what Rohan had said. He hadn't thought about that. Ryder seeing Kai hurdle through the open window, his Coyote brother jump into the road to catch him. The one-two punch of moving steel.

"I got Kai, and I got my brothers." He softened his defensive anger.

Ryder bobbed his head, didn't look at him. "Yeah. Always."

And then he was gone, and Ryder had been right. All Calhoun had now was time to think. He wanted to avoid the dark hole his thoughts jumped into, but he feared he was going to drag Jory in there along with him.

THE TEAM HAD saved the mother and baby, and Jory was once again grateful for the big-city level-one trauma hospital where she had had the chance to do an extra year of training just for situations like this—unexpected and dire complications for what had first appeared to be a common medical event—giving birth.

She peeled off her gloves, washed her hands, sucked down a bottle of water and then made herself another coffee. Her first instinct was to go to Calhoun and demand to know where and when he'd been given her brother's medallion, but she had a chart to finish on the emergency and rounds to complete.

She needed to think, and she didn't want to confront

him with a very private conversation in front of his friends. She probably needed a witness every time she was in his room, but she didn't want an audience.

Her training saw her through the next hour, but her focus wasn't absolute because it often drifted off to a stunningly handsome, enigmatic man in room 310 who just might help her find her brother. Had he been a soldier? Had Calhoun and her brother been friends?

It was a little past eleven at night when she gently rapped on Calhoun's door, this time not bothering to ask Rhianna to accompany her.

He was awake. His dark honey gaze pinned her to the spot, and it was only with an effort that she walked into the room.

"Your dog on the bed is against medical advice."

Not the friendliest opening, but it could never be construed as flirty, and she wrapped herself in her professionalism like it was a scarf.

"Kai's my partner, not my dog."

"No partners in bed with you in a hospital setting," she countered, nearly wagging a finger at him, but by the way his gaze was already glinting with light, she had a feeling he wasn't taking her seriously, so she didn't need to add fuel to that fire.

*Note to self: never sleep with a future patient.*

Like she'd need that reminder. Jory had thrown caution to the wind last night with Calhoun. She didn't think a repeat was in the cards.

"No partners, ever?" He raised one eyebrow, and her insides lit up with heat like he'd flipped a speech.

"Where'd you get the medallion?" she demanded.

Regret lit his face, and Jory's legs wobbled.

"Sit," he said.

"I'm your doctor," she answered, drawing the lines.

"Doctors don't sit?"

"Sometimes. If it's bad news." She drew each word out, feeling like they might tangle in her throat. "Did you know my brother Josiah? Josiah Quinn?"

Calhoun's hands rested on Kai, who lay tucked next to Calhoun's body. He began to stroke the dog, whose expression remained alert, and his steady gaze never left her face.

Jory felt tired. She wished she could sit, pet the dog, drop her wall just for a moment. What would that be like—to have Calhoun trust her, to have his dog trust her? To be able to trust them both?

"No, Jory," he said, his voice kind like it had been last night. "I didn't know your brother. Tell me about him."

She fiddled with her medallion, nervously, wondering if she should take it off so that they could compare them, but no, she'd seen it. They were close enough.

"My dad and brother took off one Saturday when I was eight. Josiah was ten. They never came back. Never contacted any of us again."

Calhoun absorbed her words, head bent toward Kai, as if

conferring, but she knew she was being imaginative, wasn't she? But she'd heard that dogs and their handlers could have an almost spiritual connection, and Jory wanted to cry as longing pierced her. To have a close friend. A lover. Family. Someone who got her, so she wasn't always outside in the snow with a storm barreling down.

"I'm sorry, Jory."

She'd expected more questions.

Calhoun sat up in bed, sheets pooled around his waist, looking like an athletic celebrity 'It boy' prepared for a photo shoot. She'd see designer underwear ads featuring A-list actors who looked less physically perfect. Never had any patient post-trauma and post-surgery glow so determinedly with good heath. His expression was somber. She had a feeling he was worried.

She braced herself for his answer. "How..." She licked her dry lips. "How did you get the medallion? Did...did you serve with a Josiah Adam Quinn?" She balled her fists, unable to ask the follow-up.

The room was silent. Jory lowered herself into the chair on the bed.

This was bad. Worse than she'd thought even though she'd thought plenty about where her father and brother might be, but she'd always held out hope once she'd gone to college. Josiah would find her when they were adults. For whatever reason her father had taken him and raised him, Josiah would find his sister. He'd been a wonderful big brother. Kind when no one else had been.

"Any coffee for a wounded warrior?"

She didn't have to look at his chart. She knew it by heart. She also knew he would ignore medical advice.

Coffee. Of course he wanted coffee. But then so did she, and he could probably use the distraction as much as she could.

She grabbed the straw from his water bottle and jammed it into the hole in the lid of her coffee. She shoved it at him.

He looked at her handiwork. "Seriously? Why not get me a sippy cup while you're at it."

Sippy cup. Kids. Condom mishap. Heat flushed her cheeks and she stared at Kai instead of Calhoun.

"And that reminds me though I haven't forgotten," he said softly.

Jory slumped in her chair, hand up. "I don't want to talk about it. We're talking about my brother's medallion."

She jerked up as another, less ominous thought occurred. "Did you find it at a pawn shop or something?" Although the medallion had no value since her great-grandfather and then grandfather had destroyed the historic coins with their 'artistry' and desire for the family tree to appear more…epic?

"We need to talk about the condom. I don't walk away from responsibility." An expression fleeted across his face, and Jory stared, fascinated.

"Did you take the Plan B like you said?" His voice sounded as neutral as a robot's, and guilt whispered through her.

"No," she admitted.

For a moment he said nothing. His gaze never wavered, and she wondered what was going on in that handsome, far too complicated head.

"Is there a medical consequence for you if you do take it? Side effects?"

She rolled her eyes. "There's always a consequence for the woman," she snapped without meaning to.

"I meant health wise. I imagined it would be uncomfortable."

"It's an emergency contraception pill that contains a synthetic hormone levonorgestrel, which prevents ovulation." Probably more than he wanted to hear and hearing herself say the words was a slap in her face because she, Dr. Jory Quinn, career woman who'd never once thought she'd marry or have children, had felt paralyzed taking a course of action that she would have unhesitatingly—and had—recommended for a patient.

She sat there waiting another dose of judgment.

"I would imagine that you would need to take the pill soon after having sex."

His voice was horribly neutral, and Jory felt it like a lash.

She nodded. "I'm still within the window of time," she said, wondering if he expected her to run down to the pharmacy right now and pop the pill in front of him. And why didn't she?

"I feel…I feel…like a stranger to myself," she admitted to him, not meaning to. "I've always supported women and their choices for themselves and their families. When I was in medical school, I volunteered at a domestic violence shelter and also for a rape crisis hotline, and I helped many women access the Plan B and other medications."

So why hadn't she swallowed it with her latte from the staff lounge when she'd come in tonight? She looked at him as if he'd have the answer.

"I'm not sure of the right thing to say," he said, his expression shuttered.

"You don't have to say anything," she said. "It's my situation."

"Our situation." He stepped on her words.

"It's unlikely that there is a situation," Jory shot back, standing up and then sitting back down again.

Frustration was stamped on Calhoun's handsome features, and he pressed his lips together as if not wanting to say something that would piss her off, which was funny because Jory's emotions were all over the map and she couldn't begin to grab one to react to.

"Tell me about my brother."

"I CAN'T."

Her midnight eyes flashed—first shock, then anger.

He could watch the storm of emotions in her eyes all day. It countered how dead he felt inside. No. Now that he had Kai with him, he knew he could reengage with the world. It was alone he shut everything down. And Jory—not his teammates—threatened to pull the lid off.

"But you have his medallion. There were two presented. Father to son. Only I was a girl, so my grandfather made another. It was the one time I felt..." she ducked her head as if trying to hide her feelings "...special," she whispered.

There was a wealth of feeling in that last world.

Calhoun's father had been like that—a man who wanted a son. The son would be lavished with attention. The girls ignored. Only it hadn't gone that way at all. His shriveled heart pinched a little, and the ache in his side burned for his angry sisters and for his father's brand of attention, but he shut down the memories.

He was built tough.

Honed in fire and steeped in insults and scathing disappointment.

The army had ground him to a fine point of a weapon and unleashed him. He could handle cracked ribs and missing organs.

"I was in the army. Special Forces. Our team leader..." His words sounded like gravel in his throat.

Jory handed him her coffee again. Her kindness and rapt attention spurred him on. He took a deep draw of the coffee. It had a lot of milk in it—something he wasn't used to. It felt like a luxury.

*One day out and I'm injured and going soft. Distracted.*

On a mission, that could get him and his team killed. He only had one mission left, and he'd nearly blown it before it had started. Lost condom, distracted thoughts. He hadn't commanded Kai to stay. Kai had acted on instinct and so had he. Bitterness squatted on his chest, accusing. Maybe he was as dumb and soft as his father had claimed.

"Our team leader was Jace McBride. He was weeks from mustering out and coming home to Marietta, but he didn't make it home. He left a list of unfinished business, and each of us—we call ourselves the Coyote Cowboys because we'd all grown up ranch…" His mouth twisted up. If his brothers had seen the 'ranch' he'd grown up on, they would have laughed him out of the brotherhood. "We all came to Marietta to finish what Jace planned."

He was tired. His head was woozy. His ribs screamed with every movement, and he couldn't suck in enough air.

Jory was on her feet. She tilted his bed back at a slightly lower angle. Rinsed out the straw and added more water and ice chips.

She held the cup for him, and he drank greedily.

"You had blood loss from your damaged spleen. Not devastating as the hospital was so close, and the first responders were picking up their breakfasts to go at the Java Café a block away, but your body has suffered a trauma, Calhoun. You will need to rest, and if you won't take any meds for the pain, that raises your blood pressure. Necessitating rest and fluids. Infection is still a risk, and without a spleen, you won't have the same immunity to viruses and bacteria, necessitating rest—more than you're probably used to needing."

He wanted to rest. Close his eyes and just turn off. But that wasn't fair to her. Or Jace.

He had a mission. One last responsibility for someone else and then he could lead his life as he pleased.

Unless Jory was pregnant.

His eyes snapped open.

He truly was the F-up his father had sneeringly proclaimed.

"We all had tasks. There were five. We each drew one out of Jace's helmet and had a year to complete it. I was delayed a few more months on a mission with the temporary new team leader."

"What's my brother's medallion have to do with your task? Did you serve with him? Did Jace?" She had sat down, but now jerked to standing like someone had pulled her strings. "How did Jace or you get the medallion? Did my brother die in battle, and the medallion is all that's..." Her eyes teared up, and her voice dropped to a whisper. "Left? Oh. God."

Jory bent over, her chest to her legs, and sucked in breath after breath, and he hated that he couldn't go to her. She'd made it clear she didn't want anyone to know that they had a history though it was 'blink and you'll miss it' brief.

"I knew Jace McBride." She sat up again, wiping at her face, trying to compose herself. "Well, not really knew him, but his family had a ranch near our farm. They had more land and were more successful, but when I was a kid, their fortunes seemed to decline—not as fast or far as ours, but still. The cattle herds they ran got smaller each year. We'd stopped cattle soon after I was born."

"But how did he get the medallion? What is your task?" She was as bewildered as he was, only he had suspicions that grew with each piece of the puzzle Jory inadvertently provided.

"I don't know how he got it. Jace left a list of tasks, but not much information because he knew the details."

"Keep drinking the water." Jory sounded every inch his doctor.

"From what I surmised from trying to get intel from my teammates, their tasks were straightforward. Be a godfather to a friend's kid. Walk a sister down the aisle at her wedding. That sort of thing."

Jory didn't blink, but he could see her thoughts race across the sky of her eyes.

"Mine was more obscure. Open-ended."

*Creepy.*

"What was it?" Jory was on the edge of her seat, body angled forward, her pointed chin thrust out as if she suspected it was going to be bad, and she needed to be braced for the hit.

He wondered if she'd had to steel herself for a rolling barrage of storms growing up as he'd had to do. There was strength in her, even though she was physically small. Her spirit—her life energy, her quick brain felt expansive.

"What did your piece of paper say?"

"Find the bodies?"

# Chapter Nine

*FIND THE BODIES?* Jory repeated to herself, stunned.

Not an order but a question. Why had Calhoun phrased it like that? He wasn't a high school girl who turned statements into interrogatives squeaking up at the end of each sentence.

But Jory hadn't been able to quiz him any more that shift. She'd had more admissions from the ER, and another patient who'd had an emergency appendectomy. Being busy had helped to keep her mind off the potential ramifications of Calhoun's words.

Find the bodies?

Maybe Jace hadn't been sure?

But why had he thought there'd be bodies? And whose? And when had he found the medallion? And why had none of the McBrides come forward twenty-three years ago with any suspicions of foul play?

*Foul play.*

It sounded like a mystery novel, not her life.

But when her father and brother had taken off, it seemed like eventually the whole town knew, and had drawn the conclusion that Jesse Quinn was with a woman or gambling his way across the country.

No one had taken her mother's concerns seriously—especially not the police or the sheriff's office.

Never once had Jory heard anything that intimated that her father and brother had been killed and buried.

She shivered.

She'd checked on Calhoun through the night, taking his vitals because Rhianna had been freaked out by the dog's focused stare, and Jory hadn't minded because if Calhoun woke, she wanted to ask more questions, though she wasn't sure where she would begin.

And now she had a dilemma.

She was off shift. Calhoun would probably be released today as he'd push, push, push to get out of the hospital and his former…what had he called them…Coyote Cowboys would help him. The brotherhood. Just thinking that made her feel more alone. But that likely accounted for the huge coyote in hunt mode he had over one pectoral and across his shoulder that she'd—

Jory cut off that thought. Her lusty explorations of Calhoun's body needed to remain in her vault of memories.

But now she couldn't just let him drive down Highway 89 like she'd intended. He might have information she could use to keep searching for her brother. She'd started doing social media searches in college—only setting up her own sites hoping Josiah would be looking.

But he hadn't.

And maybe he'd never really left Marietta.

No, she was going to have to get more information from Calhoun. If he intended to track down the mystery of her father and brother's disappearing act, she intended to be by his side.

She debriefed her colleagues, and then hesitated. Should she change into street clothes—meet with Calhoun as Jory or as Dr. Quinn?

And while she nibbled her lip in indecision, Rohan arrived at the nursing station well before normal visiting hours.

"Hey, Jory, can I talk to you, real quick?"

"Yes, but I can't discuss Cal…Mr. Miller's case with you."

Rohan grinned. "That big lug is bulletproof, and no he's not going to follow doctor's orders, but I have a plan that might keep him minimally contained."

"That sounds as if you're skirting legal limits."

Rohan laughed, and the nurses who were entering for their shifts as the others prepared to leave all looked up, and Jory felt like she'd been doing something unprofessional, but Rohan waved his hat in the air that he'd likely taken off when he'd entered the hospital.

"Ladies, gentlemen," he said expansively. "Thank you all for your skill and service to the community of Marietta."

"Rohan, are you going to challenge Chelsea Collier Flint for mayor in the next election?" Rhianna teased. "Bye, Dr. J, see you tonight."

Jory waved and smiled wanly, wondering if she should object to the nickname. It sounded cute, not professional, but it also seemed like a sign of acceptance and though she was only here for a couple of months, her worried heart warmed a little.

"I wanted to nail down if you've decided for sure if you plan to stay at the house for the duration of your time in Marietta?"

She nibbled on her lip. How much did Rohan know about Calhoun's plans or his task? He too must have had to do something, and curiosity stirred.

"You said you had some things you wanted to sort through," Rohan reminded her as if she might forget she was supposed to dig through her past.

He looked so appealing, as if he wanted her to take the house, but why? And then she wondered if he was maybe wanting it for Calhoun's recovery.

No way. Her heart jumped into her throat.

*But he was no longer a patient.*

And he wasn't in any shape for a repeat performance.

*Am I?*

The night with Calhoun had woken something in her that she wanted to go back to sleep. She didn't want to crave a man. Wait for him to call or come home. Her father's disappearance had devastated her mother. She'd had to prop up colleagues who'd lost their sense of purpose when heartbreak hit.

She couldn't risk financial future or heartbreak just for good sex—even excellent sex.

"Sorry to hit you with this now, Jory." Rohan looked sincere, but he smiled, full of confidence. "You're probably exhausted after a long shift. I just wanted to get Calhoun somewhat settled so he doesn't overdo it, but I'd have better luck keeping the sun from rising."

He did want Calhoun to stay at the house with her.

Her stupid heart leapt, and her hormones practically gushed.

*Stand down.*

Jory pulled her attention away from her own troubled doubts and focused on Rohan. He looked really worried about his friend, and she felt like she'd split open wider. No one had ever worried about her since Josiah and her father had disappeared.

And she was surprised that she felt a stab of disappointment that she wouldn't be staying at her old house—ridiculous because the Graff was really too expensive, and she felt too shaken to launch a temporary apartment hunt. Maybe the hospital could help.

"Rohan, it's your father's house now. Of course your friend can stay there. But he probably shouldn't be alone for at least a few days. He's showing no signs of infection, but…"

"Exactly," Rohan verbally pounced. "He shouldn't be alone, and so I was thinking that if you'd decided the house suited, you both could be roomies. Calhoun could recover. He's got something to do for a friend," Rohan said evasively, "and my dad is hoping for his help on something for the ranch when he's back to one hundred percent, so he'd be gone during the day once he's healed up, and you'd be gone most nights."

*But not all.*

Why was that her first thought? She had no idea she had such a lusty libido. She stared at Rohan, trying to think of an objection, but she was picturing Calhoun lounging shirtless on the couch, and her mind just spun and spun, and her mouth dried, but the rest of her went liquid.

"It sounds great to you too." Rohan slapped his hands together, and she jumped. "Perfect. You put my mind at ease. We'll get Calhoun moved in when he's sprung. Let me know if you need help moving. The brothers will do a grocery run for y'all—the least we can do. Food preferences?"

His words rushed over her like an open fire hose, and she was surprised he didn't pull a pen out of someplace on his body and start taking notes.

"Wait. What?"

"Win-win." Rohan smiled, and she had a dirty suspicion that when he used that smile, pretty much no one said no to him.

"But I didn't say yes," she objected.

"Say yes."

She opened her mouth to say no. She had reasons. A lot.

But Calhoun might have answers she needed. And her lifelong frugality was shouting the word 'yes.' It wasn't like she was what her oma called a 'hot dish' that Calhoun would want to take bites of.

"I'll think about it," she tempered her reply, but Rohan's green eyes flared.

"I'll take that as a yes."

CALHOUN SNAPPED THE leash on Kai before he steeled himself to exit Rohan's truck. He hated that he had to concentrate to maneuver his large body out of the truck. Worse, he mentally counted the steps to the small farmhouse, and it seemed far away. He couldn't remember ever feeling this weak. He was exhausted just from the drive from the hospital, and he ached like he'd gone on a twenty-mile run across sand with a full pack. He hated it more that Ryder had felt the need to follow them out of town, fifteen minutes on the highway and then another twenty on several gravel roads. The last one rose up into the foothills of the Absaroka Mountains.

But the hardest to take was leashing Kai because they weren't on a mission, and Calhoun felt like he should have total confidence that he could control Kai, but yesterday when Kai had launched out of the window it had shaken his confidence.

And now Rohan was driving him out to the northernmost area of the ranch where they'd soon be moving their herds to summer grazing. He said there was a farmhouse, and he had what Calhoun suspected was a pity job offer. Ryder followed, driving Calhoun's truck, and Calhoun suspected, determined to ensure that Kai settled into the new digs.

He had no intention of becoming a project or a burden on his brothers, but he hadn't imagined the turn of the twentieth-century farmhouse would be so appealing. Small. Rustic. Clean lines. Wide covered wraparound porch. Huge oak tree providing shade and a windbreak and what looked like a large back patio with part of it covered. Two barns in the same white and green squatted as if waiting for approval.

"I can bunk in town," he said, but he didn't want to do that to Kai. Charity was hard to swallow, though, yet he was loath to tell his brothers about his trust fund. It sounded arrogant AF and would forever drive a wedge between them—othering him like he'd been othered all his life until he'd graduated West Point with honors and then had taken a different direction with his military service.

"No need," Rohan said. "My dad wants a presence on this part of the ranch. A caretaker to keep an eye on the cattle, the fences, the wildlife. Someone who can handle some isolation. We have drones, but cattle rustling is always a threat."

Calhoun shot him a look, seething with Rohan's reasoning. "Isn't rustling high tech now—done on a computer rather than cutting fences?" He thought back to his father's ranch, and it had been years ago since he'd been involved. "Animals just don't get loaded up at point A or unloaded at point B or entered into the finance system."

"Yes, but not always. Seriously, Calhoun, you're doing us a favor. A small salary comes with the caretaking along with a place to live, and when you're at full strength, we have plenty of need for assistance on the ranch during spring, summer and fall."

Rohan cleared his throat. "Also, the Coyotes and I have a business proposition when you're feeling more yourself."

If he didn't lie down soon, he was going to hurl. His stupidity yesterday was seriously humbling him, and he wanted to be alone to pull himself together. His ribs ached as did his right hip. Even his shins hurt, and he couldn't draw a deep breath.

Look at him like some delicate Victorian miss with the vapors needing a fainting couch. He despised weakness. It bit too close to the bone and reminded him of his father.

"I'm paying rent," he grit out.

"You can rock paper scissors Jory for who's going to pay. She's as stubborn and proud as you."

"Jory?"

*WTF?*

"I'm not auditioning for whatever Montana bachelor auction you Montana idiots are rockin'," he said, stung by their clumsy attempts to set him up so he was ball-and-chained like they were.

"Who am I to fight fate?" Rohan grinned.

Ryder carried Calhoun's duffel bags into the house as if they weighed nothing, and Calhoun's anger at his body's weakness hit like a rogue wave, nearly taking him down.

Kai sat beside him, attention on his face, and he schooled his features, and tried to draw deeper breaths to calm himself, even though his right lung screamed in protest.

At least Kai hadn't attempted to follow Ryder.

*God, I'm jealous of Ryder's closeness with Kai.*

When he should be grateful.

A cloud of dust appeared down the road.

"Our cue to leave. Good luck, brother," Rohan lightly squeezed his shoulder. Even that screamed invalid.

Ryder sauntered out of the house. "This is a sweet set-up," Ryder enthused, his long stride eating up the distance. "Is the barn finished too?"

"We'll talk about that later," Rohan said, his voice a little cool, but Calhoun was hurting too much to pursue it now. Plus, he was seething at his brothers' clumsy attempts at a setup.

His life was as far from a rom-com as a man could get.

"You need help into the house?" Rohan asked as the three men and Kai tracked the approaching cloud of dust.

"No."

"Don't be so pissy," Ryder advised, not fazed by Calhoun's 'tude. "This will be solid practice to blow a little dust off your very dusty wooing skills."

"My what?"

"Exactly."

"Is Jory really coming?" How'd they persuaded her? She seemed as keen to forget their one-night stand as he was.

"That's up to you." Ryder slapped him on the back and he staggered.

He bit back an F-bomb, not wanting Ryder and Rohan to know how much he hurt and how much they were getting to him. They'd never leave. And all he wanted was to be alone with Kai.

"Behold destiny," Rohan intoned as Jory in a dusty—practically vintage—Subaru pulled to a stop next to Calhoun's truck. She peered at them through her windshield, eyes wide.

"It's a beautiful morning to embrace your future," Ryder said. "You're welcome."

IT'S NOT LIKE she had a choice.

Not a true one. Jory turned off the engine of her Subaru Sport, and tried to keep her expression neutral.

Three men and a lethal dog blocked a path to the house as if she was the uninvited guest in her childhood home.

She rolled down her window, her gaze drinking him in

when she really should be eyeing the alert dog at his side.

"You still have a death wish? You should be in bed."

"Our work here is done." Ryder laughed and high-fived Rohan like the idiots were still in high school.

Jory scowled and tried to look tough as she got out of her car.

Calhoun's gaze could only be described as locked and loaded and yes, guilty as charged. She'd read way too many cowboy and military romances growing up.

"Hit the road, boys. Jory and I need to talk."

She expected a snappy comeback. Maybe Calhoun got one as Ryder saluted before he squatted beside Kai, stroked him while looking deep into his eyes and talking softly.

That gave her a moment to get her game face on—she hoped.

"Let's talk," she said after his two friends drove off.

"I'm listening."

She was supposed to start? The irony of a man truly prepared to listen, and she didn't have the nerve to say what she was really thinking. Okay then.

"Grey's and the Graff was still a one-off. I'm your doctor. I've worked too hard to achieve my skills and training. My career is all I've got, all I might ever have, and lust is not going to derail me." She drew in a deep breath.

"Agreed."

She blinked. She had more to say about her brother and trying to find out where he was, and his quick acquiescence threw her.

"To what part?"

"What happened at the Graff stays at the Graff."

"Like Vegas." She nodded her head and plunged on. "And I want to know…"

"But you are not my doctor here. You aren't in charge of this mission."

"Mission?"

His cut and tatted arms had been crossed as she'd spoken to him, but now he uncrossed them and held out one palm, the metal glittered in the mid-morning sun, mocking her, reminding her that her great-grandfather had been a man who dreamed big for his family. But failed over and over, no matter the reminder he'd hung around his son's neck, and his son's son after that.

"No one likes to have their past dug up, Jory. But that's my mission, and I intend to see it to the end."

She staggered back against her car, her body going cold and her ears ringing. She felt sweat prickle on the back of her neck. Now that he'd brought up her biggest fear, she felt flattened. "I hope…" She couldn't continue. Her mouth was so dry, and her heart thundered in her ears. "I hope you aren't speaking literally," she whispered.

SHE LOOKED SO shocked, so vulnerable, the impulse to

comfort her was visceral. But he had to remain objective and focused so he could do the job, honor Jace's last wish and get out of happy-cute town before his brothers trapped him into whatever business here they were dreaming up. Dreams had a way of turning into nightmares in his experience.

He wouldn't be a good partner to take on. Whatever he tried to achieve outside his family would turn toxic—either it would be sucked in, chewed up and spit out by his family, or swallowed whole leaving nothing behind. He'd seen it happen to an aunt and later a cousin—they'd tried to step away, start something new, but everything had been slowly, painfully destroyed, and then they'd been sucked back into the family even with the fragile trust broken.

He was the only one he knew of who'd escaped.

*Hard to argue and manipulate the US military.*

But he'd already decided he'd help his brothers—have a no-paper-trail claim on their business. And then there was Jory. He'd have to ensure that when he left, he wasn't leaving any...loose ends.

"Tell me what you know."

They were in the house now. He kept the front door wide open. When he pulled up the sashes on the four windows lining the room, his ribs screamed in protest, and his small suture tugged. He hid his wince and braced his legs that threatened to shake as if he'd run ten miles uphill with a full pack instead of climbed the stairs to the porch.

How the hell could he be so weak when the day before

he'd been at the top of his game and over, under and inside the woman who sat tucked in the corner of one of the cheery yellow sofas?

Yellow?

It would be filthy the first week of July with all the dust the passing cattle would kick up.

Kai followed him around the room, sniffing.

"We're safe here," he murmured to Kai, relatively. Jory presented a different kind of danger.

"Jory, focus," he barked, and since looming over her likely wasn't helping the flow of information—she wasn't a prisoner he needed intel from—he stalked to the opposite couch. This one was a more appropriate tobacco bluish brown that would hide the dirt.

"I don't understand any of this," she murmured.

"Start with the medallion."

She looked at him, her delicate features clearly troubled. "It doesn't make sense."

"That's my job."

"Your job is to make sense out of confusion?" A hint of fire entered the velvety black of her irises. "Because you're the man? The big brave soldier riding in to save the day?" She grimaced. "I want a coffee," she murmured. "I need to sleep. But I need information more."

She sounded like she was talking to herself, which was adorable. He had the urge to get up, cross the room and sit beside her and pull her into his lap. He wanted to feel the silky brush of her black curls and waves against his skin again. He craved the connection and had a sick feeling she was going to need it, if what he suspected was true.

Jory gave the impression she was alone in the world. They had that in common.

But there were her ground rules. Despite the pain he was in, a smile tugged at his lips. He could blow by those ground rules in a second because Jory was a passionate woman. But he was not a man who stayed. Not for a woman. Not to build a business with friends in a small town where it would be too easy for his family to find him.

"Jory, tell me everything you know about your father and where he might be. You said he walked out on your family when you were a kid." He spoke the words low, but he still heard the whip of demand in them.

He expected her to bristle and demand to know what he knew, which was annoyingly little.

"When I was eight, my dad dropped me off at a Saturday afternoon rehearsal for the school spring musical at my elementary school. It was a long rehearsal—called the cue-to-cue—for the lighting blocking, so we were supposed to bring a sack lunch and dinner in case we had to stay late because the show was the following week. We ran the cue-to-cue and then we were supposed to eat and then get in our costumes to run the show again as a dress rehearsal, but I didn't bring anything to eat, and I didn't have a costume."

Her face and tone were blank, flat. But he could practically feel her childhood pain, resentment, humiliation, hunger. He too had been hungry, but it had never been for food. He'd never lacked food. Clothing. School supplies. Sports equipment. Activity fees. He'd been pushed to excel over and over at everything.

"One of the other moms—Sarah Telford—brought me a takeout dinner from Main Street Diner. Fried chicken and mashed potatoes and green beans, and it smelled so good, I just wanted to…" her fingers fluttered near her face "…keep inhaling the scent, but I was so hungry that I just started eating it and couldn't stop and then after I wondered if perhaps I was supposed to share it with her."

Even now in the light filtering through the oak tree's leaves as it danced through the side windows, her cheeks colored a little.

"Then she made me the costume to be Lucy in Narnia. It was a blue velvet dress with a big white bow and a collar, and it fit and was one of the first things I ever wore that was new."

Jory stood up.

"Sorry. That wasn't the information you wanted." She balled her fists and pressed them to her eyes, and he felt like the biggest jerk in the world. He was pushing her to go further than she wanted—something he'd learned at his father's knee. "I'm not sure why I even said that. I haven't thought about any of that for years." Her voice had an accusatory note. "Sorry."

"It's fine. Keep going."

But she stalked off to the kitchen and he heard her moving quietly around.

He stayed where he was, scratching Kai's ears, waiting for Jory to pull herself together, even though everything inside of him urged him to follow her, get the whole story, learn as much about her family dynamic and what could have happened to her father—an accident? A crime? He dragged in a shallow breath and then another—his right lung still needed to heal. He needed to stay calm. Whatever secret Jace wanted him to uncover, it had lain dormant for years and could wait a few more minutes.

Jory returned with two steaming mugs.

"Sarah must have done the shopping for you." She paused, her nose scrunched. "For us. She definitely bought coffee, but also lots of tea. I remember that was her go-to. She used to always bring an electric kettle and a basket of different teas to all of the school events for the volunteers, but she'd also let the kids drink the herbal teas. She'd do a couple of dunks with an herbal tea bag and add milk or honey. I always chose…peppermint. She said it helps with energy, tension headaches and bacterial infections. Without your spleen you're going to need to take better care of your health. Do you know the function of the spleen, Calhoun?"

He held the tea and her black gaze. He liked the way he said her name.

"Since we are living together…"

"We are not living together."

He raised his eyebrows, and then deliberately looked at his two duffels near the front door and her suitcase and large backpack that Ryder had placed in the living room, leaving them to pick their room or rooms.

*Interfering and idiotic cupids.*

"Temporarily," she admitted returning to her side of the room and her couch as if they were adversaries and the bell had rung for round two. "I'm in town working for two months as a hospitalist. I am a traveling doctor. This was my childhood home, and I have very few positive memories or associations."

"Then why come?"

He was letting her go off topic deliberately. He wanted to know more about her. Since he suspected he was now hunting for Jory's father and maybe her brother, he had to tread lightly. Perhaps Jace had been wrong. Perhaps whatever he saw or thought he saw was part of a nightmare, or a misunderstanding. He'd need to cast a wide net for clues.

Jory made a face and took a sip of her tea. "Rohan can be persuasive."

"Say it. He's a pain in the ass."

Jory's poofy lips tilted up, and he found himself staring, his tea mug close to his mouth, nearly forgotten.

"Part of his charm," Calhoun said, hoping to see her smile again.

"He was so lovely in high school. So handsome. Total

cowboy. Polite. Kind. Helpful. Smart." She blew on her tea. "He used his superpowers for good. He could have been a total arrogant jerk, and yet he wasn't. He even gave me a ride home from school a lot of times because my mom and oma would forget to pick me up and the activity bus didn't go so far out. I tried to be invisible, and yet he'd always find me and make sure I had a ride home and never made a big deal out of it. And he was so popular and well liked no one dared tease him about it—not that there was anything going on. He'd had the same girlfriend since seventh grade."

He sipped his tea, thoughts churning, and his emotions so complicated he didn't want to try to extract one to examine.

"Jory," he began, reluctant to bring the conversation back to where it needed to be, but she hijacked the silence.

"So you came to Marietta as a favor to a friend—Jace McBride. You have the dubious honor of completing his final request."

He stilled. The mug to his lips, the peppermint fragrant in his nostrils, but he was powerless against the tension that tugged at him. The way Jory summarized his mission sounded beyond dubious, and he felt that Jory had been hurt enough by the past. Did he really want to dig it up, likely literally?

"What did Jace say exactly?"

"He didn't say anything," Calhoun stalled. Sipped the tea finding it oddly soothing although everything in him recoiled from the next words that would necessitate action, and he had the feeling Jory would be hard to keep clear of what he was going to try to do.

"He had a list written. Mine was the medallion and a note. I told you what he said." He didn't want to go into it again, but he really had to. "There was a bit more." He kept his voice flat and recited: "Find out if the bodies are buried at the northeast border to McBride and Telford property."

He waited for tears. Confusion. Questions. He had no idea how Jory would react. Plunking down her tea and standing up with authority wasn't it.

"Did he say why he thought there were bodies buried on the McBride land?"

Calhoun shook his head.

"Okay, then. It's a long border. We better get going. I'll need at least five hours of sleep before my shift tonight. Can Kai sniff out corpses after this long? Is that why you brought him?"

He stared at her appalled.

"There's no we," he objected.

"My father and brother never picked me up from that rehearsal. The truck was never found so it was assumed that they'd left town—deserted me and my mom. This was twenty-three years ago. If they never left Marietta, I want to know. Besides, you're in no condition to do much of anything, especially dig.

He shot off the couch, stung. No one had questioned his

abilities in years. He'd slammed the door on the sneering contempt and mocking cruelty when he'd secretly accepted the scholarship to West Point and honed himself into an independent weapon.

"Let's get one thing straight." He closed the distance between them, blood thrumming hotly and Kai at his heels primed for action. His instincts shouted at him to prove a point. Shake her. Grab her arm. Get in her face. But no that was his father. And he would never be that man. Not ever.

He tipped his finger under her chin and faced her down, inches from her plump lips that he still remembered the taste of.

"Don't ever doubt that I'll hold, that I'll get the job done, Jory. Not ever."

And because he was feeling wild, uncivilized, he took what he wanted and kissed her.

# Chapter Ten

JORY MELTED INTO the kiss.

She was tired of lying to herself that she didn't feel the pull between them, that she was strong enough to resist. The desire and connection were novel, and almost unbearably welcome, and the ache and need so consuming that she dove into the kiss like it was the Aegean Sea and she'd arrived for a long-anticipated vacation.

His arms were steel around her. His body heated tungsten and his mouth jolted her back to life.

They had to stop.

*Why?*

*He's injured—just beginning his recovery.*

*I'm his doctor.*

*Not anymore.*

*I don't know how to make connections.*

*I want to. I'm so lonely.*

Her good and bad angels shouted at each other, and the need stamped in her last two thoughts shamed and scared her.

Her hands roamed over his back, delighting in each muscle pair—latissimus dorsi, supraspinatus, infraspinatus, teres major and teres minor.

"You're so incredibly made," she noted reverently. She speared her fingers in his thick hair that was dang perfect. "So damn beautiful."

He laughed. "That's my line."

"I'm not beautiful," Jory said with certainty.

It hadn't bothered her before this moment. There had been no point to beauty. It couldn't help her get love from her family. It wouldn't bring her daddy and brother home. It wasn't a vehicle to drive her out of Marietta. It wouldn't earn her a degree, assist plotting a career that would finally lead her to financial stability and respect.

But now with his arms around her, his most masculine part a tempting thrust against her yielding body, and his mouth creating a cascade of heated sensations coursing through her blood and nervous system, Jory wished she were beautiful to Calhoun.

And that snapped her out of her sexual stupor.

Beauty and sex and connection were sirens singing her to crash on the jagged rocks lining the path to her future.

Calhoun was here to do a job for a friend and then he and his dog would leave.

She too had a job to do. Work. Get a recommendation. Close her Marietta chapter forever.

She didn't want to want him, and she definitely didn't want to miss him.

"This is crazy," she whispered against his lips, as he lifted her and pressed her against a wall so that his erection was hot and hard and aggressive against her wet core.

"Good crazy."

"Crazy's never good." She'd stop kissing him after this last kiss. It would have to be enough. It would have to last.

She bit down on his lip. "We have to stop."

"Do we?"

They did, didn't they? She searched for a reason. She had been so sure, but now that her hands were around him, tracing his muscles, and grinding on him, she couldn't find her brakes. But then she heard his breathing fracture.

"Oh my God," she yelped and jumped out of his arms. "You're injured. You just had a splenectomy. Four of your ribs are cracked and your lung was punctured."

She backed up. Her hands out. "Calhoun. I could have hurt you," she whispered. "I'm so sorry."

"I'm not," he said, but she could see he was pale under his flushed cheeks. "Okay, I am, but kissing you offered up something more than a banshee screech of pain, so I'm not sorry. And one part of me is definitely working." He stroked his palm down his pants, his dark-honey eyes still lit with desire.

Her stomach bottomed out, and her legs felt weak.

"Don't," she said shakily.

"You can take over. We can move to the couch."

The invitation in his eyes, combined with his words, was shockingly seductive, and for once she wanted to kick caution aside.

And that piercing longing was reason enough for her to hold on to her no.

"I had ground rules," she reminded him, although she'd forgotten them.

The heat doused in his eyes. "Your house. Your rules."

"It's not my house."

"Rohan said…"

"No. Not anymore. After my father and brother left, it never felt like home. I left here after high school graduation, and never came back." She sounded bitter. She hated that. "What are we going to do so this—" she waved her hand between them "—doesn't happen?"

"You work nights, right?"

"Four nights a week. Twelve-hour shifts. Sunday through Wednesdays, but maybe five nights some weeks, depending."

"I'll be working—" his mouth twisted "—during the day so you'll be able to sleep, and we can avoid distractions."

Practical, but boring.

*Boring is good.*

"You need to rest."

"I need to fulfill my vow to Jace and help my brothers with a memorial celebration of his life. The goal is Memorial Day so tick-tock."

"You were just in an accident," she said mulishly. "Just because you were a badass soldier and now are in Marietta to play cowboy doesn't mean you're immortal."

"I know I'm not immortal. I'm counting on that. I'll rest

when I'm dead." He palmed the keys to his truck. "Now I got a job. Kai, let's roll."

Jory scrambled after him, seizing the keys out of his hand, and she was surprised that it was so easy. She tucked them in her back pocket.

"You rest." She glared at him. "Tomorrow after my shift we'll start the hunt to look for…clues? Do you even know what you're looking for?"

His eyes looked like fire, and his face had the expressiveness of a rock.

He narrowed his eyes. "This is my mission. My search. There is no we."

"There is now, Cowboy. Pick a room. Get some rest. Plenty of time to hunt for clues and ghosts."

JORY WOKE UP to the smell of a something sizzling on a grill. Her stomach rumbled. Calhoun didn't comprehend the concept of rest, but then again, she too rarely 'took it easy.' Too much to accomplish in a small window of time. She took a quick shower out of habit, a bit shocked at how nice the bathroom was. When she'd been a kid, the family had all shared one bathroom. Now her childhood bedroom had its own bathroom with an antique desk that had been converted into a vanity, and a matching mirror had two globe lights on either side.

"Not my house," she murmured, but still the tension and dread that had balled in her belly when she thought of returning to Marietta had dissipated.

She dressed in jeans, a T-shirt and button-down oxford-style shirt tied around her waist and, as usual, she didn't bother with makeup beyond moisturizer with sunscreen. She went downstairs and froze at the bottom step at the sound of a female voice chatting happily, confident of belonging. Jory's heart sunk. Once again she was on the outside, looking in, even in her old house that no longer belonged to her.

*Calhoun moves fast.*

But that wasn't fair. They'd agreed to one night, and she couldn't change the rules now, but that kiss…

She steeled herself to walk into the kitchen and face Calhoun. Maybe Rohan hadn't meant the groceries for her, but she had to eat something before she headed to work. She had a couple of hours. She'd thought they could discuss a strategy for finding more clues about what had happened to her dad and Josiah.

But did she really want to learn the truth? Was it better to think her father had left her? Chosen Josiah over her? Or that they were dead?

She brushed away the hot tears.

The truth was always better.

Jory's mind stuttered, unsure if she was ready for the truth, but she definitely wasn't letting Calhoun set off on some damn quest that didn't include her.

"Oh, hello, you must be Jory. I'm Shane."

An Amazon, no a supermodel, looked up from chopping vegetables, wiped her elegant hands on a hand towel and strode forward, hand out, dazzling smile decorating her face.

She shook Jory's hand. "Welcome home."

Jory blinked at the tall platinum-haired beauty, dazzled by the turquoise blue of her eyes. Those must be contacts, right?

Some women definitely won the genetic lottery.

"How'd you meet Calhoun?" Jory asked warily.

"I haven't really. The boys took off with Kai looking hot, enigmatic and stone-faced flipping me the 'need to know' attitude so Willow and I thought we'd start dinner early so that you could eat before you headed to work."

"That was a super-stealth stink bomb. I think Jacie is eating dog turds at the stable. I thought breast milk ensured less stinky poops. Oops! TMI. Hi, I'm Willow." A petite woman with a huge smile and a long, dark ponytail that nearly brushed her ass strode into the kitchen, holding a baby.

"Don't worry. I washed my hands." She laughed as she shook Jory's hand.

She looked like an advertisement about Montana cowgirls and motherhood. The baby girl had bright blue eyes and a mop of curls and looked to be just exiting the bobblehead stage of infancy. Jory had an unexpected pang.

What if the condom mishap with Calhoun led to a baby?

She'd been in denial about that possibility, and yet

weirdly passive. What if this was her one chance at motherhood?

"She's a cutie," Jory said, feeling awkward. She'd wanted to cook something since she finally had a kitchen, but the impromptu dinner party made that tricky. Hopefully there was some bread, apples, jam and peanut butter. That was usually her go-to.

"Thank you. I'm lucky Huck was so busy doing the bro handshake with Calhoun, that I could finally pry Jacie out of his arms. That man. You'd think he invented fatherhood the way he puffs out his chest."

Willow paused for breath. "You may not really remember me. We didn't really know each other too well growing up, but we were ranch neighbors."

"Ranch is a stretch," Jory said.

"Us too," Willow confessed easily. "Welcome back to Marietta. I'm Willow McBride. Did the howling wake you?"

"What?" Jory blinked.

Willow and Shane laughed. "The boys. They were all on a Special Forces team near the end of their service and had this team name of Coyote Cowboys. They have tats, a handshake and a greeting where they end up howling like they're drunk sorority girls."

Jory laughed at that image.

"Gotta keep them humble and in line," Willow said.

"Or they'll think they have all the answers," Shane said. "So you and Calhoun?"

The question dangled and Jory flushed, grappling for an answer that didn't have 'hookup' in it.

"Oh, I gotta get the biscuits," Willow saved her. "Hold my little stink bomb."

Before Jory could respond, she was holding the baby, who wore a light pink ruffled onesie with a pattern of horses on it.

"Hello," she said softly, falling into the curious expression in Jacie's eyes. "I'm Jory."

THE TRUCK LURCHED to a stop, and Huck popped out before Cross had even cut the engine.

"It's fantastic. You need to see the views. The scope. There's some huge chunks of granite that tumbled down the mountain range millennia ago. We could do bouldering, rock climbing," Huck enthused, continuing to walk away from the truck.

"How are you?" The reflection of Cross's unnerving silver-gray scrutiny speared him in the rearview mirror.

"Good." Calhoun swung open the passenger door and carefully got out of the truck. He couldn't believe he'd taken a nap. A nap. He hadn't napped since he was two—maybe. "Beat up but nothing a couple more days won't handle."

Kai jumped out on his heels, but he heard Cross's derisive snort.

"You so worried about me, why drag me out on this field trip?"

He still felt sluggish. He'd lain down to catch his breath and to try to ease some of the pain, but he'd woken up hours later and only because Kai alerted him they had company.

Not even a week out of the service and his instincts were shot.

"We wanted you to see this," Cross said. "We want you all in."

He looked out over the section of Paradise Valley that rose up toward the mountain range, with one craggy peak dominating. Off to the right an alpine lake glittered in the May sun.

"We need you," Huck said. "We all need this. It's what Jace wanted."

"A mountain?" Jace had dreamed and talked big, but he'd been realistic.

"Our future."

The reverence and certainty in Cross's resonant deep voice along with Huck's hope had him reaching down for Kai's massive head, which tucked in under his hand.

"I told you I wasn't planning to stay in Montana."

He'd be too easy for his father and extended family to find, and he'd left that vociferous greed, toxicity and narcissism far behind.

If he'd expected them to protest, he would have been disappointed.

Cross gave him a scathing look. Huck sort of smiled.

"I rode into Marietta on my bike. Thought I'd camp one night. Say my piece the next day to Jace's high school friend and ride out that afternoon. But Fate got her teeth in my ass," Cross said.

"With an assist from a blonde, blue-eyed beauty," Huck added dryly.

"Like you resisted Willow for longer than a hot minute."

"Probably less than that," Huck said amiably.

Calhoun looked at his two friends. They looked well. Happy. Huck seemed to have fully healed, and there was a lightness in his body and face that hadn't been there when Calhoun had served with him. And Cross had always seemed supernaturally serious and still—more ancient warrior than a modern man, but now he teased Huck, and the expression that he fixed on Calhoun was serious, but open, almost pleading.

"We found a new path," Cross said. "We're all in—Ryder, Huck, me and Rohan. There's even a…cousin of mine I recently met, Laird Wilder, who occasionally leads outdoor adventure groups when he's not brewing whiskey, and he's willing to merge with us. We want to offer something more intense—survival-oriented. There's some land coming up for auction we have a shot at."

"Or we can lease, but we want to buy so we can make some adaptations."

Calhoun didn't listen to the words as much as he homed

in on how they said it, how they looked.

Happy. Hopeful. What Jace wanted.

"We all got ranch jobs—so this would be more like weekend warriors or some week-long adventuring camps a few times a year, but we need someone to run the business—the financials, marketing."

Calhoun stared at them. "Me?"

"You're the only one of us who has any college," Huck said, all reasonable.

"You and Kai would definitely be out in the field," Cross said, as if having a desk job was the problem, but that didn't begin to cover his objections.

But he could see how much his brothers wanted this. Ryder had tried to talk to him about it, and he'd blown him off. Rohan had hinted. And now the pitch from Huck and Cross. They wanted him all in. A team again. For a moment he let the idea percolate. A home. His brothers. A job that challenged and interested him and would suit Kai.

A woman of his own. Friends.

He was shocked at how much the dream beckoned.

But then his father would viper his way in somehow, poison it all, turn everyone against him. Hurt his brothers.

But the land. He could stake his claim on the land for his brothers. Ensure they had their dream.

"I haven't even finished my task for Jace," he stalled, not yet able to nut up and tell them 'no.'

"You'll get it done," Cross said quietly, no doubt in his

voice.

"But we wanted to give you a taste of what we're thinking." Huck's voice rang with enthusiasm. "Nothing full-time, but something we can build on, keep our skills and instincts fresh. Maybe employ other vets. Wolf's thinking about getting out. We can build a legacy for ourselves and family and honor Jace. He wanted us to have a business together."

Calhoun turned away from the view of the beautiful valley bathed in the shadow of the watchful mountain. He had no intention of having a family. Building a legacy. Everything the Lael-Millers touched thrived financially, but was shadowed, allowing the rot to spread, and with nature and 'nurture' colliding, who could guarantee that he didn't have the same black thumb?

"Let's get your girl dinner before she heads to work. We can talk some more when Ryder and Edi arrive."

"Jory's not my girl." He sounded defensive and felt like a liar.

The look Cross shot him said it all.

They drove back to the farmhouse. Kai, as if sensing his dark thoughts, leaned against him, instead of sticking his head out the window.

When Cross pulled up to the house, Calhoun was jolted out of his brooding because Jory sat on a porch swing with an infant cuddled on her lap. He winced getting out of the truck, feeling like his insides had been jostled into a new place.

Jory met his gaze, and he had no idea what she was thinking, but for him, it was pure panic. What if their condom mishap resulted in a baby?

She said she hadn't taken the Plan B yet and though it seemed a logical choice, it was hers.

He barely knew her, and yet he yearned to know more. And that was dangerous.

And while all the nos played in his head, the baby let out a cooing sound when Huck ran up the steps, arms out, smile wide, and Calhoun had an icy premonition that quitting Jory and Marietta and his brothers and their hopes and dreams was not going to be as straightforward as he'd anticipated.

# Chapter Eleven

On Wednesday afternoon, Calhoun shoved his truck in park but made no move to get out.

"You're in pain," Jory said softly. "I told you it was too soon for you to be up and about. We can drive along over the old property lines when you're feeling better."

"My body, my choice."

"You're lucky you're injured, Mr. Not Funny, or I'd poke you in the ribs for saying that."

He still didn't get out of the truck, and Jory, the chain of her brother's medallion woven through her fingers, bent her head like she was praying. Dumb. Whatever they were trying to discover had happened over two decades ago. And how could there be any clues on a rarely used ranch access road? The Quinn and McBride cattle runs were buried in decades of dust.

She felt her own medallion warm against her flesh.

Did she really want to know?

"You don't have to do this with me, Jory." Calhoun's voice was soft with compassion. "It's my vow, not yours."

Briefly she flirted with the idea of asking him to let it go. Drive away. But Calhoun had as much quit in him as she did, although she would have rather stayed at the house this afternoon and made him an early dinner before heading into work, blanking out the past and her missing father and brother.

Even though injured, he looked invincible, compassionate, and everything inside of her wanted to press against him and be held, be told that everything was going to be all right, and she'd believe it if he said it.

But she hadn't gotten this far by being a coward. Blindly she reached for the truck's handle and hopped out gracelessly. Calhoun swung himself out on the other side, Kai jumping out smoothly next to him.

She wanted to pet Kai. She always did. But he was a service dog. Jory wasn't sure if it was all right to touch him. But she loved watching them together. Attuned. The hole in her heart deepened. She kept telling herself that once she reached her financial goals she could have a home, a garden, a kitchen, a dog, friends.

But when? The goalposts kept moving.

"Kai is so majestic."

"He is. At rest and working."

"I know he was injured. He seems fully recovered," Jory noted. She'd seen the scars, but with his fur grown back they weren't that visible, and then Calhoun's last word, pinged on her consciousness.

Awareness rushed over her, startling in its harsh brutality.

"Is Kai a…a…corpse-sniffing dog?"

"No, not really," Calhoun said after a long moment where the early afternoon breeze hurtled down Copper Mountain with enough force to send Jory's soft waves and curls bouncing into her eyes.

Impatiently she pushed her hair out of her face.

"Your hair's beautiful." He reached out and speared a curl with his finger. "I love the color—so midnight yet with touches of indigo in the sun, and the curls are so playful as if hinting at a nature you try to deny."

Jory's throat closed. Helplessly she looked up at Calhoun, but the sun was behind him, shadowing, yet haloing at the same time, like he was concurrently an angel and a devil.

"We weren't going to do this again," she whispered, helpless against the longing that swept through her much like the afternoon breeze.

"Weren't we?" he murmured, distracted, and his voice went through her like heated honey, and she shivered, even as her body woke up. "I'd forgotten why."

So had she—well, she remembered the initial reason. But he'd been injured, and she'd been his doctor briefly. And now they were improbably staying in the same house. There must be reasons, but Jory couldn't dredge up one beyond the low buzz of alarm that she didn't know what she was doing.

"I'm way out of my depth," she admitted.

"Keep swimming."

She wanted to laugh—take life as lightly as he seemed to.

"I've always been cautious," she admitted.

"That's no way to live, Jory."

His smile broke her heart a little.

"I know." She looked at the toes of her boots. Tried to picture her mom as a confident, starry-eyed teenager, beautiful, determined, swinging herself up in the saddle to guide a thousand pounds of champion animal speedily around a course of barrels.

"That's why I went out that night I met you instead of staying in the hotel room like I always do."

"I'm glad you did." He cupped her face in his rough hands and his voice went gravelly. "But I don't want to hurt you."

"I know." She covered his hand. There was so much more she could say, probably should say, but instead she turned her cheek and kissed his palm. "But now we're looking to see if…" She didn't want to say it.

"What do you remember about the day your dad disappeared?"

"My dad and brother were having a boys' day." Jory frowned. Her dad and brother had often done things together—'boy things,' her brother would tease her. Never once had her father taken her out to do something special.

"They dropped me off at the school. They never picked me up. They ate lunch at the Main Street Diner. The server Flo said my dad seemed preoccupied and rushed. He kept looking at his watch. He didn't eat but bought my brother a burger and fries and an ice cream sundae, which was really a big splurge, then they left. My dad gave her a big tip, which considering we were always poor and often had nothing in the house to eat but bulk cereal, was totally out of character."

Calhoun listened and it felt strange to tell him anything about her childhood. No one had ever asked her about her family, and she hadn't confided.

"My dad had been a rodeo cowboy. He was pretty good, but…" She pulled away, but he reeled her back in, and she let him. It felt weak to let him hold her, and yet she didn't have the will anymore to pull away.

He smelled awesome. And if felt wonderful to be held.

"He'd disappear for weeks, supposedly competing but not always. He was a bit of a…" She dragged in a shaky breath trying to remind herself that she wasn't defined by her father, by her family, but the childhood shame still squeezed her heart. "Hustler. He gambled. Did other things. Rode bulls brilliantly but lacked discipline and focus and often lost his earnings slinking home with less money than he'd left with.

"The police didn't take my mom seriously when he disappeared. They knew his reputation. He'd spent more than a few nights in the county jail. They told her to go home, that he'd turn up again like a bad penny."

Calhoun hissed a breath. "Jerks."

"The police weren't the only ones who thought they'd turn up again," she said. "No one was worried but my mom. Even I thought they'd come back. I was mad. He missed our musical." She frowned. "I wasn't worried until later. Much later."

"Thank you for telling me. I wish my father had pulled a disappearing act," he said. "Sorry, Jory. I don't mean to minimize the pain for your father's disappearance."

"It doesn't make sense," she said looking across a field. "My dad's truck was never found. And they wouldn't be here," she said. "I mean why? This wasn't our land."

She dragged in a deep breath.

"It was a long time ago," she said. "I don't think I really want to try to find them," she admitted, ashamed. "But maybe it would bring peace to my mom and oma, to know that they weren't deliberately left behind, but..."

Her mom was finally forward-facing. Excited about her future. Starting over.

"What if finding out what happens puts my mom back in a dark place? She missed my dad and brother so much I think she forgot I existed." Jory tried to keep her voice neutral. "That's why my oma moved in with us. She was worried about my mom and me."

He didn't say anything.

"I don't think they're here," she said. "Not that I've ever had a vibe about anything—I don't know, ghosts—before."

"That's right." He smiled, but his eyes were dark with emotion, and she had a feeling he was thinking a lot of things he wasn't willing to tell her yet. "You're my scientist."

Like hitting a nail with a hammer. She wished she were

his. And that was not going to work in her favor. Never once had wishes or hopes delivered, only determination and working hard.

"I am, and I'm also aware that you promised your friend," she said sadly. "A promise is a promise. And I don't think I can let this go either, but Calhoun." She looked up at him, strong jaw, sensuous but firm mouth. He looked as alone as she felt. "I don't want you to have to do this alone."

"I…" A shadow crossed his face and he shut up.

She wondered what he'd decided to hold back.

"I'm just not sure where to start my search," he said frustrated. "I need a plan."

He was probably anxious to get out of Marietta and start the rest of his life post military.

"*We* need a plan," she reminded him.

"I promised you dinner," he said, taking a last visual sweep of the land, and Jory bit back a sigh.

She'd defined the rules of their not-a-relationship. She couldn't change her mind now, but for a moment, just a small one, she let herself pretend that the dinner was a date.

AT THE MAIN Street Diner, Jory ordered the pasta primavera with roasted chicken and a salad for later in her shift, but Calhoun's order of chili and a grilled cheese sandwich made her mouth water.

"I'll give you a bite." He smiled after the server, Flo, tucked her pen behind her ear and the order pad into her apron pocket and walked off to get their drink order of ice tea—on the house for first responders and vets.

"How did she know?" he marveled, looking at the woman who had been a diner institution when Jory had been a kid.

"She knows everything. I can't believe she still works here," Jory said. "Or that she recognized me."

"You didn't swarm into the diner with your friends following a Grizzly football game?"

"No, never." Jory looked around the diner, almost awed to be here. She'd forgotten the high school team had been 'the Grizzlies'—that's how much school spirit she'd had.

"I didn't have any friends. We were poor. But worse, my family had a bad reputation. As far back as anyone remembers, Quinn men were in trouble and in and out of jail and other dubious scrapes. Kids were warned to steer clear of us—not that it bothered Josiah all that much. He was smart. Funny. Athletic. Popular. Everyone loved him."

She played with the condensation on her water glass, hating to review the past, but when Calhoun suggested he drive her into work since he was going to meet up with his friend Ryder, before he pulled out of town for a couple of days, she'd said yes. Calhoun promised to pick her up in the morning—a hassle, she'd argued, but he'd been unbending. She figured he had as much trouble doing nothing as she did.

Kai, who lay under the table on a folded blanket, sighed and rested his head on her foot, and Jory felt a spark of triumph.

"Did you talk to your mom about your dad's disappearance when it happened?"

Of course he wasn't going to let it go. She played with her water glass. "It was all she talked about. She haunted the police department and the sheriff's office trying to get information. No one took her seriously, at least not for a while, but then one deputy helped Mom a little. I thought it was because he was sweet on my mom, and maybe he was. My mom was beautiful." Her lips twisted. "So was my dad, but…"

She shrugged and remembered something Carol Bingley had said to her once when trembling, she'd brought in her thin résumé into the pharmacy hoping for a part-time job.

"Sometimes an apple does fall from a peach tree," she recounted derisively.

Calhoun, a muscle ticking in his granite ledge of a jaw, shifted his focus to her just as Flo bustled up, with two ice teas.

"Let's hope that's true," he muttered, his hand, on the table, briefly brushed over hers, and it took all her willpower not to link her fingers with his.

"Welcome home to Marietta, Jory," Flo said. "Heard your mom and grandma are living in California now. Bad timing now that you're back." She smiled sympathetically.

Jory didn't know much about Flo except what she'd overheard from kids: "Be careful at the Main Street Diner because Flo has ears big as a rabbit and knows everything that happens in town." But Flo had always been well liked because she didn't gossip too much and had always had a generous spirit, especially to kids.

It was Flo who'd recommended she apply at Monroe's when the diner didn't have any openings, and Flo who had given her a sandwich and a cookie more than a time or two—'left over from the lunch rush'—when she'd been loitering on Main Street waiting for a ride home.

"The timing works out fine," she said. "My mom and oma are happy. They have a big lot close to the town so they can walk to a lot of places and still have a few fruit trees and large vegetable garden for their canning."

"Your mom's corn salsa and tomato and tomatillo salsa were delicious. We carried it in the diner for years."

Jory stared at her, astonished. She remembered her mom, crying, sitting by the window and staring blankly down the long, empty, pitted gravel road. But then, she'd been away from home for over two decades.

"We're going to miss it, but I have their business email, and I'm hoping that once they get settled in, we can order a few of their products as garnishes. Your linner…" She paused and looked at her watch. "Well it's almost five so I guess I can call it dinner, will be up shortly."

"I didn't know my mom and oma had a small business," Jory said softly. "When my dad and brother left, she just crumpled in on herself after six months had passed and the police finally started looking but found no clues."

Calhoun drank deeply from his ice tea, his gaze bright and laser-honed on her.

"Have you thought about the repercussions if you join in the search?"

"No. Yes. No."

"Thank you for your straight answer." She squeezed some lemon in her ice tea. "So what do you think—that my dad had a car accident and he and my brother died, but no one found the truck or their bodies?"

That seemed impossible to believe. "I mean Highway 89 goes over the mountain range into Bozeman, and it can be treacherous in winter, but they took off in April."

"If they took off."

She unwrapped her straw and methodically folded up the paper, not meeting his knowing gaze. "My dad was in and out of our lives," she said softly. "No one was surprised he left. Taking my brother with him was new. A kid on the road is a hassle, but he and my dad were tight."

"Carjacking gone wrong?"

Jory's mouth dropped open. "In Marietta?"

"You mentioned your dad got into a few scrapes with the law and that Flo said he seemed in a hurry. Maybe he…"

"Committed a crime with my brother riding shotgun?"

Jory stared at him.

"Lotta open country out here. Rohan mentioned his ranch and a few others are experiencing an increase in cattle rustling—high-tech. Organized. That was part of the reason they bought the property from your mom—to have a presence at the north end of the ranch near the highway."

"And you're the presence? You're not fully healed. You just had major surgery. You can't tackle cattle rustlers." Fear speared her, the outrage at his suppositions about her father forgotten.

"Jory, I'm a soldier. I have training. But I'm not going vigilante. I'm used to working in a team. The Telfords have high-tech surveillance equipment, cameras, drones, which I've used before. Kai's trained, but I think they're more worried about wildlife, and that it's a pity hire."

She'd started to relax "Yeah. Pity. I'm sure that's it."

"But I will help them while I'm here."

She tensed again. The ticking clock.

*But I'm leaving too.*

The reminder didn't provide any comfort. She was already in too deep even as she told herself she was only dipping her toes in.

Their food arrived and Calhoun tucked into the chili that was fragrant and heaped with melting cheddar cheese. Jory smiled, and Calhoun tore off a hunk of his grilled cheese sandwich—pepper jack and cheddar—dipped it into the chili and held it out toward her to take a bite.

Jory looked at the food and into his eyes.

She leaned forward and took a bite, savoring the blend of tastes as much as the moment and the brush of his fingers against her lips.

She chewed, swallowed and sat back, her heart pounding, and judging by Calhoun's expression, the moment had significance to him.

"I feel like we are crossing a line," she said when she could speak.

"Jory, we blew across that line the night we met."

RYDER WAS ALREADY in the parking lot of the May Bell Center, the place where he'd served Jace's community service hours. Ryder had completed the commitment, but still volunteered one afternoon a week. He'd parked his rig—a truck and a large trailer—sideways in the lot.

Kai shivered with anticipation; his gaze targeted on Ryder.

"Yeah, you get to say hello." He rested his palm on Kai's head, needing the contact.

Ryder was looking down—at his phone maybe—and hadn't acknowledged him yet, but Calhoun was convinced Ryder knew he'd arrived. You didn't last a decade in the army—more than a handful of those years in Special Forces—without being totally aware of your surroundings.

Calhoun steeled himself—his body hurt less than yesterday, but he still felt like crap. Jory had urged him to return to the house and rest, and it was embarrassing how much he wanted to do that. But no, he owed Jace and his brothers his best.

He pulled the chain out of his pocket and looked at the flat medallion—some kind of coin with two stones in it and something etched on the back. Not much of a clue, but still he'd asked Jory if he could hold on to it, and he promised he'd take care of it and give it back so that she'd have both, no matter what they—no he—discovered.

"Gonna say hello or just stare at a shiny object?"

Ryder stood beside him, aviator-style glasses protecting his eyes from the still-bright sun and Stetson angled down hiding his features.

"Talk about losing my instincts." He was shocked that Ry had gotten the drop on him.

"Kai clocked me." Ryder stroked along Kai's back, scratching him under his red service vest. "Edi's ready."

"For what?"

"She's going to introduce you to Mrs. Johanson. It might be nothing. She's in the early stages of vascular dementia, but she's still mobile and Edi's got her eating better and socially engaged and attending the exercise classes. She and Edi's gran, Lydia, are a pair." Ryder's deep voice was warm with affection.

"You're really happy?" Calhoun asked, and it sounded

more like an accusation.

A tall, slim woman in royal-blue scrubs exited the building out of double glass doors and jogged over to them. Kai quivered, and he moaned in excitement. The woman's ponytail swung drunkenly behind her, catching the rays of the sun.

"Hey." Without hesitation Ryder swept her up in his arms and kissed her. "You and mini behaving?"

"I am, and we are not calling our daughter Mini Me."

Calhoun stared, feeling like he was in one more foreign country where he didn't speak the language—and he spoke several. He could see now what looked like the beginnings of a pregnancy in Ryder's wife.

"We had an ultrasound. It's a human."

Edi lightly whacked him on the chest with her palm and then held out her hand. "Hi, I'm Edi."

"Calhoun. Congratulations."

She glowed, and her gray-green eyes sparkled with happiness and her mouth that looked a little too big and plush for her narrow face seemed to be fixed in a permanent smile.

"The final Coyote Cowboy is home," she said softly. "I'm so happy for you all, Ry. And you, Calhoun. The Coyotes have all been checking their phones like teens waiting for word from you."

Guilt slapped him. He hadn't bothered to try to get in touch. He hadn't wanted to leave the army. But he hadn't wanted to stay. It wasn't the same without Jace and Kai and the others. He'd felt one misstep away from death.

"It's good to be here."

"You come out to say goodbye?" Ryder tugged playfully on Edi's ponytail and then wrapped it around his wrist to reel her back into his arms.

"Yes, but then I'm heading to the hospital in a bit. I have two clients there, and I'm going to meet with the new hospitalist about a couple of her patients who are in the orthopedic wing and another who had a stroke, and they're rehabilitating hoping to release to the May Bell Center in the next few days."

A shadow crossed Ryder's face. "Babe, you need to take care of yourself and our mini. I told you I got this. I'll earn the extra money we need."

Calhoun's attention pricked. Ryder sounded serious. Was there a problem? Did he need money? Was something wrong with the baby?

"We'll take care of it." Edi turned in to his body and kissed his jawline, and then her fingers lightly touched his lips. "I feel fantastic. All my energy's back and then some, and I want to work extra and earn more when I can."

Calhoun could tell Ryder didn't agree, but he smiled anyway. "I got to get on the road. Short haul to Billings. I'll text when I get there, and I'll be home Sunday late afternoon. You're coming to the ranch for dinner." He gave Calhoun a hard look. "Bring Jory."

"Jory?" Edi's brows rose, and then her lips tilted into a

classic smirk. "The new hospitalist? She's who I'm meeting. You already know her? I should probably warn her that you Coyotes are potent." Her fingers reverently brushed her abdomen.

"I got it hole in one." Ryder's hands covered Edi's hands so that their hands were both protectively over their unborn child, and Calhoun wasn't sure what he felt—too many things at once he definitely didn't want to analyze.

He was not normally superstitious but learning that all of his brothers had found love when they were completing the task for Jace, had him antsy. And now Ryder was alluding to a condom mishap.

Edi laughed and kissed Ry's cheek. "You're not supposed to brag about an oops," she said, her voice indulgent with love. "And you can't compare making our baby to a round of golf."

"It was not an oops. I was trying to play in the majors, way above my pay grade. How else was I supposed to catch you? Oldest trick in the book."

"You are so bad." Edi shook her head, smiling, her entire demeanor shouting that she not only thought Ryder was so good, but exquisitely perfect, and Calhoun wondered, just for a painful second, what that would feel like.

"Drive safe," she said as she extricated herself from his arms. "I love you."

"Can we talk for a second?" Calhoun said, his voice coming out more intense than he meant.

"What's up?" Ryder asked alertly.

"I can take Kai into the lobby area. Some of the residents are waiting to greet him," Edi offered.

"What?"

"Oh. It was part of his training," Ryder said, looking a little bashful. "I used to have Edi hide around the May Bell Center and Kai would find her, and some of the residents wanted to play, and I thought it would be good for Kai to be familiar with their scents in case anyone wandered off, and it was a game but training and also the residents really enjoyed the contact."

Ryder looked unsure for a moment, like Calhoun would be pissed that he had been using a highly trained military asset for an emotional support animal, but instead Calhoun choked up at Ryder's gentle and generous spirit.

"I figured with us all starting a business together, Kai would be going out on the adventures in case any of the rich wannabe survivalists get lost out in the woods. And you'd mentioned wanting to volunteer for search and rescue. Edi and I are picking up our dog in June after Jace's memorial service. We're going to train him for search and rescue, and Edi plans to bring our dog—we're calling him Copper, for the mountain—to work a couple days a week to engage with the clients."

Ryder was serious about the business idea that Rohan and the others had briefly floated.

"Shall I take Kai?" Edi asked, and he realized he had

Kai's harness handle in a death grip.

"Yeah. I'll be right in," he said.

Edi snapped a leash on Kai and jogged back into the building.

"You need money?" he asked Ryder. "Is the baby okay?"

Ryder's open, happy expression shuttered.

"Baby's good. I can take care of my family."

Yeah, he could have been more subtle. "Then why's Edi working extra?"

Ryder scowled. "She doesn't need to."

Calhoun said nothing more. The breeze from Copper Mountain rolled down, chilly in the spring afternoon that was edging toward evening.

"Edi's gran is in the early stages of dementia so we will need to move her into the memory care wing at some point, which doubles the cost. Edi gets a break on fees by working here. It's still hefty, but with the new business starting up, we'll be fine."

He had to get that land for his brothers. Invest. They needed money, not him.

"She'll take maternity leave," Calhoun said, feeling like if he could use the money he had just sitting around in a trust earning more and more but with no purpose, it would ease his guilt over having it. "You'll have childcare costs when she returns to work." He thought physical therapists made decent bank, but she'd want to spend time with her kid.

"I can take care of my family."

He put his hand on Ry's shoulder, grip tight because Ry tried to shrug him off. Damn. He'd offended his brother.

"I know you can," he said.

And Calhoun would make sure that Ryder and his new family and his other brothers and their families were cared for as well. He set his shoulders and breathed in deeply through his nose, even though his ribs screamed in protest.

"Tell me about the lady who asks you about the bodies," he commanded.

# Chapter Twelve

CURSING HERSELF AS idiotic for being vain, Jory snuck in a shower toward the end of her shift. She used her special shampoo and conditioner on her curls and scrunched them into place and lotioned her body, reveling in the light vanillaish scent of the shea butter.

She slid into a gray pair of stretchy jeans, cuffed them at her ankles and slammed her feet into her lug-soled black Chuck Taylor All Stars. She rarely bothered with makeup, but she did moisturize her face and add a bronze-tint sunscreen that added a little glow and sparkle. Then she lightly slicked her lips with moisturizing and sunscreen gloss.

She deeply regretted accepting Calhoun's drive into town yesterday because now he'd have to pick her up so early in the morning. And worse, she was nearly sick with nerves about seeing him. Her heart thumped like she was in a horror film, not exactly sophisticated or sexy.

She ran into both orthopedic surgeons Witt Telford and Wyatt Gallagher near the nursing station.

"You clean up good. Hot date?" Dr. Gallagher casually asked as he looked over his patients' charts.

Jory opened her mouth and closed it, and her skin prickled with heat.

"I think that's a yes." Rhianna had already pulled off her sweater and packed up her backpack, which she flung over her shoulder.

"It's not even seven in the morning," Jory denied.

"And that's stopped anyone, when?" Rhianna demanded.

Twin smirky smiles met her denial, and Dr. Telford looked up from his chart examination, his expression puzzled.

"What did I miss?"

"Nothing," Jory assured him, schooling her features into a professional mask. And racked her brain for something relevant to say, but she'd covered all patient details, and Witt was looking at the charts.

"Our new hospitalist has a hot date at dawn," Wyatt said.

"What is this, an episode of *Grey's Anatomy*?" Jory asked coolly.

"She's defensive, so she'd hiding something," Rhianna said, straight-faced.

"Have fun," Witt said politely and then he quizzed her about a few things on one of his patients and both Jory and Rhianna also slid back into professional mode.

She and Rhianna walked out of the hospital together, and it felt companionable, even though Jory's stomach excitedly hopped at the thought of seeing Calhoun.

Lust. That's all. No 'feels,' as Rhianna would say.

Heat and excitement crashed together in Jory like the timpani section of an orchestra when she saw Calhoun parked in an emergency lane and standing next to his truck. Wearing worn Wranglers, a deep-blue Henley shirt pushed up to his elbows and a black straw cowboy hat shadowing his features, he was mouthwatering. Kai sat at attention, his ears cocked adoringly.

"If that's not a hot date that's a crime against womanhood, Jory," Rhianna said. "Seize the frickin' day I say. And bonus. His sidekick's a cutie too."

Jory couldn't speak. She stopped walking because her legs stopped working.

"Dr. Telford's 'have fun' is way too mild for what you need to do with that Hottie McHottie cowboy."

"We're just roommates," she squeaked.

Rhianna waved cheerily at Calhoun. "Just. Yeah. Right. He looks like he's going to eat you for breakfast, and I'd pull up a chair and say dig in."

"Rhianna." Jory was shocked. She'd never had friends to joke around with. She'd been painfully teased in school, and mostly ignored in college except in study groups.

The nurse laughed. "I want you to stay in Marietta and at the hospital, Jory. I like working with you. You're smart and an awesome doc, and I think we could be friends." She stopped and gave Jory an unexpected hug, which Jory was too stunned to return. "I hope we can be friends." The teasing smile was gone, then it was back. "Have fun." She winked and peeled off toward her car.

"Good shift?" Calhoun slipped her backpack off her shoulder and over his.

Even though he'd been a patient three days ago, his movements were fluid, and his expression not twisted in pain like she'd seen the past couple of days.

He looked delicious.

"Yeah. Not too busy. A couple of ranch hands were brought into the ER after getting caught on the wrong end of a bull they were trying to unload."

"Not Ryder," he asked quickly. "Or Rohan or Huck?"

"Your friends? No. From another ranch. Nothing broken. A nasty puncture but no organs damaged. Just bruised and a dislocation that I handled as the ER doc was busy with another patient. I did learn some new curse words."

Jory walked beside him toward the truck. The air was warm and fragrant with grass, and evergreen and a hint of snow from the mountains. She felt energized, bubbly. Even the air felt buoyant.

"You can share in the truck. I brought you breakfast."

Jory nearly stumbled over her feet. He brought her breakfast. No one had ever done that before—not even a coffee before Calhoun.

"Thank you," she said, her voice rusty.

Calhoun opened the door and put his arm out apparently so she could use it as a boost up.

She placed her fingers on his arm, and she felt the zing to

her nipples. He looked at her, his dark-honey-colored eyes shaded by the hat but still blazing with heat that also kindled heat inside of her. Her hunger burned and had nothing to do with food. With just a look, a touch he could set her on fire, and Jory despaired she'd never be the same. Never. But she didn't want to go back to who she'd been before. Alone.

"What's happening?" she whispered—not what she'd been planning to say.

"I say we let it." Calhoun's expression was dark, carnal, and looked like how she felt. "I'm so tired of fighting it, fighting fate."

What did fate have to do with it?

Did she dare? How could she not? It would hurt when he was gone, but at least she'd have something lovely to remember instead of a giant nothing—just school, studies and work.

Jory jerked a nod and brushed her fingers against his cheek.

He kissed her fingers, sucked one into the heat of his mouth.

"You mentioned ground rules when we first arrived at your house."

"The Telfords' house," she reminded him. "I'm good at rules."

"I say we make some changes."

She could barely speak around the rush of fear and lust and excitement.

"I'm listening," she said, shocked that this was her life now. Other than the one night she'd stepped out of her routine Sunday night at Grey's Saloon, she'd never so much as poked her head out of her shell. Now she was tossing her shell into a corner and scuttling free.

"I'm not looking for anything long term," he said, each word enunciated like a bullet falling out of a clip. "I can't promise that. Some things…have changed, maybe, but I have no definite plans, and I won't make promises I can't keep. I don't see myself as a man who…" His face tightened, and he shrugged as if trying to rid himself of an unpleasant thought. "I don't want to risk putting a woman in the cross hairs like that."

What the heck did that mean? Calhoun wasn't dark or dangerous. He'd been nothing but respectful of her boundaries and person, but he was trying his best to be honest, and she should be too. This was where she should say she wasn't looking for a future with him or any man, but she wasn't sure that was true anymore.

Did she really want to go through her entire life alone with only the hope of a dog as a companion once she had her financial footing?

Not Calhoun. He was too big of a reach, and it was clear by the way his gaze drilled into her that he meant every word. But maybe another man someday? The physical therapist she'd met with early evening yesterday, Edison Martin-Lea, had married Calhoun's friend Ryder, and they'd met in the least likely of circumstances, while Edi was still consumed with grief from losing a baby, her marriage, and her grandmother's slow decline into dementia.

And yet she'd reached for joy.

"I need to know before we go any further, Jory, that we are on the same page. I don't want to hurt you. You're sweet. You're vulnerable."

"I'm strong," she countered. If she told him he meant more to her than fun and sex, he'd shut this down, and Jory was tired of playing it safe.

"I know that," he murmured skimming her lips with his, and she rucked her hands behind his head and speared through the thick silk of his hair and lied.

"I understand your rules and the sentiment behind them," she said.

There was something soaring about Calhoun. He was like a golden eagle catching thermals while she stood on the ground, admiring, longing. He could dive down to earth, but eventually he would rise up and fly off again.

"I accept them," she said rather primly. "We can have fun while you're in town or while I am, and whoever leaves first we'll wish them the best."

She sounded so emotionally healthy.

*Ha!*

His eyes searched hers, and she wanted to kiss him to get this awkward part over with.

"There's something else," he said gravely, and Jory vibrated with tension. He hadn't touched her yet, but she could smell him, feel his energy, and her body felt liquid with longing. "Did you take the Plan B? I read it had to be taken within seventy-two hours. Today is the last day within the range."

She nodded. Yes, it was. And she hadn't taken the Plan B, and it was her body and her choice and yet Calhoun too had a stake in it.

"It delays ovulation so it's not technically an abortion, if you were morally worried," he added.

He clearly was. And that told her two things. He was responsible. And while respectful of her independence and agency, he meant what he said: he wasn't sticking around.

"Your facts are correct, and I bought it from the hospital pharmacy last night before my shift began." And it was still wrapped and tucked in her backpack. It had been hard to do it without any other staff being around.

She felt Calhoun's shoulders relax. "That's good," he said.

"You don't need to worry," she said, barely recognizing herself and the conversation—not one she thought she'd ever have. "I wasn't exactly in the window of my ovulation."

"Isn't it a cycle, so it's the same every month?"

Jory forced a laugh. She was unfairly regular and had never once had a cramp or mood swing, much to her roommates' dismay over the years.

"Not for everyone."

She was practically becoming a politician with the way she was dodging his questions. She wanted to tell herself they were out of the woods, but the woods was where she unexpectedly wanted to be.

But why? Just to hold on to the dream for another week or two—that small tendril of hope unfurling like the first new leaves of spring.

It wasn't fair to Calhoun.

It wasn't fair to the possible baby to not get to know its father.

She would take the pill when they got home.

His eyes searched hers. "It's your body, Jory, but I gotta tell you I don't want kids." He swore, leaned across her and placed his Stetson on the back seat and then ran an agitated hand through his hair. He looked across the hospital parking lot.

"Never wanted. I don't want to pass on…" He jerked his arm wide.

"Never?" she whispered astonished—not that she'd thought of having kids. The financial burden was daunting. And what if something awful happened, and she couldn't love them anymore like her mom had barely seemed to notice her half the time after her father left?

But Calhoun radiated health and confidence and masculinity and drive and kindness. A man like him seemed destined to be a father, and a good one. She could see him coaching his kids' little league or soccer, taking them for ice cream following a game—unlike hers.

He sighed. "Sorry to hit you with everything. I can get intense. You must be exhausted." He opened the back cab door for Kai, who scrambled in.

"I'm fine," she said. "Do you have a genetic predisposition to..."

He barked a laugh and started the truck. "You would think that. Just boundless greed, narcissism, lust for power and a skill for being a gigantic dick, excuse my language. Sorry." He ran a hand through his hair, and then lightly brushed her shoulder. "Not a good way to start your day with my chest-beating rant."

"Beat away." She was puzzled, but didn't like to see him distressed or down on himself. She wanted to distract him from his dark thoughts. "It always takes me a couple of hours to wind down from a shift before I go to bed. "I thought we could..." She broke off smelling something mouthwateringly delicious.

Calhoun grinned as if he hadn't been so intense a moment ago. He opened a bag and handed her a steaming, fragrant croissant sandwich.

"Spinach, egg, cheese and bacon. Food of the gods. You're not vegetarian judging by how you eyed my chili yesterday."

Jory unwrapped the sandwich and closed her eyes as she took a bite. A hunk of egg fell off, and she caught it.

"Can I?" she asked tilting her head toward Kai, sitting up

in the back.

"Not sure if Kai could fall for you any more but go ahead."

She handed the morsel to the dog, who took it daintily from her fingers. He licked his lips, and Jory smiled. "Yes, it is that good," she agreed and broke off another piece of egg, avoiding the bread as she wasn't sure if dogs should eat bread. She thought not. Kai licked her hand as if thanking her, and she stroked his sleek head.

"He's so beautiful and sweet."

Calhoun laughed. "He's a fierce and highly trained former officer, but his service to our country is over, and I want him to still have a purpose but also to be a highly loved-up dog."

"Me too." She smiled at Kai, giving him a bit more of her egg.

"You don't want to spoil him," Calhoun said, but his voice was full of indulgence. "It's your breakfast."

And Jory had to bite back the more than idle comment that she'd love to spoil them both. Not that she knew how, but she wouldn't mind learning.

THEY SPENT ABOUT an hour driving gravel roads north of Marietta because Calhoun wanted to look at all the properties and roads he'd been googling and looking at using a hunting app. He was trying to get a direction for what could have happened to a father and son—how they could have been killed—hit, shot, murdered, but why? Drug deal gone wrong? Gambling debt? A rancher taking the law into his own hands?

But what had happened to their truck?

And as Mrs. Johanson's mind began to unwind, was she really partially remembering anything she'd seen twenty-plus years ago? And why hadn't Jace said anything to his family? He would have been a kid—a young teen.

None of it made sense, and he felt cross-eyed from looking at aerial photographs.

"The Wyatts' ranch is, I think, at the highest elevation and still considered to be in Paradise Valley," Jory noted at one point. "I've never been up there, but the views must be even more spectacular than from here."

Calhoun was floored by the beauty, gaping at it all like a tourist, and Kai had his head and half his body out the window sniffing.

"What's that lake over there?"

"Miracle Lake. My mom and dad took us ice-skating there a few times. They have a little skate rental booth and hot apple cider, coffee and hot chocolate, but I don't know if it's there anymore."

"Do people swim in the lake?"

"Crazy people. It's glacier-fed, but yeah, kids go up there to swim. Families go to float on rafts or hike—there are some trails, picnic. Fishermen swear by it. Lots of couples make out up there."

Her cheeks pinked—whether from alluding to kissing or insinuating that they were a couple, he couldn't guess, and her thinking of them as a couple flashed all sorts of danger signs, but he was going to plow through them with a recklessness that had him wondering if he hadn't escaped the Lael-Millers' greed and selfishness as much as he told himself he had.

"I had something a little more comfortable in mind back at the house," he said. "But maybe we could pack a picnic one afternoon when you're not working and take a hike."

Jory's eyes shone. "I'd like that. In late spring and summer there are a few trails I've heard of but never hiked. That would be fun. Kai would like it."

He frowned. It sounded like her childhood had sucked. So had his, but he'd had many outings and activities even though he'd worked hard learning all areas of the family's businesses.

"In the winter there's snowshoeing and cross… Oh."

Her light dimmed, and it felt like she'd flipped a switch in him. He wouldn't be in here in the winter. But maybe she might.

The Coyotes would be here, working out their business plan, building their own small empire, and his gift would help to make that happen. He'd already checked out the rules for the sealed bid on the upcoming auction and contacted his trust's executor and investment broker. He'd also seen another hundred-acre parcel that looked intriguing. Having that much land would allow his brothers to expand the business over the years, and if not, they'd have one hell of an investment to sell and split.

"Do you want to see Miracle Lake?" she asked, and he realized he'd gotten lost in his thoughts.

"Let's go home." He covered her hand, and she flipped hers so that they were palm to palm.

The significance of the word he'd used hit him as did the light in Jory's eyes, and just for a moment, he let himself relax, pretend he could be someone else.

"I like the sound of that," Jory said.

He nodded, not trusting himself to speak.

Jory leaned across the middle console and kissed him, and he kissed her back with a hunger that felt consuming. He'd planned to wait until they made it back to the house, but his body had different, more urgent ideas, and the way Jory's fingers tugged on his hair and stroked his shoulders added to his heat until she came to the wrap around his ribs.

"Oh. I forgot." She pulled away, but he crushed her to him.

"I'm fine—better than." He kissed her again, but then Kai's muzzle was there, and Jory was laughing. She kissed Kai's snout.

"Sorry that you're feeling left out, Kai. You are a sweetie, but I prefer kissing the big guy, but we'll be more circumspect about it."

Kai wagged his tail and settled back in his seat as if he understood. Calhoun looked at Jory. She was full of surprises, and he was finding that too damn appealing.

"IT'S WEIRD TO be back here," Jory said. "I didn't want to take the assignment in Marietta, but it was all that was on offer, and I wanted the money since my mom and oma didn't feel ready for a visit."

She frowned. "But I'm glad now." She hoped the driving wasn't too much for him. She'd offered to take over, but men and their trucks… He'd asked to head back to the farmhouse a different way, and Jory had already directed him to take a wrong turn once, but he didn't seem to mind.

"It's been a long time since I've been out here," was her apology. "I feel like I've been running away my whole life," Jory mused, letting the air from the open window dance the curls around her face because Calhoun had said once he liked her hair. "From the embarrassment of being a Quinn, from poverty, from the gossip about us, from my mom's devastation when my dad and brother left."

She was quiet then and kept her hand tucked in Calhoun's. He was so easy to talk to, and she felt safe—as safe as a woman could be with a man who had one foot out the door.

He shot her a look. She wondered if he expected her to say more. Did she want to? She'd revealed more about herself to him than she had anyone else, but he hadn't shared too much about himself.

"I know a little about that," he said. "I didn't grow up poor." He grimaced. "But my dad was a hard-ass." He shook his head and blew out a hard breath. "Unreasonable and uncompromising. It was all about him and the family name, the legacy, and I was the male." He sucked in a deep breath and made an effort to dial himself back.

"He never would have served his country or anyone else. I took the scholarship to West Point to piss him off as much as I did it to escape."

*Wow, West Point.*

Jory didn't know much about Ivy League schools or top-tier anything, but she knew West Point was an honor, and her heart swelled with pride for Calhoun's quiet accomplishment and strength of purpose.

"We never spoke again. He wanted me to go to UC Davis—a few hours from home. Work in the family business. Live the life all of the other Lael-Millers had built."

Jory wondered what the business was, but Calhoun looked broodier than she'd ever seen him, and while she was thrilled he was opening up, the past brought him no joy.

"I imagine a lot of families want to pass on their legacy, but I can't imagine not being proud of a child who wants to strike out on their own path. I left after graduation and didn't come back. I couldn't even if I'd wanted to because there was no money, and I had no car. I worked my way through school but did send my mom and oma money when I could. And I called." They'd been duty calls, but she'd be lying if she didn't accept that she'd craved a connection.

She nibbled on her lip. Was loving someone weakness or strength?

*I can't love Calhoun.*

He'd made that clear. And yet she was more than halfway home.

"You're a better person than I am," Calhoun said. "My dad piled all my stuff on a funeral pyre while I was at my graduation and giving my valedictorian speech." His mouth twisted, and his eyes narrowed. "He lit everything on fire as I arrived home, just so I could watch it burn."

Jory stared at him, eyes wide. "If this were an awful contest, you win," Jory said, laying her head on his shoulder.

"I saved a few things—my lacrosse kit, laptop a few clothes. Drove out the gate for good. The old man cut me off and made a big deal out of it, and I just felt finally free."

Jory kissed his shoulder. Breathed him in. Her heart felt heavy, but at the same time, she felt lighter, as if she still carried a burden but could see a shady glen up ahead, dappled with shade and sunlight and something cool and tasty to drink where she could finally lay her burden down and sit and just be. Take time to savor the moment and rest up for the next fight life threw at her.

"I wonder if it's possible to be fully free of our pasts."

"I intend to do my best."

"Then maybe we both need to stop running," Jory ventured.

They were quiet for a moment, but it was comfortable when Jory had expected Calhoun to insist he wasn't running. But no, he was honest enough and confident enough to not pull out some masculine bravado.

Calhoun slowed just as the truck came over another rise so they could see a slightly different view of the valley.

He brought her hand to his lips and kissed her, nibbled on her fingers, sending her stomach and thoughts tumbling even as he looked straight ahead.

"Maybe it is that easy," he mused, playing with her fingers. "Which way?"

The question felt rhetorical, even though the rough gravel road split off in three directions, one of them not looking often traveled. It was beautiful here, even in a state celebrated for its rugged beauty.

"Left," she said.

He turned and then smiled, tangling his fingers in her hair. There was no sign of the bitterness that had gripped him. His eyes were clear with a touch of heat, and her blood rose to match.

"You soothe me."

"I want to make you mad with passion."

He laughed. "That too."

He made another directed turn onto the gravel drive leading up to what used to be the back side of their property.

"Lots of memories," she murmured. "Josiah and I caught the bus here. This used to be Quinn land, and also McBride, but both families sold off five-acre parcels to some townies who wanted to have some land for a bit of farming. "The Kagels, the Greberts. Hmmmm who else? Oh, the Johansons. She was always nice, baking muffins or cookies for the kids waiting for the bus."

Calhoun slowed and looked at her.

"She worked at the bank in town." Jory looked around. "The drive is nearly grown over. I wonder if the house is still there or if anyone still lives back here. Maybe not. Maybe the Telfords bought what was left of the McBride land that was back here. My daddy and old Mr. McBride used to argue a lot."

"Any other families out here when you were a kid? Were they interviewed when your dad and brother disappeared?"

He sounded like a cop. So much for moving on, but would she respect him, if he broke a promise to his friend?

"The McBrides. The Boylens—that was deeded to Jason McBride when he married Amanda Boylen—now McBride. The Johansons leased from them. And a small part of the Telford Ranch speared through it all, and when Taryn Telford took over from his father, he was a really good rancher, and worked hard to put the original Telford Ranch back together again, and then some, but a lot of the families made it easy for him. And the economy."

Calhoun looked out the windshield.

"I told you, the cops didn't think there was a problem so I doubt they talked to anyone, but I'm sure my mom talked to Mr. Johanson and Mr. McBride. Do you want to walk around?" she asked, not sure what he thought he would find decades later.

He was quiet for a moment. Jory put her hand on the door handle, prepared to help in whatever search Calhoun needed to make to honor his friend.

"I want to go back to the house and take a couple of hours to make love to you." He shoved the truck in park and kissed her, lips lingering, and his hand sliding under her T-shirt so that she had no doubt about his intentions.

She moaned as his hand cupped her breast.

"You're not wearing a bra," he ground out. "If I'd know that I would have taken the highway back to the house and done recon later while you were sleeping."

"No can do, Cowboy." She could barely breathe or speak because she didn't want to miss a millisecond of this. "We're partners in your quest."

"You are so damn beautiful." He kissed his way down to unbutton her shirt and lift up her tank. His tongue stroked her nipple and he bit down lightly. "Delicious."

"No one's around." She reached for him.

"Another time," he promised. "I want to spread you out like a feast and devour you until you scream my name, but with my stupid ribs and dumb stitches the truck fantasy will have to wait."

Jory laughed a little even as she whimpered when he found a particularly sensitive spot. She stroked him through his jeans.

"I want to taste you too," she whispered boldly.

He groaned in her mouth, and his hand cupped her. "Take off your pants," he hissed, his hand already on her zipper working it down.

They were out in the open on a rise and in the middle of a road on someone else's ranch and Jory didn't care. She kicked off her shoes and wiggled out of her jeans, and then Calhoun's fingers were stroking her, and inside of her.

"Angle your seat back. I want to make you come while I'm driving back to the house."

"We'll crash." She angled the seat back.

"Spread your legs."

Despite what they'd done at the Graff Hotel, Jory felt she'd never been so bold. So openly dirty, and the excitement pulsed through her like a laser.

"You're so wet," he marveled, stroking her and then bringing one finger to his mouth to taste her.

"Sweeter than honey. I'd love to have you on toast."

Jory blinked, shocked. No one had talked dirty to her, ever.

He drove, eyes on the road, but his fingers edging her closer and closer to an explosive orgasm before he'd dial it back down. She held on to the seat, bucking against his hand and begging—shameless, she thought when she could think.

"Calhoun," she breathed. "I need you. Now."

She tried to grind against his hand, set the rhythm she needed, but he pulled away.

"This is my rodeo," he said darkly, and she stared fascinated at the way his cheeks were streaked with red, and his breathing was as ragged as hers. "My rules."

"Then my turn," she insisted.

"Absolutely," he promised.

She wasn't even aware the truck had stopped until Calhoun was out of the truck and jerking her door open. She spilled out into his arms, and his jeans were down, and he had a condom sheathing him even as he braced her against the side of the seat, jerked her legs around his hips and plunged into her hard and fast. Jory, clutching the armrest on the door with one hand and part of the seat with the other, cried out his name as the long-teased orgasm finally hit and continued to wash over her as Calhoun rode her. Jory fell back against the seat, giving up all control as bliss blasted through her, and she looked up at the brilliant blue sky as Calhoun drove them both over a sharp edge she'd never imagined in her wildest late-night fantasies.

# Chapter Thirteen

JORY SLEPT AND Calhoun palmed his keys. Kai rose up expectantly from his bed, looked at Jory and then cocked his head at Calhoun. He'd always loved that expression on Kai's face. There was eagerness, but a touch of cynicism as if Kai thought Calhoun's idea was ill-conceived, but as his ride or die, he'd always give his best.

Relief that Kai had made it washed through him and he squatted to give the dog some love. This morning's errand wasn't dangerous. His gaze lit on Jory, naked, hair all over her face, sprawled across the bed. She looked cute and tempting and abandoned, and for a moment, he imagined joining her.

A nap.

He rose up, wincing now that Jory wasn't awake to see him and, after a pause, he snagged the wrap and Velcroed it tightly around his ribs. After another pause, he wrote Jory a note. It felt weird to share where he was going. He'd never done it with a woman before. He just left.

As he drove back into town, his mind seesawed about the note. Had he done the right thing? Would he have told one of the Coyotes? Unlikely. But he and Jory had crashed through more than one barrier, and leaving the note had felt necessary.

"Don't overthink. It's just sex."

Excellent sex. Amazing sex. But still sex, yet as he heard his excuse, it rang hollow. Jory was more than a bed romp, and he was going to have to wrestle his doubts about keeping it simple back into a dark corner of his mind.

"Head in the game," he murmured, something Jace had often said as if top-secret missions that could blow your body to bits at every second were some sick game.

Two hours later, armed with pictures on his phone and a few hard copies and a raging headache, Calhoun loaded two bags of clothes from the western-wear store into his truck, and googled directions to the Telford Ranch. He'd been invited for lunch and a meeting with Rohan and his dad to discuss the caretaker position, ranching needs and potential for cattle rustling. It made him feel like he'd slipped back a century or two.

He frowned at the shopping bags that Kai sniffed suspiciously. Rohan had texted him a 'supply list' that he'd want 'if you choose to accept this mission.' He'd even included the *Mission Impossible* theme music.

It was weird to see the former, almost silent, sniper whose countenance had usually had the expressiveness of a granite wall be so playful.

But now he had two more pair of jeans, a Carhartt vest and barn jacket, four western-style plaid shirts, work cowboy boots instead of the fancy ones Wolf had bought all of them to commemorate Jace, and a Stetson that he wore angled down on his forehead to block the sun. He probably looked like he was cosplaying a cowboy.

The manager, Joanie, had teased him a little, asked if he'd model for the shop's social media, and he'd had to stifle the temptation to rip her phone out of her hand.

His quiet 'No' had unsettled her—probably something about his delivery, and the alarm that had flashed in her eyes had had him moving across the store and picking out a few more Henley-style shirts that he hadn't planned on purchasing. He hadn't meant to scare her, but he didn't do social media for a reason.

He still didn't feel comfortable with so many purchases. Calhoun had lived light for so long, and he didn't have any specific plans, other than waiting to see how his submitted auction bid worked out, so many clothes were wasteful. He was about to get in his truck, when he saw a real estate sign. The auction had been online, but Styles Realty looked local. They'd know if anything was coming up for sale in the future or if there was someone who could be nudged to sell at the right price.

Locking his truck and with Kai on his heels, he crossed the street—this time looking both ways like he was seven years old again.

Half an hour later, he had information and a loose plan.

It was the best he could do to take care of his brothers.

*And maybe yourself.*

Usually, he ignored his inner voice that often seemed to tempt him away from the path he'd carved out with grit and sweat and blood and loneliness, but today, it gave him something to think about.

A house.

A business.

Civvy friendships that involved socializing, not just guarding his brothers' backs.

A woman.

His mind screeched to a stop.

Jory was as isolated as he was. She kept reminding him that Marietta was just a job to her. Temporary.

Temporary with pleasurable fringe benefits. And he needed to get to the Telford Ranch for his meeting so he could catch up with Jory later. It was her first night she wasn't working, and he wanted to make it special.

"Unless I discover that there are bodies buried out there," he muttered, and then he turned up the satellite radio station so that he could listen to Dave Grohl of the Foo Fighters sing and shout about 'One of These Days.'

"Amen," Calhoun said as he listened to the lyrics.

CALHOUN TURNED OFF the truck and stared through the windshield, eyes narrowed. Jory wiped damp palms on her sundress—the only one she owned—and wished she'd worn jeans. Two of the women bringing bowls of covered food out of the small farmhouse to the extra-long picnic table wore jeans and T-shirts, but Jory, who rarely socialized, had thought she should make more of an effort.

Her mouth felt dry, and it was hard to swallow.

"Are you sure I was invited?"

"Of course." He slanted her a look, and she felt like she had a giant button on her chest blinking 'insecure.'

"All the Coyotes are here at Jace's mother's home to begin to plan his memorial—he had a funeral, and the town came to honor his service. We also want to honor him our way, but of course we will include his mother in our plans."

It was some comfort perhaps that he seemed as reluctant to get out of the truck as she was. She didn't really know anyone here other than through one brief meeting, except Rohan, and she wasn't sure how she was supposed to act around Calhoun. Were they together? The spectacular sex over the past couple of days sure made it feel like they were.

But she knew he could walk away at any time.

"Let's do this." Calhoun swung out of the truck, and Jory opened her door at the same time. Kai bounded out, and before Jory was fully out of the truck, Calhoun was there, catching her as she slid to the ground.

"That's my job." He smiled, and her heart settled into an easier rhythm, and when he curled his fingers through hers, she relaxed even more.

And then everything happened at once. Ten Nubian goats came running from a fenced-in area near a small barn, bleating and jumping up on hind legs to get attention. Another truck arrived—with Ryder and Edi—and soon Jory was swept up in introductions, greetings, feeding and petting the goats, and then washing her hands and tossing the last salad and scooping out little balls of goat cheese, rolling them around in olive oil and spices and then putting them in a halved and cored cantaloupe.

"Wow." Jory looked at the appetizer. "I've never seen anything like that. Gourmet."

"My mom and aunt are really going to town on the goat cheese." Willow smiled fondly at the two older women who had been organizing the salads and sides.

Calhoun and the other men grilled steaks and chicken outside.

"Mandy and I started a little business. We've been experimenting with different herbs in our goat cheese and with consistencies. We will have our own booth at the farmer's market. Huck and Calhoun are going to help us set up the booth tomorrow." Willow's aunt Barbara had looked a little stiff and stern when Jory had first walked into the kitchen to offer to help, but she smiled now as she opened a second fridge and showed off their different-sized wheels of cheese and also the plastic containers with small goat cheese balls marinating in infused oils made by Shane, the wife of another of Calhoun's friends.

"Tomorrow is our first day," Willow's mom Mandy trilled. "We don't know what to expect, but Barbara has been doing a lot of social media for our business—taking pictures of the herb garden and of course the goats. They are quite popular on Instagram."

"They have a huge following." Willow laughed and kissed the top of her mom's head. "They blew by my followers in less than a week, and this time last year, I was still a championship barrel racer."

The energy in the room dipped and everyone quieted. Jory immediately thought of how this year had unfolded. Last May, Jace had been alive. All of Calhoun's friends had still been part of a Special Forces team. She'd been working in a busy Helena hospital and in the process of helping her mom finally selling what remained of their land to Taryn Telford so they could buy something smaller and have a fresh start.

Had she done the right thing persuading them?

Had any of them?

Maybe there wasn't a right answer to so many life events. People just had to make the best decision on the information they had at the time.

And now that she was back, temporarily, she'd realized how much she'd shut herself off from everything but her studies and her work.

*I'm making changes.*

She looked out the window at Calhoun listening to some

story one of his friends was telling. She couldn't help feeling she was making too many changes too quickly.

It was thrilling, scary and yet, she didn't regret it. She was tired of being alone, and she was the only one who could take the next steps with or without Calhoun on her side.

CALHOUN HADN'T REALIZED how dysfunctional he still was from his previous life as a civvy. In the military life had been prescribed. Rules. Regulations. Expectations. If a soldier didn't adhere to the rules they could die or get team members killed or be dishonorably discharged. He hadn't done much socializing in the military except in a bar with his brothers.

Sitting around a table, handing around platters of food 'family style' was something new. Dinners when he'd been a child had been a minefield with his father calling the shots. Here everyone seemed friendly, especially Huck's mother-in-law. She asked questions, listened and told stories about Jace.

"I think I'm more F'ed up than I realized," he murmured to Jory as she took a wedge of corn bread for her plate, divided it, and put the bigger piece on his plate.

He stared at the still-steaming bread. Such a simple gesture. It should not choke him up.

"How so?" Jory asked licking a little butter off her fingers before looking guiltily down the length of the table and wiping her hands off on her napkin. That too was sweet.

Kai had already been fed some cut-up chicken, sweet potato and a roasted carrot. He now lay, relaxed, head on his paws, under the table, and Calhoun's tension eased more. Kai was safe. Content.

*I am too.*

The thought startled him.

"Dinners at my house weren't like this growing up."

"Mine either," Jory said. "It's nice. I feel like I'm in a magazine ad."

"My family is large, extended and turned family dinners into emotional war zones. Fighting. Manipulating. Undermining."

It was rare for him to share anything about his past with anyone.

Jory ran a finger along the back of his hand. "I'm happy you aren't there anymore, Calhoun. You are meant for friendship, not strife."

For a moment, he was too choked up to speak, lost in the velvet midnight of her eyes.

"Well." She ducked her head a little and tucked an errant curl behind her ear. "As peaceful as a pack of coyotes can be."

She looked down the row at everyone and then over at the goats who kept bleating for attention. "It's so alive here. So vibrant. I don't think anyone could be lonely here."

Her wistful look nailed him in his chest. Jory wanted

this. After a lifetime of feeling on the outside, she was finally on the brink of stepping inside. And he could help her with that—find out what happened to her father and brother. That might help her to heal the rift with her mom. And maybe with closure she might decide to stay in Marietta. Build her career. Make friends. Buy a home. Find a man. Make a family.

*You could stay.*

It wasn't the first time he'd had the thought.

But when he looked at his brothers, laughing, talking, breaking bread, their wives and children by their sides, he wondered if he could dare take the risk.

"How's your father keeping, Rohan?" Mandy McBride asked into a rare lull in the conversation later in the evening when they all sat around a fire pit and ate their ice cream and brownies for dessert. Cross and Shane also had the fixings for s'mores and their daughter Arlo was holding Huck and Willow's baby while she and Lucas, Rohan's adopted son, played a modified game of keep-away from Arlo's dog, Beast, by kicking a small rubber ball between them.

He and Jory sat next to each other on Adirondack chairs, Kai between them, watching the game but not budging.

"Not cool enough for you, huh Kai." She scratched his ears.

Rohan answered, "He's good, Mrs. McBride. He's taking on less of the day-to-day ranch work now that Boone and I are both working the ranch, and we have more teams for the stock-contracting business so he's not so much on the road. He's more focused on the bull breeding with Kane Wilder.

"We also have another experienced ranch hand coming on board." Rohan looked hard at Calhoun.

"Ouch." Jory laughed. "That look burned."

"Look at you, defending your man," Gin cried out, nudging her husband, Rohan.

"It's so good to have all of you here, isn't it, Barbara?" said Mandy McBride. "This is what we imagined when we moved back home to our original homestead. Having a small farm, a manageable business to supplement our income, and friends. Jace is so pleased." She leaned back in her chair, smiling, eyes closed as the fire crackled.

"It's happy here, now." Mandy opened her eyes and looked around at all of them. No one had yet to speak after her use of present tense. "Not cursed."

"Mom, the McBride Ranch wasn't cursed," Willow said shooting a quick look at Rohan and mouthing *sorry*.

"It wasn't always, though it wasn't a happy place. Too many restless spirits, but there was a darkness, a malevolence that started creeping toward us, strangling the happiness. It started twenty-two, no, twenty-three years ago."

"Mandy, let it go." Her sister patted her hand. "Let the monsters sleep."

"I'm thinking more of ghosts," Mandy said as if this were a normal conversation to have with her dead son's friends. "I didn't want to sell the land to your father, Rohan, because it's cursed, and your family has always been so happy, but when he came on the land and walked around and talked to me, I could feel the darkness slither way. He has too much light and life power, and his family wasn't planning on living there."

Calhoun tried to think of how to phrase a question that wouldn't make him sound insane.

Willow looked at Arlo and Lucas who'd joined the circle, squishing together in the one chair and roasting marshmallows.

Huck put his arm around his wife and whispered in her ear, but Calhoun's attention homed in on Willow's mom. He'd heard she was a little…off. Spacey. Not dangerous. But just…marching to a different beat, polite people would have said. 'Stark-raving psycho hippy-dippy hippie' his dad would have growled.

"Why do you say that, ma'am?" he asked.

"Mandy," she corrected with a smile. "You boys are always ma'aming me. It's so sweet but aging. I'm fifty-four, not seventy-four. I had Jace the fall after I graduated high school. But I felt the difference in the land when Jace was in middle school. It changed him too. He was always sensitive. It was a shadowed, creeping dread. Jace went quiet. Started fighting with his grandfather, and his father stepped in too harshly. Jace pulled away from us. It was the curse that had settled in the land." She nodded sadly. "I'm happy to be back here on the original homestead of my grandparents. They were strict and quite exacting but never cruel or unkind."

"Another marshmallow." Willow popped to her feet. "We also have herbal teas and decaf coffee."

"Decaf," Huck huffed.

"Not for you," Willow said sweetly. "I want you up all night."

Cross and Rohan roared with laughter and fist-bumped a rather stunned-looking Huck, but Calhoun kept his no doubt speculative gaze on Mandy.

He didn't believe in curses. But if Jace had seen something or participated in something unsettling and had been vowed to secrecy twenty-some years ago, that could account for his hostility, shutting out his family and years later vowing to discover the truth. He said he'd been wild in high school. He'd been in trouble with the law, earning him a mountain of community service hours and a strong suggestion of joining the military.

He had the pictures of the old property boundaries. Maybe there was a clue there or on the back access road Jory had shown him. And then there was the truck. It was easier to hide a body, even two bodies, than it was to hide a truck. But there was a lot of land out here. And small, struggling ranches had a lot of privacy and run-down outbuildings.

"You look like Kai when he's alerting," Jory commented.

Guilt shot through him at the same time his protective instinct rose. She wanted to be part of the search for truth, but he didn't want her hurt.

"Thinking it might be time for a s'more." He kissed her palm. "Can I make one for you?"

He rose up so he could avoid her too-discerning gaze and tried to still his churning thoughts as he gathered s'more supplies.

Tomorrow he'd continue to hunt, he promised Jace. Tonight, he was going to savor his friends, aching because the man who had brought them together could no longer join them.

# Chapter Fourteen

JORY WOKE UP, warm, relaxed and with a sense of floaty well-being that felt delish but utterly unfamiliar.

*Don't spoil it by analyzing and worrying.*

"Good morning," Calhoun's deep voice rumbled against her sternum.

"Good morning." It was Saturday, the fourth morning she'd woken up next to Calhoun, and she still felt like she'd won the princess lottery.

That would make him laugh and reveal too many insecurities. Even though she reminded herself how far she'd come, she still felt like the same anxious, lonely girl.

But the way he was smiling at her, unguarded and with rising desire, banished her worries.

"For a man who was badly injured this week, you don't seem to require a lot of rest and healing," she commented, thrilled with how hard he was against her thigh.

She traced his sleeve of tats. She especially loved the coyote howling at the moon. It was large and vivid, and she felt like the eyes were watching her. Calhoun had told her the tattoo artist had modeled the eyes on Kai's eyes, only he'd been called Duke then.

She kissed his rock-hard pectorals, making sure she didn't put any weight on his ribs. "Alien DNA?"

"My secret's revealed. I'll have to hold you captive."

He rolled over her, intent stamped on his hewn features, and as they kissed, Jory accepted that Calhoun already held her heart prisoner, and she'd handed it to him.

LATER THAT MORNING, Calhoun and Jory rode ATVs to the farthest area of the Telford property.

He powered down the vehicle, frowning a little at the sudden silence. It seemed a crime against nature to make such a racket on a beautiful Saturday morning, and if he did help the Telford family, he'd do so on a horse. There was plenty of room in the barn for horses. Rohan had said having horses on site had always been part of the plan.

Jory worried he was pushing himself too hard, but he'd been nowhere near full throttle, and his body was itching to power up. He was tough, but he wasn't stupid. And while he could afford to sit around and do nothing the rest of his life, he had no intention of taking that route.

But did he want to do this—be a ranch hand on another family's ranch—build up their legacy instead of his own? He frowned. Legacy sounded like his father. His family. Something he'd run fast and far from.

And if he did stay, could he protect his friends and their

fledging business from his father's meddling?

Could he fly under the radar? He'd avoided all social media. Perhaps his father had forgotten he existed.

"What's wrong? It's beautiful up here," Jory noted. "I've never been out this far from town, and we were considered to be out in the boonies then."

She paused, and he tried to tame his troubled, racing thoughts.

"But why are we here?" she asked tentatively after a silence. "You don't think my dad and brother were out here do you? We didn't have any livestock. We leased the land for grazing. It wasn't a lot, but it was consistent."

He heard the shame, the hurt of a girl who'd worked so hard to pull herself out of poverty, and his admiration swelled. She'd suffered, but she was kind and strong.

"The summer pastures are up here, and I've been asked to keep an eye out on the fencing, predatory animals, humans too. Montana ranches are getting hit by cattle rustlers who've gone more high tech."

"Have you decided to take the job?" Jory's eyes rounded. "Is it dangerous?"

He smiled. No one had worried about his safety. His father and family had expected him to suck it up, his teammates to get the job done. Jace as team leader had always made sure he and the others understood the parameters of a mission and were prepared.

"Baby, I am the danger." He lowered his voice, playing

with her a little.

She narrowed her eyes at him. "Okay, tough guy. This is not a cowboy movie role audition. This is rural Montana. I grew up here. It can be very dangerous. And high-tech cattle rustlers…" She broke off, and he remembered that she said her father and other men in her family had been in and out of prison for crimes such as cattle rustling.

She was really worried. Something in his chest twisted and broke free, leaving him warm and breathless.

"I'll be prepared," he said, deliberately not mentioning the weapons he normally carried, and the AR-15 Taryn Telford had told him to carry. "There are cameras that monitor much of the ranch, and I'll be sending up a drone to monitor the more remote back areas during the summer, but they'll also need me for other ranch work at certain times."

"So you're going to take the job?" she pressed, leaning forward on the seat of her ATV.

And there it was. The question he'd been avoiding.

"I haven't said yes, long term," he admitted. "But I'm willing to help the Telfords out while I'm here."

Looking a little broody, Jory removed the thermos of coffee that she'd brewed before they'd headed out on their drive along with an insulated package of still-warm biscuits she'd baked in a skillet this morning.

Calhoun had been jonesing for a biscuit, and he'd also been oddly touched by Jory's casual domestic gesture. Jory poured him a steaming thermos cup of coffee and handed him a biscuit that had been buttered and spread with homemade raspberry jam Jory had found in a cupboard.

"What are you thinking?" he asked, curious, and then took a bite. "Damn. Delicious."

Jory sipped her coffee, looking southeast over the valley.

"There's something about Paradise Valley. Marietta. I thought I knew it, but after being here a week, I'm not sure what to think. Everyone has been so kind. Interested in what I'm doing—how my mom and oma are. Your friends' wives have included me."

She took another sip of coffee. She'd yet to take a bite of her biscuit. "I thought I was running toward something—a new life—and when I took the job here, I realized I'd been running away."

"And you want to stop running."

"It sounds so easy." Her voice was thoughtful as she stared at the view. "When most things worthy of being achieved are difficult. Are you running from something, Calhoun?"

The question shouldn't surprise him. Jory didn't sound accusatory. This woman got him in a way that both peeled off his skin, and yet comforted him.

"Yes." He didn't want to lie to her or himself anymore. He finished his biscuit and reached for another. The sun was up now, warming his shoulders. He felt so alive—a woman he was beginning to trust as well as like by his side, Kai on his six, coffee, a biscuit, a beautiful morning. He was savoring it all, but Jace was six feet under, and Jory's father and brother might be somewhere he might never find them.

No. He would find them. He owed Jace. And now Jory. Closure.

He took another biscuit and held it out first to her to take a bite.

"Yes. I ran away from my father, the family expectations even as I told myself I was running toward something. Not very manly for a cowboy turned soldier turned back to cowboy."

"Accepting yourself, flaws and strength, being honest so that you can change if you want is very manly." Jory took a bite of the biscuit and smiled as she chewed. "And womanly, but don't worry, Big O. Your secret is safe with me."

He laughed, and a little more tension eased out. He finished the biscuit and sipped his coffee.

"It's beautiful here," he said, looking at Jory instead of the view.

Jory handed Kai a sweet-potato-based treat that she'd baked this morning. Calhoun tried to hide his rising smile. Jory might claim that she felt alienated, but she was making an effort to belong.

Did he have the courage to do the same?

"You never answered my question about the job," she said, breaking pieces off her biscuit and nibbling them. "You didn't say yes, but you didn't say no."

Seeing her plush lips so near her fingers made him remember what they felt like on his skin and on his dick.

He leaned forward. Kissed her.

"You're right. I didn't." He took another long swallow of coffee.

"Calhoun, you don't need to protect me from whatever you're thinking you might find."

Yes, he did. She mattered. He couldn't pretend to himself that she didn't.

"Stop stalling."

"You really up for this?"

"Up for what exactly?" she challenged, one dark brow arched. "Trying to find clues to my father's disappearance? I didn't see any shovels in your truck. I'm not up for that, and neither are you for another few weeks." She gave him her doctor look. "But yes, Calhoun. I'm in."

"DOES ANY OF this look familiar?" Calhoun asked after they'd been walking for over an hour in two different areas spanning different ranch access roads. They'd started—with permission—near the McBrides' former land on a potholed, sort of still-gravel narrow lane that paralleled the highway and led to several different properties. It had all once been McBride, but it had been broken up years before she'd been born.

"Yes, all of it does," she called back to him. They'd driven by it a few mornings ago. "This road parallels the highway at a few points. It was the bus stop Josiah and I would run-walk the mile and a half from the back end of our property. If it was really snowing, my mom would drive us down or my dad would in the tractor." She shivered even though the morning sun was warm.

"This wasn't the main road to our ranch, but it was a convenient shortcut to get to town. Hard on the axel of the truck though, and we didn't have the money or equipment to regrade it. But when the weather wasn't bad, it was faster, and a much easier walk."

Calhoun didn't look at her as she explained. Instead, he'd pulled a pair of binoculars out of a pocket and was looking in several directions.

Why that was hot was the biological mystery.

Did her ovaries think Calhoun and his binoculars could hunt her and any potential offspring some dinner? She cringed guiltily. The hunter versus gatherer myth had exploded. He didn't want kids, and she hadn't taken the pill. She'd insinuated that she would, but then she and Calhoun had been savagely ripping each other's clothes off—they hadn't even made it into the house the first time. And then Calhoun had turned her into sexually quivering jelly. He'd blown her body, her mind and her intention.

And she wasn't sorry.

But she also wasn't unrealistic. They were having fun, but he wasn't hers. He hadn't committed to staying.

*But neither have you.*

And if she did have an unplanned pregnancy—unlikely, the statistics weren't in her favor—she'd deal with it them. Calhoun would likely be long gone.

There wasn't a future for them.

Did she want there to be?

*Yes.*

And even though it didn't make sense, she had a secret hope that she would have a baby.

*Someone to love.*

Nervous about the course her busy brain had taken, she glanced guiltily toward Calhoun. He stood still, about fifty yards on the opposite side of the narrow track. His back was to her, and his head was down.

He'd been working while she'd been dreaming.

Kai had been running a search pattern, between them through the weed-choked fields along the road, but now he sat where Calhoun stood.

"Find anything?"

CALHOUN STARED AT the two small, rotted homemade crosses, close to the ground. They'd once been painted white, maybe, but now they were weathered to a silvery brown. One cross's nail was loose so the cross part hung drunkenly down like a person trying to push themselves off the ground back up to standing.

Two.

Damn.

He'd wanted Jace to be wrong.

But the location made sense. Isolated road, only traveled by a few locals. He could see a house from here, tucked back from the road and partially obscured by a grove of aspens. Mrs. McBride had said that they'd partitioned and sold four five-to-ten-acre plots to several families on the backside of their property thirty years ago in an effort to stay solvent.

The grove of trees would have been smaller twenty-plus years ago. It wasn't a county road. It had been a ranch road.

Kai had alerted, which shocked Calhoun. Kai hadn't trained as a cadaver-dog, but he had found victims in rubble from bombings or blasts so maybe it wasn't as big of a stretch as he'd imagined.

What did he do next?

Call the cops? Tell Rohan? Dig to see if there were bodies here? Even his hardened stomach lurched. Was this a crime scene? And how was Jory going to react?

He looked over at her. She'd been taking pictures of the carpet of wildflowers that grew out of the weeds. She'd told him their names, her face shining with happiness—glacier lily. And few-flowered shooting stars. She'd yipped with wonder to find a few arrowleaf balsamroot. They looked like small, slightly pale daisies to him.

Jory had strung some flowers through Kai's service harness.

'Very handsome,' she'd intoned before heading back to her side of the road to walk around, her gaze focused more on the mountains and hawks riding thermals rather than looking at the ground.

*Because it's not real to her.*

Heart in his throat, he looked down at the toes of his new cowboy boots—he was surprised at how easily he'd made the shift from tactical boots—rested against one of the crosses. Was he standing on a grave? A secret one? And what had happened? What could thirteen-year-old Jace have witnessed? A hit-and-run? A hunting accident?

But why say nothing and then vow to find the bodies decades later?

'War changes a man.'

Something his history professor his first semester at West Point had said.

He sure as hell wasn't the same seething-with-resentment-and-fury hothead he'd been at eighteen.

"Did you find anything?"

Calhoun heard the question, and he quickly looked up. Jory smiled at him. She now had a few purple flowers tucked in her curls, secured by what he thought was a jeweled bobby pin.

She looked happy.

Free.

*Persephone ascending.*

"No."

JORY SANG A Taylor Swift song as she grilled the paninis. Calhoun had been working on his computer, and also looking at the hunting app on his phone that showed him the different property lines. She quickly tossed a salad, cutting up a few raw vegetables—carrots, cauliflower, tomatoes. She added a crumble of goat cheese that Willow's mom had gifted her.

Willow's mom had told her about the farmer's market on Saturdays. It was a wonderful addition to Marietta, but was it worth it to drive that far for fresh veggies when she could grow so many here if she repaired the raised beds and mulched the soil?

She stopped singing.

This was no longer her house.

No longer her property.

She wasn't staying in Marietta.

*But I could.*

She wouldn't have the money for a down payment on anything until she paid off her student loan and started the long haul of building her savings back up again.

"Well, are we?" Calhoun asked standing up from the farmhouse table where he'd been working on something.

"Huh?"

Gosh, he was handsome. He'd been quiet on the drive back to the house, but before they'd made it through the door of the house, he'd started kissing her, and they'd made love on the couch.

Life was just about perfect.

"Are we out of the woods?"

She flushed. She always loved to sing on her own—in the shower, in her car, out for a trail run with her headphones in. She must be getting comfortable with Calhoun to do it while cooking.

"Don't distract me." She still held the chopping knife and quickly put it down as he continued his stalking advance. "I'll burn the sandwiches."

"Think you're about to do that without my help." He grinned and opened the panini maker. "Perfect." He looked at her, an expression fleeting across his handsome features that she couldn't quite place, but it made her tummy feel gooey, and her hunger for food turned to her hunger for him.

"Lunch first," he said, his voice graveling, and the heat in his dark-honey eyes, matched the flame kindling in her. "I need to keep my strength up."

She could barely swallow much less speak so she nodded and unplugged the appliance.

"It's weird that the house is so tricked out," she said as Calhoun plated the sandwiches, and added the rosemary and thyme potato wedges she'd baked. She brought the sandwiches to the large farmhouse table. "It's way nicer than when we lived here except for the veggie beds. My mom had a green thumb when I was a kid. She canned salsa, marinara sauce, corn salsa and beans and baked a lot until my dad and brother left."

She shot a quick look at him. He felt different somehow. The sex with him before making lunch had been even more intense than last night, but she felt like part of him was distant, working on something.

*Don't invent trouble.*

It would find her soon enough.

"The house was functional but showing a lot of its age and wear-and-tear. It's stylish now," she said looking around, and breaking off a piece of her sandwich. "Do you really think your friends are going to run an outdoor adventure company from here?"

He bit off a big bite of his sandwich and chewed, his expression thoughtful. "They are in the brainstorming stage," he said. "We're going to meet here Sunday night when you're at work to talk about it. Sorry, I should have asked first before I invited them here, but…"

"It's not my house," she said. "It's the Telfords' now. They own the property. They remodeled and upgraded the house and the barn and the outbuildings. I'm not even paying rent although I pushed the point." She tore off another small piece of her sandwich and nibbled. "Besides you live here too. They are your friends. You can have whoever you want over. What?"

"You are so adorable. You eat like a…a pixie, although I

don't know what that is, but it's cute how you break up your food."

"Drove my dad nuts." She swallowed and wiped her damp palms on her jeans. She'd always broken up sandwiches or bread or bakery items in pieces. She'd been teased about it—called chipmunk.

"It's sweet. And never in a million years would I have thought…" He broke off, and she held her breath waiting for him to say more. But instead, he took another huge, manly bite, and she thought the moment was lost, but for a second, she thought he might feel more for her than sexual desire.

*Jory, you are in trouble.*

"I was thinking, after lunch we could head over to the Telfords' ranch and take a couple of horses out. Rohan invited us. You ride, right?"

"Yeah," she said softly, sadness settling over her. She'd always had to borrow horses. She'd wanted to compete in a mustang rescue project. It was the only way she could have ever had a horse to care for, but their barn had been deemed too rough, and they didn't have enough money for the feed and veterinary care.

That was the thing about coming home. She was reminded of all the small and big hurts that had piled on her, and yet also the moments of beauty, like the flowers in the fields this morning.

"I never had my own horse. I desperately wanted one

but…" she gestured toward the window "…our property didn't look like this then. There wasn't any extra money for luxuries and a lot of times no money for basics."

"So a ride will be welcome."

"It's been a while, but…are you sure you're up for it?" She tried to keep the excitement out of her voice.

"We'll find out." He finished his sandwich and reached for another half. "It's been a while for me too, but if I'm going to help at the ranch, I need to see how well I'm healing, and if I'm ready to ride. The ranch has ATVs but a lot of work is done on horseback, and if I'm going to be patrolling, I'd like not to announce my presence with noise you can hear a mile off. Plus Kai will prefer working with horses."

"Then let's ride."

# Chapter Fifteen

"I LIED TO Jory."

Four sets of eyes focused on him. Nonjudgmental but waiting for more. He hadn't even meant to say this much, but he'd trusted them with his life. And he would quite possibly be trusting them with his money—not that he thought he'd ever use his grandmothers' trusts they'd left him, so any potential loss would not keep him up at night. But he wanted his brothers happy. Safe. Together.

But he still wasn't ready to jump in the picture frame with them.

He ran both hands through his hair.

Damn. He really was going to break the pact. Ask for help, even though Rohan kept checking his email for news of the auction. He didn't bother checking his email. If he didn't win the bid, they most likely wouldn't. And even if he won, that wasn't going to go over too well that he'd outbid them so that they could keep their money for start-up costs.

They wouldn't like knowing he came from obscene money and that he'd never once mentioned his family.

"Jace left a medallion along with his task." Everyone perked up at his confession, even Kai, who lay across his feet, head on his paws, adoring gaze on him. He reached down and touched Kai's head and stroked his ears, as much for his comfort as for the dog's.

Ryder who knew that much clearly waited for more.

"He wrote 'find out if the bodies are buried at the north-east border to McBride and Telford property.'"

The air went electric, and it would have been funny if it hadn't been so dang tragic and serious. His brothers were hard to shock.

"Bodies?" Ryder choked out.

"What the hell?" Cross sat forward. "What else did he write?"

"That's all. And the medallion."

"What's that got to do with Jory?" Huck asked. "Why'd you have to lie?"

"Jory has a medallion just like it."

Even Ryder hadn't known that. Rohan's green gaze was laser-sharp. "Holy shi—" He broke off. "That's why you were asking my dad about all the changes in the property boundaries and the roads when he started buying up land again."

"And you kept digging for more information about the curse that Willow's mom said darkened the McBride land over twenty-years ago," Huck added, also sitting forward.

"Twenty-two, maybe twenty-three years ago, Jesse Quinn and his ten-year-old son lit out of town," Rohan said slowly into the unsettled quiet. "No one thought much about it. Jesse had been a rodeo star in his day, the quintessential cowboy—always on the road, hard life, hard living, booze and buckle bunnies, in and out of county jail—nothing big but nothing good either. He was devoted to his son, but not so much his ranch or working."

"Wait, do you think…?" Huck didn't complete the sentence.

Calhoun frowned. Jory had thought a lot about her father's and brother's disappearance. And her mom, by all accounts, had never fully recovered, but who would? Not everyone despised their offspring.

"Where's the medallion come in?" Ryder asked.

Calhoun sucked in a deep breath. "I think Jesse and his son never left town. I think they died in some kind of an accident, and Jace knew something about it when he was a kid. Maybe he saw something. Heard something. Maybe he was there with his dad or granddad. I don't know. Could have been a hit-and-run. Hunting. Jace didn't say anything, but it ate at him enough that he was determined to figure out what happened once he moved back home."

Everyone seemed too shocked to say much.

"But I remember Jace said he was wild in high school—got in trouble a lot. The military straightened him out. Maybe seeing a man and his son die is what changed him. Maybe he suppressed it, but as he matured, became a leader, thought about coming home, he wanted to make amends." Calhoun felt foolish. Who was he to psychoanalyze anyone?

He waited to be mocked, but everyone just sat on the couches, staring at the floor.

"Jace's granddad drank," Rohan said after the silence stretched out. "Maybe he was driving under the influence and hit and killed them."

"Someone would notice a wreck—and what about his car?" Ryder speculated.

"I found something." Calhoun pulled the medallion and chain out of his pocket and swung it back and forth like he was a cheesy party hypnotist.

The air in the room chilled.

"Yesterday morning I drove out along a back access road that Jory said the four of five families who'd purchased land her dad had subdivided and sold to try to stay afloat, used when they were heading into town even though it wasn't really an official road."

He paused. Took a swig of his water. "Kai and I were on one side of a field on a narrow track and Jory was on the other. Road hadn't been used in a while since it was all Telford land now. She was so innocent." He could picture the sun shining on her blue-black hair, haloing her, the smile that teased her generous lips when she looked at him. "Not really thinking we'd find anything, I damn near tripped over two small, very weathered crosses."

He had everyone's attention now.

Cross swore under his breath.

"Could be for pets—farm animals," Huck suggested halfheartedly.

"What's your next step?" Ryder asked. "Do we dig? Call the sheriff? What does Jory think?"

"I didn't tell her. Didn't want to upset her before I had to," Calhoun said. "Do you think we should…?" He stopped a little stunned by how he had automatically included his brothers.

"Sheriff," Rohan said decisively. "I'll go with you. We'll tell my dad about our suspicions first. We'll let the sheriff's department take it from there. It may be a crime scene even if it's decades old. They'll probably have a process—maybe a cadaver-sniffing dog. I've heard some are so good they can smell skeletons after thirty years. That's probably better than digging up a bunch of dirt, disturbing potential bodies and evidence and…wow."

"Kai alerted," Calhoun confessed, proud but disturbed.

"Damn." Rohan whistled through his teeth and he picked up his phone. His features more closed off than usual. Calhoun saw that he too had an email.

Just what he needed. More drama and tension with his brothers.

"We lost the bid." Rohan looked at his brothers. Calhoun saw their quickly masked disappointment. Surreptitiously he read his congratulatory email and then the list of next steps.

"It's okay," Rohan rallied. "We can still use part of the ranch. My dad can lease us some land, and we can modify our plans. We'll start small. Build."

"About the land and the business," Calhoun said slowly feeling like he was lined up in the cargo hold of a plane, just realizing that he hadn't packed his own chute or checked it properly, and yet he was next up to jump. "There's something else I didn't tell you."

"What?" Cross seemed to be the only one able to speak.

"My full name."

"Huh?" Ryder roused himself. "You related to Thor or something? I always thought you'd make a good Viking."

"Otis Calhoun Lael-Miller V."

"What's that mean?" Huck squinted at him.

"That Lael-Miller with the ranch that spreads over three state lines? And has their wine served at presidential inaugurations?" Rohan clipped out.

"Guilty," Calhoun confessed, feeling like everything he'd tried to build was about to tank. "It also means you got the land." He held up his phone, shocked when Cross knocked it out of his hand and swore at him.

"There's no you," Cross growled his gray eyes glowed like hot mercury. "There's only us. Brothers. We. All. Coyote Cowboys. You're in the pack. You don't got another option."

Four serious gazes stripped him of his attempt to other himself for their protection.

"All in or all out. That's the way it's gonna be," Huck's voice rasped at him.

"We do it together or we don't." Cross's silver-eyed gaze drilled into him.

All four of them nodded, solemnly, and he remember the same nod when they'd stood in the circle, Wolf handing around Jace's bloody helmet. They'd agreed then to travel to Marietta. Carry out Jace's task. Memorialize Jace. Make his life and his death matter.

"What do you think the business plan is about?" Rohan demanded. "It's in honor of Jace. He wanted us to be together. To help each other. To build new lives. To work the land, but have a side hustle where we could use our skills and knowledge and spend time together. Jace wanted that for all of us."

"He'll be with us in spirit, man. I know it," Huck said.

Calhoun wanted to flip them off. Make a joke to dial down the intensity. Instead he felt like the cracks in his ribs expanded.

An unexpected smile bloomed on his face. "Then I suppose it's good that I put an offer in on another hundred fifty acres."

The expressions on their faces—the shock, the awe—as they processed, the excitement answered his own dumbed-down questions. Yes, he was staying. Yes, he was all in. Why the hell would he go anywhere else?

Ryder cleared his throat. "So just to clarify…"

"We got the land we wanted and a bonus hundred and fifty acres."

Ryder jumped up and everyone followed suit and soon they were chest-bumping and grappling with each other and Ryder tilted his head back and howled at the ceiling and Calhoun's once-heavy heart slipped free of one more chain.

He'd have to tell them his father might approach them—serpent in the garden and all that—but for now he just wanted to enjoy this moment with his brothers, all of them, and him belonging, no more secrets.

JORY FINISHED HER shift by sharing notes with the incoming hospitalist. She would usually run into one or two surgeons making their rounds before heading to their clinics or offices, and today it seemed like a party. Drs. Sam and Wyatt Gallagher reviewed charts and discussed patients with her, but they spent even more time talking to her about how it felt to be back in Marietta. How she liked the hospital. Sam had even winked at her and said she'd seen her coming out of Sage Carrigan's Copper Mountain Chocolates with a large box with a copper bow. Like it was a question she wanted an answer for.

"They were mixed truffle style for a barbecue I was going to," she said primly, a little shocked that Sam had noticed her on Main Street.

"I was more interested in the hottie," Sam said.

Rhianna, also finishing up her shift, had laughed. "Good

luck getting deets out of this one. I've been trying for the past two weeks. She makes clams look chatty."

"I was being professional," Jory said.

Rhianna laughed and gave her a quick hug that shocked Jory, who stood stiffly for a second before reminding herself to hug back.

"You can still be professional and have a life." Rhianna drew an X over her own chest. "I promise."

"You can also keep your personal life personal," Wyatt said.

"As if you aren't all about the chatter in the OR." Sam nudged her brother-in-law with her hip. "Don't act so pious."

Wyatt grinned.

Dr. Witt Telford approached them. "Good morning."

"Exhibit A," Wyatt said. "A highly professional and skilled physician who doesn't believe in being chatty or sharing deets."

"I ran eight miles this morning and ate oatmeal with blueberries and walnuts for breakfast and changed the twins' diapers."

"Hopefully after the oatmeal, not during," Rhianna said, and Wyatt thought that was so hilarious he bent over laughing and Sam pounded on his back as if he were choking.

"Welcome to the madhouse," Sam said. "I don't think the ridiculousness is contagious."

Jory looked at the three physicians. They were clearly comfortable with each other—taking the piss out of each other, her grandfather would have said. Her father would have used more colorful language, and it felt good to start remembering details of her childhood, not just the loneliness.

"I wanted to run something by you," Sam said. "I'm done here. I'll walk you out."

Jory was surprised but pleased and happy she'd taken a shower a few minutes before the end of her shift. She'd changed out of her scrubs, but still had her ID tag and her white coat she'd earned at the beginning of medical school. She'd started doing that so she'd be fresh when she arrived home where Calhoun would greet her along with Kai and a hazelnut latte he'd made for her.

"I heard that you'd mentioned that you were hoping to get a dog," Sam said.

"It's been on my mind," Jory replied, surprised that one of the doctors had heard about it. "Traveling around the state so much gets lonely, but my contract with the locums company expires at the end of this contract with Marietta General, so I could take a hospital staff job in the future for more stability for me and a dog."

"That's good news," Sam said.

Jory was surprised by her enthusiasm. "There's a shelter in town, but I haven't had time to look. I've enjoyed spending time with Kai, my…" How to classify Calhoun. Her college roommate would have called him her F*** buddy, but Jory shied away from that. Was he her boyfriend? They'd not made a verbal commitment to anything, and Calhoun was so far from a boy it was laughable.

"My roommate has a Malinois. Kai was a military service dog. I've loved spending time with him. Calhoun's training him for search and rescue. He's going to be a volunteer and…"

"So he's staying in town."

"I don't know about that," Jory said, suddenly shy. But she was hoping. Dreaming. Imagining. All in. What if they both stayed in Marietta? What if they both stayed together?

"Jory, that's good news."

"Is it?" She looked up at Sam, worried. "I don't have any definite plans, or a job offer. And Calhoun he's…he could have anyone, go anywhere. Do anything."

Jory had the idea Sam could see a lot more than she wanted to share. But instead of being intimidated, Jory relaxed under Sam's scrutiny. Maybe she'd have advice. Maybe…didn't friends help each other? Maybe she could make friendships if she tried, if she stayed.

"What do you want?" Sam asked. "That's the first question you ask yourself. Then you go for it. And as for Calhoun, he needs to figure out his life. He's going through a huge life change and coming off on an injury, but if you want him, tell him."

Jory had with her body, but not her words.

"And while you're mulling on that…" Sam smiled. "Give

me your cell. I'm going to put my number in. We have a group of women from the hospital that we get together once a month—sometimes it's a cooking class or something crafty. Sometimes a book club or we go out for drinks and dinner. You should come with us."

For a moment Jory couldn't speak. "Yes," she said. It was one more step in changing her life. "Yes, I'd like that." She handed Sam her phone who put her number in and then texted herself.

"Got it. We also have a litter of border collies at the ranch," she said. "Unexpected, but they will be ready for homes in another two to three weeks if you want to come out to the ranch and pick one."

Jory stared at Sam as the implications washed over her. A dog. Hers. Finally. Something for her to love and care for. And before she could think of all the reasons to play it safe. To be practical, she just said: "Yes."

Jory was still reeling when she got in her car. She wanted to hold on to this moment, so she tucked her phone away in the center compartment.

She'd said yes to a dog and was going to visit the Gallaghers' ranch after her shift tomorrow to pick a puppy to take home when it was old enough. It would be the end of her second week of work and maybe she could treat Calhoun to dinner. She'd heard about a steak house in town that was highly rated. Men loved steak. Maybe Calhoun would bring Kai and help her choose a pup so they could ensure the dogs were a good fit.

She was moving way too fast, but for a moment, she let herself, allowed her to savor the spurt of hope.

She closed her eyes and crossed her fingers like she was eight again and wishing, wishing so hard for something, though none of her wishes had ever come true. She'd wished for her father and brother's return. She wished her mom would see her. Comfort her. Have fun with her again. She wished she knew how to make a friend. She wished people could see beyond her family's poverty, deadbeat dad, and see her without pity, judgment.

As an adult she'd made the life she wanted, but she'd been lonely.

"And I'm doing something about that too."

She made up her mind. She was going to tell Calhoun what she felt for him, let him know she wanted a future with him.

"No fear," she whispered—it was something she'd often said when she was going to try something challenging, and she'd been full of fear, which she acknowledged and then pushed to the side.

But she was done being defined by the past.

Jory started her car and drove home, her heart soaring. She was going to email the hospital medical director about the possibility of a permanent position at the hospital—so many of her colleagues had asked her about staying on. Time to find out if she could.

Inspired, she peeled off the highway earlier. Her Subaru could handle the rough road. She'd go the back way, pick a wildflower bouquet to bring home to Calhoun. Walking along the back access road a few days ago with Calhoun had been a little traumatic and yet cleansing. She'd forgotten the rugged beauty and nature. She'd been such an unhappy child, so lost in her loneliness and dark thoughts and determination to escape she hadn't appreciated anything around her—the people, the kindness, the riot of natural beauty, the power and intensity of the seasons.

She bounced around for about a mile, happy she hadn't stopped for a coffee because she'd be drenched when she saw a cluster of emergency vehicles and yellow tape.

"Oh my God," she whispered pulling over into the weeds.

She couldn't breathe. Her heart thundered in her ears.

Leaving her car on she flung open her door and started running. Calhoun! What had happened. Had he crashed his ATV? Fallen from a horse? She ran. Screamed, maybe. Somebody was yelling, and then she saw Calhoun look up. He stood in a cluster of other men, looking grim.

"Jory, don't look." He ran toward her, and she was so relieved that she stumbled, and everything went gray and fuzzy and sideways.

CALHOUN CURSED AND swept Jory up, ignoring his stupid ribs and the pull of his incision that was mostly healed but still sore.

She didn't need to see this.

He'd texted her that he'd gone to meet up with Rohan at the ranch so she wouldn't worry about his absence. He'd hoped they could get a definitive answer before Jory learned what he'd been doing the past couple of days when she'd been at work.

Now she'd think he'd been lying to her.

*I have been lying.*

But Jory was his to protect.

"Hey, baby." He put her in the driver's seat of her car, feet angled out toward him. He saw her water bottle, pulled a bandana from his pocket—something Ryder had told him he should always have on him, which he'd thought was lame, but in hindsight helpful.

He dampened the cloth and wiped her forehead and wrists and leaned her forward, so her head was below her heart. He'd never seen anyone faint before, and if he did again, it would be too soon. Anxiety choked him.

"Hey." A paramedic knelt down beside her, first-aid kit in hand. "What happened? Did she faint or fall? Did she hit her head?"

He tried to get in position to examine Jory who showed signs of coming around, and Calhoun could barely swallow his irritation. He had thought having the paramedics and fire department accompany the sheriff vehicles was overkill, and now it was pissing him off, which was irrational.

"Does she have a heart condition?"

"No," Calhoun snapped, terrified. "I don't know. I don't think so. She's a doctor at the hospital in town."

Doctors had to get medicals to practice, didn't they? She would have told him if she had any health issues.

*Yeah, like you told her all about your life.*

He got out of the way, reluctant to not be the one to hold her, but he wanted her to get the care she might need.

"Shouldn't she be awake by now?" he demanded. He was being a jerk. "Sorry."

"No worries. If it were my girl, I'd be panicking too."

Calhoun didn't panic. He was highly trained and cool under fire. Yet he was panicking. Kai nosed his way past Calhoun and between the door and the paramedic to nuzzle Jory's limp hand and then lick her face, something Calhoun had never seen him do.

Jory stirred and reached for Kai.

"Hi, sweet boy," she murmured, pulling Kai close, and he tried to climb in the car with her. Her eyes fluttered and then opened. Her gaze was cloudy, but before Calhoun could gather her in his arms to reassure her and himself, the paramedic shone a pen light in her eyes, and he had a blood pressure cuff on her.

"What's happening?" she murmured.

She stroked Kai and kissed him, and Calhoun had never

thought he could be jealous of his dog.

"Okay, big guy." The paramedic tried to work around Kai.

"Kai. Heel," Calhoun commanded. It took two commands to get Kai to return to him, and his dog watched the paramedic with an intensity that had him gripping Kai's service harness.

It took Calhoun a second to realize his own cranked tension was setting Kai off, and he square-breathed through his nose and relaxed his hold on Kai's harness and instead stroked his head and scratched his ears, relieved to see the tension leave Kai.

"Your pulse was over 140. Have you ever suffered from vasovagal?"

"No. Never," Jory said. "I was scared. I saw the emergency vehicles, and I thought Calhoun was injured."

Her dark eyes met his, and Calhoun saw the naked emotion in them.

He should look away. His own panic that something was wrong with her was still close. He wasn't ready for commitment. It was what he always told himself. He'd never be ready. His parents' toxic marriage, their social pretenses and behind-the-scenes cold, calculated fighting and undermining, their affairs—all of it had determined him to steer clear.

He'd never seen a healthy relationship until these past two weeks in Marietta. His Coyote brothers were loved up and supported, and they supported their partners. Hell, three of them already had children, and Ryder and Edi were expecting.

And what if he and Jory…instead of dismayed dismissal of the concept of an unexpected child, he wondered if perhaps they had been lucky, or unlucky that first night together.

"Are you expecting?" The paramedic casually asked Jory the question he'd been unable to voice. "That can cause dizziness and fainting and rapid dips in blood pressure."

"It can?" Calhoun demanded. He wasn't caring for Jory properly. He didn't know the first thing about pregnancy. He didn't even know if she *was* pregnant.

"I don't think so?" she said softly her voice raised in question, and she didn't meet his gaze.

"Are you late?"

"That's pretty personal," Calhoun said tensely.

"Just doing a health check," the paramedic said easily, as if accustomed to partners growling at him.

Partner. Were he and Jory partners? Were they going to be parents?

He felt like he might be the next one to pass out because life was moving way too fast, and this was out of the service when he'd expected everything to calm and settle down.

"You should take a test and make an appointment with your doctor just to be sure there's no underlying health concerns." The paramedic stood up.

"I don't have a doctor." Jory smiled wryly. "But I'll get a

checkup," she conceded. "I felt great though. Happy. Then when I saw all the vehicles…here…" Jory pulled herself up using the car door. She swayed and Calhoun reached for her. "I thought you were hurt."

"I'm fine."

The paramedic jogged back to the grouping of his colleagues while an excavator from the Telford Ranch, driven by Taryn Telford, began digging up careful scoops of dirt.

"Calhoun, what's going on?" she asked.

"Are you late? Are you pregnant?"

He heard his father's voice in him. His father's tactics. The best defense is a stronger offense. He hadn't told Jory what he'd been doing this week. He hadn't told her about the crosses, about his visit to the sheriff with Rohan, the call to a dog handler in Bozeman who had a cadaver-sniffing dog. How the dog had spent less than an hour crisscrossing the field before alerting by the crosses, just like Kai had earlier in the week while he, Rohan and a deputy had watched.

Nor had he told her that as he patrolled this newer area of the Telford Ranch that had been slowly added over the past couple of decades, he'd been doing more than orienting himself to the summer cattle pastures. He'd been looking for abandoned outbuildings. And he'd found several—one with an old blue truck covered in a tarp. A deputy had run the long-ago expired plate and in the DMV archives he'd learned the truck was registered to a Jesse Quinn.

He hadn't told her any of that.

He hadn't shared.

Something else his father had excelled at.

Hell, he and Jory weren't partners. He didn't know how to be.

It took him a moment to realize she hadn't answered. Instead her gaze was glued to the activity.

"What's happening?" she asked and then pushed off her car, her stride determined.

"You don't want to go there, Jory. You don't need to see this."

"What is *this*?" she stopped and demanded. Her eyes were huge. Her olive skin pale with a sheen of sweat.

"I think I might have been right," he said slowly. "I think your dad and brother never left town."

His voice didn't sound like his. His ears rang, and his voice sounded tinny, defensive. His heart thundered like he'd been running. "I think there was an accident, a cover-up. I think Jace saw something as a kid and went back to see and found the medallion around a cross in the ground."

"What?" she whispered. "What? What are you…you're just telling me now that you think…you think that my father and brother are really dead? Dead and buried in a field where I waited for the school bus!"

Her voice rose.

"You think…all the years I waited for news? I searched? I hoped? You think they were here the whole time?" she screeched.

He nodded and reached for her. She pulled away from him.

"No. No. You're wrong. That wouldn't happen. If someone we knew hurt them, it was an accident, and they would say something. They would have called for help. You're wrong."

She began walking toward the scene again, her fists balled up, arms swinging, petite body angled forward in fierce determination.

Calhoun hurried after her, and Kai left his side to walk beside Jory, his nose nuzzling her fist, which opened so he could slide his muzzle in between her fingers.

Calhoun heard a shout and then another. The arm of the excavator hovered over the beginnings of the hole it was digging. Dirt spilled from the claws and so did the grayish white arm bone of a skeleton, dangling in front of the gathered crowd.

Jory skidded to a stop and fell on her knees. Her keening cry pierced his heart and his soul, and he realized in his stupid, I'm-the-man-protecting-my-woman move, he'd left her utterly vulnerable and alone.

# Chapter Sixteen

"JORY, YOU DON'T need to be here," Calhoun said for probably the tenth time, his face shadowed by his Stetson, but she could see his shuttered expression, the tenseness.

She said nothing, just kept her arms crossed over her body, holding herself together like she'd done her entire childhood. Her father hadn't left her behind. Her brother hadn't forgotten her. They were dead. Dead. Dead. Dead. She'd have to tell her mom. How would she react? Would it send her back into that hellish dark place where no one could reach her? Where she'd remained for months barely responsive to Jory's attempt to tell her something about her day, get her to eat, take care of the garden?

The rhythm of the operation had changed. The spectators were pushed back even farther. More first responders arrived—fat lot of good they would do now. Maybe if someone had listened to her mother…

"Let me take you home."

Home. She didn't have a home.

She tilted her chin and stared at Copper Mountain. It was still there. Strong. Majestic, Silent. Watching over the valley. In a way, Copper Mountain was the only thing in her life that had never let her down.

The medical examiner arrived. More people. Women from the barbecue.

"Jory," Willow said softly, pulling her into a full-body hug even though she had her baby in a front pack. "Jory, sweetie. I am so very sorry."

Jory's face was brushed by dark, downy hair, and she caught a whiff of shampoo, powder and milk.

She squeezed her eyes shut as the hug went on, and then she was clinging to Willow and her baby, but she couldn't see them because they were blurry, underwater.

She shook, and the tears fell, and she couldn't stop them. It was like a lifetime had stored up all her tears, and Willow had pulled the plug.

"So sorry," Willow said, her arms on her back and they rocked in the early morning breeze.

She was aware of Calhoun taking a side step away from her and then another.

Good.

She didn't need him.

She didn't want him.

He hadn't told her what he was up to. He'd acted like she had a right to know what he knew or suspected about her father and brother's disappearance, like she was part of the plan to discover what had happened, when all along he'd been working alone. Or with his friends.

And she was not a part of his group, not really.

Only Willow hadn't abandoned her, even though they had only recently met.

Shane arrived. Her long blonde hair flagged behind her in the morning breeze and her long stride quickly closed the distance.

"Jory, how awful. I'm so sorry." Shane too enveloped her in a hug, and Jory for the first time she could remember didn't feel alone, didn't feel like she had to pretend everything was fine, and that she was strong enough to handle whatever life threw at her.

"Let's go to the house," Willow said.

Jory must have shown her distaste of that idea.

"My mom's place," Willow said.

"But..." Jory shuddered and looked toward the growing group of men, thankfully blocking the beginnings of the hole, where two people in white protective suits stood on the edge conferring.

"We can't do anything here," Shane said, her strong hands on Jory's shoulders. "Mandy's house is close, and she has tea—I'm desperate for a cup." Shane smiled.

Jory looked from Shane's beautiful face, oozing sympathy and practicality to Willow's encouraging smile. "Come. Let's get away from here. I'll let Huck know where we are if the police want to talk to you. This will take a lot of time, and then there will be the DNA tests." She waved her hand.

"You won't know anything for sure for some time,"

Shane said, "so it's best to pace yourself. Let us take care of you."

Somehow it was worse to hold on to hope.

"I'd finally given up," she whispered. "I finally felt like I could move on. I was even thinking—" She broke off seeing Calhoun's attention was lasered on her, and despite her shock and grief and fury, that skittery thing her heart did when he looked at her kicked in.

"Never mind. Doesn't matter. I'll go to your mom's." She couldn't put up a fight, and she didn't want to be alone, and she definitely didn't want to hear whatever manly, lame excuse Calhoun would dredge up.

Willow smiled and looked relieved. "Good, because Jacie is going to want to be fed soon, and I think if I pull my boob out in front of half the crew of Marietta's finest, Huck will lose a little more of his mind."

Shane laughed, and instead of being offensive to her storm of emotions, the sound settled Jory. They were treating her like she was normal, like her feelings were normal and mattered, but weren't embarrassing.

"Part of me wishes you'd do it, Willow, and another part thinks Huck would be a little smug—Mr. Yeah-Boys-Look-What-I-Got."

Willow put her arm around Jory, and Jory walked with her away from the hole, and away from Calhoun's discerning stare. It was too late for him to pretend he cared about her now. He'd been here to fulfill a vow to his friend. Mission accomplished. She'd just been a perk.

Shame and anger spun in her gut, and she wanted to run back and slug him.

"Don't blame you, but you'd hurt your fist," Willow said cheerfully.

"I said that out loud?"

"You muttered, but also Shane and I have been there." Willow grinned. "We're married to Coyote Cowboys. We know how those blockheads try to think. Calhoun doesn't have much training yet," Willow observed cheerfully. "But I know you're up for the job to keep him from beating his fists and going all 'I'm the man' on you too often."

"But it is beyond sexy when they do," Shane said, a secretive smile on her face.

"Don't I know it," Willow said. "Huck already nailed me with number two. That's how competitive he is. He just had to get his own genes out into the world. That man." Willow smiled and kissed her baby's head. "He needs a warning label slapped on his ass. They all do, fair warning. Potent AF."

Still smiling a little slyly, Shane opened the door of the Jeep. Jory had to use the handle above the door to haul herself in.

"Get a runner, Shane. Not all of us are statuesque," Willow said. "And don't think I didn't see your secretive smirk. I'm calling a dish and deets meeting soon." Willow wagged a finger at Shane. "After Jory's had some time to process. I'll meet you both at my mom and aunt's. I have the car seat."

"I have my car," Jory said, looking around, but realizing they'd walked in the opposite direction.

"I'll drive. You've had a shock. Your car will be fine. One of the boys will drive it home."

"No. I'm not staying there." She'd been in the process of buckling up, but now she stopped and let the seat belt slap back into place.

"Okay," Shane agreed. One of them will bring your car to Mandy's. Give me your keys."

"I can drive."

She had to get a room at the Graff again. Find a rental. Pack her stuff. Call the hospital and try to pick up an extra shift. Call her mom and oma. Her to-do list scrolled before her, settling her as her mind switched to work mode.

"Jory." Shane bent down. Her turquoise eyes shone with kindness and strength. "Let us take care of you. Plenty of time to make plans when you have all the information. Until then and after then, we're team Jory."

Jory hiccupped a 'thank you,' and more tears spilled.

Shane closed the door, briefly conferred with Willow, and then she strode back toward the group of men. Calhoun separated himself from them and met her halfway. Shane handed him the keys, said something briefly and then turned around.

She could see Calhoun starting to follow, but Shane looked over her shoulder and held up a hand with a flip of attitude and hair toss, causing Calhoun to skid to a stop.

Good. She didn't need him. She didn't want him. But as Shane got in the Jeep and started the engine and shifted into gear, Jory felt like Calhoun had a grip on her heart, and it stretched out like a ribbon unfurling behind her in the rising sun.

JORY FLAILED, ARMS wide. Her mouth opened to scream, but no sound emerged, just a gasping, terrified rasp as bony fingers crushed her windpipe and then she was falling into a deep, dark hole. The soil had crumbled under her feet and she'd reached to grab Calhoun, but he'd stepped back, arms crossed, not intending to help her.

She jerked awake and struggled with a quilt wrapped around her so she could sit up. Her head ached. Her eyes felt gritty, and her face felt swollen. She'd been asleep. She tried to orient herself. Where was she? The Graff? The house? A sliver of orangish light slid under the outlines of the white shutters so it was still day, but…she'd fallen asleep.

"Good evening, Jory." Mandy rapped briefly before opening the door and entering the small, feminine room with the daybed where Jory had apparently taken a nap. She remembered now drinking tea with Shane and Willow. She'd held Willow's baby, and Willow's mom had sat with them chatting as if Jory's world hadn't imploded.

"I brought you some lemon ginger tea and a biscotti.

Shane made those. She loves to bake, and I think she puts something magical in everything she does. She makes these tea blends."

"Thank you." Jory sat all the way up. Her fingers traced the pattern on the quilt. "I'm sorry to barge in on you and then fall asleep."

Had everyone else gone home? Of course they had. They couldn't spend the day waiting for her to wake up. How would she get her stuff and check in to the Graff? Was there even a room?

"I work nights."

Yeah, that was the excuse for her rudeness.

"Yes. I know. But you needed the rest to reset, and now I think it's time we say goodbye."

"Yes, of course." Jory quickly put her tea down on the nightstand and scrambled to her feet. "I'm sorry."

"No, no. Drink your tea. It's good that you don't work tonight. I wanted to wait for the day to be sliding into night, but not too late. I was young when I married and had Jace. And my family was troubled. My father-in-law drank. He was descending into a dark place. My husband was busy trying to save the ranch. He was a good man. A hard worker, but it seemed like nothing would go right. It felt dark to me. Cursed. I felt…" she looked at Jory placidly "…souls trying to talk to me, but I couldn't hear them fully. It was like whispers, mumbles, but they were lost, desperate to find their way home. Now I think I know why, Jory, and we want to help them. You can help them."

"Huh?" Jory looked around the room a little weirded out. Where were her shoes?

"So many deaths," Mandy mused, sipping her tea, and Jory's knees weakened, and she sat back down on the bed, facing Mandy who rocked gently back and forth in a rocking chair that looked as if it was old, but had been refinished. Of course. She would want a chair to rock her first grandchild. Maybe she'd rocked her son and then Willow in that chair.

"I'm so sorry, Mandy." She touched her knee as she rocked into her space and then back out again. The movement was soothing, almost mesmerizing. "I've been unbearably selfish. I've been thinking of my own pain. My own loss, but you lost Jace and your husband less than a year ago."

"Loss is such an unusual word to use for death, isn't it?" Mandy asked, her gaze on the ceiling that had shiny gold stars—different sizes—painted on it, and each star had a crystal in the center.

It was sweet and sophisticated, and longing swept through Jory to have her own home she could decorate instead of a series of hotels and short-stay furnished rentals. What if she found a home in Marietta? What if she had a child and could decorate a nursery? Wonder speared through her. Even in this tragedy of loss, there might be hope. Fear and excitement quivered through her, tangled.

"I didn't lose Jace. He was killed far from home, but his

spirit is here, watching over me and Willow and his brothers," she said calmly. "He likes the idea of the goats—it will keep me out of my head. He's thrilled that Willow has found Huck and that she's expecting again. I suspect he knows Cross' Shane is also pregnant, but she's keeping it a secret until the second trimester because she had an earlier loss so shshsh."

Mandy put a finger to her lips and rocked back and forth, and it was mesmerizing. She smiled at Jory. "Jace gives me strength and comfort. My husband was lost. He killed himself after hearing about Jace. His daddy did the same when Jace was fourteen. He always drank too much but when Jace was in middle school, he never climbed out of a bottle. Neither of those men have found peace yet."

"I'm sorry." Nervously Jory plucked at her abdomen. Her period would start today. Or it wouldn't. And then she'd know. And she'd have hope—life and death balanced.

"You have the sight?"

"What?"

Mandy smiled. "Your baby."

"Oh." Heat flushed through her, and she stood up. "It's way too soon. I'm not even late," Jory said. "And I'm not in a relationship."

"It doesn't work like that."

Jory sat down again, feeling so off-balanced by the conversation and her life. "I know. I'm a doctor, but…"

Willow's mom sat forward and covered Jory's abdomen.

It was such a strange thing to do, and yet Jory let her.

"You'll be loving parents. That's what you're both afraid of." Mandy took her hand away. Took her last sip of tea. "Embrace the fear. It's part of life and the one emotion you can learn the most from."

"I'm not…I'd like a baby." Jory said the words aloud for the first time. "But my life's not situated yet, and it's too early to know."

Although Jory felt pregnant. Science would tell her that she wouldn't feel any different, and yet over the years, some women had said they knew the instant they conceived. Jory didn't know what to think, but the fact that she'd wavered on taking the Plan B when it had made perfect sense to take it and not look back seemed to be a message.

"Maybe there is a balance in the universe," she blurted.

Mandy smiled. "There is, if you know how to look, but it's not presented on a plate." She stood up. "I see light in you, Jory. I think you will be a good friend to Willow and your daughters will be lifelong friends," Mandy said. "I can keep a secret if it's the right kind and for the right reason, so I will say nothing and wait for your happy announcement."

Was this real? Was this even happening? But it felt right. She followed Mandy to the door. Mandy paused, her hand on the handle.

"There have been too many secrets on this land," she said. "Too many sorrows, but a change is coming. The Telfords have open hearts and a community spirit and so much love that they will heal the land and have success.

"Barb and I have reconciled, and we both let go of the painful parts of our pasts so we can embrace a future. And now, Jory, it's time for you to do the same."

Jory wasn't sure what to think when she and Mandy walked out of the house as if she were going to visit the garden or the goats, but instead she was greeted by a semi-circle of seven women.

She knew Willow, and Shane and Gin from the barbecue, Edi from the May Bell Center, but the other three women introduced themselves—Riley Telford, a petite blonde with a mischievous smile; Tucker Wilder, who worked with Willow; and Sky Wilder, a metal sculptor, who wanted to create a 'simple memorial to mark the site for the future generations of Quinns.'

Jory was so overwhelmed by the unexpected support and the idea of future generations of Quinns visiting where her father and brother had abruptly lost their lives that she couldn't do more than a quick handwave and blink back tears.

"Let's do this." Willow slid her arm around her, and they all piled in several cars and drove down gravel roads, kicking up dust that danced in the setting sun.

Jory steeled herself to look at the gaping hole again, but it was covered by a tarp and yellow crime scene tape and barriers. The awful machine claw was gone, and bouquets of flowers ringed the site. The caravan parked up at the top of the rise, facing down because according to Mandy, who seemed to be running this odd little show, the confused spirits needed to find their path home.

They walked down in silence, and if anyone thought this was weird, they didn't show it. Jory would have thought she'd be one of the doubters if this idea had been pitched to her, but it felt right—dreamlike, but the right thing to do.

Jory thought about her brother and father dying so senselessly. She wondered if they'd been killed instantly or had suffered, alone at the side of the road frightened and in pain, hoping someone would come along to help them.

Her hand brushed her abdomen. Had her father been conscious enough to fear for his son? Had her brother died first, and her father didn't want to go on? These thoughts should have made it difficult to function, except seeing all these women here—somber, respectful and full of light and kindness, eased the ache in her heart. And as she watched the women about to participate in something they maybe didn't understand and perhaps didn't believe in, she was touched that they all did what they were asked.

Maybe together they could comfort the spirits of her father and brother. And with her new community of friends, her father and brother wouldn't be forgotten. An artist would memorialize them. Jory played with her medallion. Should she save it for her child or give it to Sky to add to the sculpture?

"I feel like my mother should be here," Jory said guiltily.

But she hadn't even called her mother to tell her yet. Maybe the cops would. Damn. Her mom should hear it from her first.

"We'll do something special for her if she chooses," Mandy promised, and everyone nodded. "This is for you and your father and brother's spirits. And this is for us to welcome you back into the arms of the community," Mandy said, her voice taking on a different intonation. "I have felt different spirits passing through or trapped on the ranch, but when Jace was a young teen, everything changed. He changed. My father-in-law changed. The feel of the land was unsettled and growing darker. I was younger then, struggling with depression and the stresses of motherhood and a husband who was always busy. I didn't understand what was needed then."

Did she now?

Logically Jory should feel full of doubt, but she didn't. And she didn't want to turn to facts or science. She wanted this community.

Mandy's sister, Barb, handed out battery-operated lanterns even though there was plenty of light—the place where sunset meets twilight, pink-gold edging toward gray and purple.

Then Shane handled out bundled herbs. Jory sniffed. Sage. It smelled pretty. Mandy lit the sticks and began to walk in a circle. They followed her also waving their smudging sticks and, at Mandy's direction, formed a large circle.

They circled three times before Barbara, Willow's aunt, collected the sage and dipped them in a small bucket of water.

"Rosemary for assisting the cleansing," Mandy said after they all had a sprig. They rubbed their hands along the rosemary leaves to release the pungent scent and then dropped it where they stood and waved their hands toward the sky. "Pine for healing."

Shane handed out sprigs of pine, and they repeated the process.

"Basil for protection. Lavender for happiness."

They again rubbed the leaves and then the blooms and dropped the herbs at their feet.

"We will plant these two red-osier dogwood shrubs to preserve your father and brother's memories. The dogwood is a symbol of love undiminished by adversity and time," Mandy said. "And you, Jory, must commit to tending to these shrubs until they can thrive on their own."

Nodding through her tears, knowing exactly what the commitment meant, she and the others took turns digging into the soil. Shane and Riley carried two bags of mulch over to the holes to enrich the soil and added water before Jory planted one dogwood. She thought she should plant the other, but Willow did, whispering that it would ease the stain on the McBride family. They all took turns watering the shrubs. Jory had chosen to flank the road leading up to what had once been a shortcut to McBride and Quinn land.

Then Willow, with dirty hands, hugged her, and this time Jory hugged back. And then all the women hugged each other, crying, laughing. They smelled of earth and herbs and life, and the doubt and pain in Jory eased, leaving her feeling lighter.

She wondered if she should make a little speech. Say something about her brother or her father. Instead, she stared at the two plants and the women all looked at her except Sky who stood off from the group looking at the living memorial with a dreamy expression on her face.

"Thank you," Jory said softly, never meaning any two words more.

"Thank you."

They walked up the hill, this time holding the battery-operated lanterns to ease away the dark.

Riley started singing 'Amazing Grace.' And on the second verse Mandy and her sister joined in and on the third verse, Jory—who hadn't sung publicly since her elementary school musical after her father and brother disappeared—joined in, holding her lantern high to light her way.

CALHOUN PACED THE length of the pine floor of the farmhouse living room up and down. Kai picked up on his agitation and sat at attention.

"Sorry, buddy," he muttered, but couldn't stand still.

And he couldn't sit. He'd betrayed Jory. The look when she'd seen the little skeletal arm exposed; her keening cry had burned and screamed through him more than any bullet ever had. He'd felt ripped wide open.

He ached for her and was furious with himself. But how should he have handled it?

'Hey, I think your dad and brother had car trouble and were walking home and were victims of a hit-and-run and buried to hide the crime.'

Just the thought of that callousness—or the desperate fear—made him want to scream out the injustice to the universe. He hurt for her. He hurt for him, selfish bastard that he was.

And she still hadn't come home.

He heard the crunch of gravel and saw headlights coming up the drive, and he practically ripped the door off the hinges.

"Jory, baby, I'm…" He broke off. It was a large black truck with the logo for some ranch beginning with a W that had pulled up.

Cross stared at him—his silvery-gray eyes felt like the slash of a blade. He cut the engine and climbed out.

"You tight?" Cross asked with what he probably thought was deceptive calm.

"No. I'm pissed." Calhoun stalked out of the house, gearing for a fight—anything to take the edge off.

"You think you can take me?" Cross looked amused, and

that lit Calhoun's fuse.

He took two more steps up into Cross's space, even though the man had three inches and probably thirty more pounds of muscle. Cross's eyes glinted before he slammed a hand against his chest like a battering ram.

"Suck it up. You're not one hundred percent, and when you are, I'll gladly take you on."

"We can do it now." Heat crashed through Calhoun when he saw Cross' evil smile.

"I'm feeling the cut of the edge myself," Cross said, taking another step into him as if daring Calhoun to take the first swing. "But you promised Jace."

Cross might as well have pulled the plug on the testosterone and fury raging through him. Calhoun swore and staggered a step back and sat on the second porch step.

"I fucked up," he admitted. "Jory wanted to help me figure out what had happened to her father and brother. She thought we were searching for clues as to where they might have gone. I kept most of my suspicions to myself. I kept what I learned to myself. Hell, I nearly stepped on two weathered, broken crosses in the middle of a field and said nothing to her. I found a truck in an old shed that was overgrown and caving in and still said nothing. I wanted all the information before I told her."

"Arrogant."

"I wanted to protect her." He ran a hand through his hair. His hand was trembling—trembling. He didn't do emotion, and he sure as hell didn't do mea culpas after his childhood where his father was a vicious junkyard dog with a veneer of sophistication, looking to tear out his gullet for the smallest of mistakes.

"Would have been just as big an idiot and done the same." Cross pinched his nose. "That's why I'm here. Fix it."

"Fix it," he repeated. "How? Why?"

"You don't think I know when a man's about to cut and run?" Cross glared.

"I can't stay," Calhoun stated without flinching even though he'd been thinking that maybe he could stay and work with his brothers. Train Kai for search and rescue, to accompany him on wilderness survival weekends with a bunch of rich idiots.

*Pricks like my family.*

He almost smiled thinking about what the Coyotes would think of his term for their target client.

"So you're going to run? Where? Why?"

Calhoun drew in a breath. Why. He'd tell Cross why. But no words came.

"Because it's easy?"

"It's not easy." His temper stirred.

"Yeah, it's easy, rich prick." Cross sneered. "You ran away from your family legacy instead of carving out your place and creating your own legacy. You walked away from your West Point education and training so you could enter as enlisted and eventually apply for Special Forces, and instead of grabbing a leadership position so you could make a difference, improve things, you chose to be a K9 handler when you probably could have been running the whole show on your ass at the Pentagon by now."

"I don't want to run any show." He sounded like a sulky kid, but Cross was just warming up.

"Then you find family—brothers. But you hold back on them—who you are, where you came from. And when we muster out and plan to build something for ourselves—lives, community, families, a business. You throw some money at us and plan to scuttle off in the dark like a cockroach. We're a team. You don't cut and run."

"I ran from Jace," he said, his throat raw. "I saw Kai take two hits, and I ran for him. Got him out of fire and patched up." Guilt curdled his blood, and he braced for Cross's rejection.

"I wasn't there. I had my own screw-up on a mission," Cross barked. "But I read the report. Huck patched up Jace. He was there. He was our best. But even he couldn't save him. Kai was an officer. He served us admirably and you saved him. Stop running."

"I'm not."

"BS. You're backing away so you can run. You're abandoning your brothers. You toyed with a vulnerable woman, made her feel special and gave her friends and family, and now you're going to walk instead of apologize for taking over the investigation into her dad and brother's deaths. Tell her you F'ed up, and that you'll do better next time."

Cross made it sound so easy.

"You think I don't want to stay? You don't think I want to hold on to Jory with both hands, build a business with my brothers?"

"Then do it."

"I can't. I don't want to bring my father's attention to anything I do. I build a business with you, market it like it has to be marketed, hook the clientele we want to hook, he'll notice. And he'll poison it all, turn us against each other, take it all away from you just because he can."

His voice broke, and he waited for Cross's reaction, which typical Cross, wasn't much.

"Sounds like a prick."

And then some.

"How old were you when you left home?"

"Eighteen. Never went back."

Cross got in his face, and eerily reminded him of Jace. "Big O, you ain't eighteen anymore. And neither are we. You think your old man can break us? Let him try."

Calhoun could hear the sincerity in Cross's voice, and he could almost hear Jace fist-bumping God and shouting 'bring it,' followed by a string of inventive curses.

"You do not want to run up against my demon seed of a father."

"Think I'm scared what some entitled billionaire thinks?" Cross made a sound of disgust. "But you do, so go make peace with the fucker and get your ass back here to build our own business empire in God's Big Beautiful Blue Sky Country."

Calhoun felt exhausted, like he'd run an ultramarathon.

"Is this your crude version of tough love?"

"I think I'd have more impact talking to Kai." Cross stalked past him and knelt down by Kai, spoke to him softly and stroked him—at least Calhoun thought that was what he was doing. He sat staring straight ahead, seeing himself through Cross's eyes—a coward, a man who ran. His father had wanted a fighter for the family, a taker.

Calhoun had joined the army as a giant FU to his family's legacy of land ownership, farming, ranching and real estate development and financial investing—empire building. But instead, he'd learned to literally fight and help build empires far from home. And he'd become a damn good runner.

"Our service for Jace is Memorial Day weekend." Cross stood up. "Do what you need to do before that, but if you're running out on us—" Cross's eyes glinted liquid mercury "—take your damn land and big banking account with you. The Coyote Cowboys are a team. We solve our problems together. We build our empire together. We fight our enemies together."

Cross slammed his way out the door and drove away.

Calhoun opened the door, thinking to call out, but the words just banged around his head. Kai joined him, and they both watched Cross's taillights disappear.

It took him another forty-seven minutes to formulate a plan—not nearly enough, but it would have to do.

He texted Cross.

*Don't count me out yet.*

And then Rohan.

*Got a demon to slay. Back in a couple of days.*

He thought about leaving Jory a note. Or texting her to see if she was okay, but he'd heard from his brothers that all of their wives, along with Willow's mother, had taken Jory under their collective wings. And what he had to say wasn't fit for a text. '*I'm sorry*' wouldn't cut it. He wanted to come to her clean, ready for the next stage of his life—with her, with the Coyotes.

She deserved him whole and looking at her when he said what he had to say and told her what he wanted.

He touched the tattoo that scrolled down his side and then went inside to pack a few clothes and enough food for Kai for a few days.

# Chapter Seventeen

"THANK YOU FOR letting me come over late," Jory said, following Dr. Sam Gallagher. "And early," Jory admitted wiping damp palms on her jeans.

"I thought you were working Sunday nights through Wednesday nights." Sam's long-legged stride toward the barn had Jory jogging to keep up. "Sorry." Sam slowed. "I walk fast. I do everything fast," she admitted, and the constriction in Jory's chest eased a little.

Getting a dog was a good second step.

She'd taken the first step—a huge step-off-the-cliff plunge by accepting an offer to join the staff of Marietta General. She still had a lot of paperwork to complete, but the offer by the hospital's director and handshake had felt official, and Rhianna's happy dance and Dr. Wyatt Gallagher's high five and down low had cemented the feeling of being on the team.

"I am," Jory said. "But Dr. Meghan Griffin's son's baseball team was in the state finals, and she really wanted to watch him, so I picked up her day shift this week."

Sam nodded. "I heard congratulations are in order."

"Word travels fast."

"Wyatt can't keep his mouth shut. Part of his charm. I also heard that condolences might be in order," Sam said softly, her hand pausing on the barn door. "Jory, I'm so sorry."

She nodded. Balled her fists in her back pockets. "Nothing's certain yet, but..." She pressed her quivering lips together. She'd called her mom to tell her about the gruesome discovery. Her mom's sigh of relief had surprised her.

"I knew my Jesse would never leave me forever," her mom said. "We had our troubles, but he was mine, and he'd never take Josiah away from me."

Jory had been the one barely holding back the tears on that call.

"I loved that man, and he loved me in his own way. He would have come home to me if he could."

Jory had cried then, because there had been no mention of her father being determined to make it home to her. But that had only strengthened her determination to build a life for herself, her new dog and hopefully her child in Marietta, with or without Calhoun.

"I always knew he'd never left Marietta," her mother had said after a few moments of Jory's stifled sobs. "That truck could have never made it out of Crawford County much less wherever that lazy sheriff thought Jesse'd gone off to that time."

She and her mom had talked—really talked for the first time in a long time. Her mom wanted a funeral when what was left of the bodies was returned, and she wanted them buried side-by-side in the town cemetery, and she wanted Jory to buy a third plot so she would be laid to rest next to her husband and son.

Jory had hung up feeling more at peace than she'd expected. The sheriff's department was investigating the crime twenty-three years too late, but Jory wasn't all that interested. What would it change? She already had her closure and next steps planned.

She focused on Sam.

"Thank you." Jory smiled. "It was a shock, but I can stop wondering and searching now and focus on my future."

"I never met your dad or brother. I haven't lived in Marietta all that long but let me know if you need any help."

"Thank you," Jory said, surprised and pleased. "I am interested in meeting up with your friends now that I'm staying in Marietta. I'm not all that crafty, and I haven't found a place to rent yet so I'm still building my cooking skills, but I do want to get some hobbies and make some friends."

"I got your number," Sam said, touching her phone in the back pocket of her jeans. "We'll be meeting on Thursdays so that should work with your schedule."

Jory smiled and Sam gave her a quick hug that Jory returned, feeling like she could definitely get used to this.

"I meant what I said," Sam said. "Let me know if you need help with funeral arrangements or someone to talk to."

"Thank you," Jory said. "Mandy McBride and her sister have offered to help as well. I think she feels guilty because the suspicion is that her father-in-law was drunk-driving and hit my dad and brother on the side of the road. They were walking home, taking the shortcut because the truck had broken down. The sheriff suspects that Mr. McBride, not wanting to get arrested, buried the bodies and hid the truck on his property."

Sam looked shocked. "That's awful."

Jory nodded. "I still feel numb, but I told my mom, and she has more peace now. And I want to focus on the future," Jory said, even as more tears fell.

Sam's beautiful eyes welled up too, and she laughed. "Look at us. We'll be a mess if we don't escape the gloom spiral. I have the answer. Puppies. You can pick your new bestie and when you have your apartment or house or wherever you choose to live, you can come pick him or her up. They are nearly old enough to go to their new homes."

With a dramatic flourish, Sam swung open the barn door.

CALHOUN DROVE ALL night and much of the next day, stopping only to let Kai exercise and take care of business and eat. He parked in the shade of a carob tree at a rest stop once he'd crossed the California border and closed his eyes for an hour, and then he was on the road again, feeling grim.

Jace would have made him detail the goals of his mission.

Hell, if he knew. He just knew he needed to look at his old man one last time. See what he'd left and say goodbye forever. Show no fear because now there was no fear. He could handle anything his dad tried to bring. He'd been thinking of his dad the way he'd been when Calhoun was still a kid, but Cross had cleared his vision.

A nineteen-hour drive should have more purpose. Calhoun's gut told him he needed to walk through that massive front door one last time.

He wanted to stop at the top of the ridge of the West Valley Vineyard and looked over the thousands of acres of Lael-Miller holdings and see the beauty and history and not the taint.

See where he came from, so he could turn around and return to what he wanted.

Jory.

His friends.

Purpose for him and Kai.

Was it really that simple?

"Is anything?" he murmured to Kai and rested his hand on the dog's head.

A couple of hours later, he bounced his way over top-dollar acreage until he found the view he'd been looking for. The weather gods had been kind. The marine layer hadn't rolled in yet so he could see the rolling hills of the vineyard and pasture lands. He could see the longhorn cattle. Typical. His dad had always wanted to make a bigger splash, throw his weight, balls and cash around.

He took a picture of Kai, with the view spreading out behind him and, before he could think too much about it, he typed in Jory's name, hesitating a moment. She hadn't reached out to him since her family's bodies had been found. But he hadn't reached out to her either.

Why the hell had he been so stubborn? Why hadn't he told Jory he wanted to renegotiate their ground rules? Be a couple? Why hadn't he treated her like a partner?

He deeply regretted pushing her to take the Plan B. It had seemed to make sense at the time, but if she'd been pregnant, he'd have an easier path to make his case to give them a chance. Calhoun had never taken the easy path though. Why start now?

*Wish you were here with us.*

He hit send and then drove back down Oakhill Road and headed to the main entrance of his family's historic vineyards.

*Still running?* flashed on his screen before he'd gone more than a hundred yards and a reluctant smile tugged at his lips.

*Never again. Home soon.*

He didn't recognize the beautiful woman, maybe in her early forties and trying to look younger, who answered the door. A wife? A girlfriend? She was dressed like she was auditioning for a *Wine Country Housewives* reality show, and Calhoun wondered if there really was such a show.

"My day just improved." She leaned against the heavy wooden door that his father had imported from some crumbling Italian medieval castle. She sipped at a glass of golden wine—chardonnay likely. "The prodigal returns. How exciting."

She took another sip of wine, and her frank sexual appraisal made his skin crawl.

"This should be interesting." She stepped back and opened the door wide. "*Entre vous*, Five."

Kai on his six, Calhoun sauntered through the doors he'd sworn he'd never darken again.

As he walked down the wide hall toward his father's office, the obvious place for a confrontation, sunlight streamed in from the open courtyard on the hacienda-style house. Hacienda—typical of early California architecture—but thinking about the arrogance of his Lael-Miller family, Calhoun would have expected his ancestors to go more luxury Mediterranean or medieval castle. For the first time, he wondered at the design choice. And why his father hadn't upgraded his permanent digs to the more prestigious Napa, where he had at last count a thousand acres of planted vineyards, a prestigious winery, showcase home on a hill and high-end guest cabins for a full 'vineyard vacation experience.'

Whatever. He'd always loved the courtyard. Orange, lemon, avocado and olive trees climbed toward the sky. His steps slowed as he caught sight of his favorite olive tree that was near the large, blue-tiled fountain that merrily splashed and caught and refracted the morning sunlight. He'd loved to climb that tree and sit in one of the middle crotches and read or do his homework. It was high enough from the ground to feel private and heavily leafed so he felt invisible.

His pause allowed his hostess to catch up. "This is where we have our morning coffee," she said. "Would you care to join us, Otis?"

"Calhoun. Not here for a social visit. He in there?" He looked down to the end of the tunnel of stucco arches and large ceramic tiles and the curved heavy wood and iron door that was his father's office, but it was really a separate living suite complete with a courtyard patio in the back to smoke cigars, an en-suite bed and bathroom, office and game room where you could be invited to play a board game or video game or be derided for an hour over some failing.

"Then why are you here?" She crossed her skinny arms and looked at him, not alarmed, but definitely curious. "Are you here to finish what Mara started?"

His curiosity stirred, and he hated that. Mara had been the eldest of his four sisters, but they'd been more like hostages trying to curry favor or survive, and it had felt so impossible. He hadn't realized that until he'd escaped to West Point. There the drills, exercise and training had left everyone reeling, but he'd felt safe for the first time in his life. The instructors were tough. But fair, with clearly set goals.

No one had punished him for clearing the bar by hitting him with it. The rules hadn't been changed mid challenge and he hadn't been gaslit, or harangued.

Should he feel guilty for not reaching out to his sisters? They hadn't once reached out to him.

*Trying to survive.*

But now he wanted to live.

"Are you?" Beautiful blue eyes, heavily extension-lashed, regarded him, and he had the odd feeling she didn't really care one way or the other. She just wanted to be in the know—or prepared.

"I've had no contact with Mara since I was eighteen."

Her shoulders drooped a little, but her smile was blinding, and he felt her attempt to appear brave.

"Okay then." She reached out her hand and lightly touched his chest, meeting his eyes. "If you change your mind about coffee, or anything, Calhoun…" Her fingers knowingly trailed down his chest and he caught her hand.

"I won't."

Though tempted to leave, he knew he'd forever regret it if he didn't look his father in the face and say…what? He walked toward the century-plus doors that had filled him with terror as a child.

What was his play?

He'd had to improvise on missions. This was no different, and as Cross had reminded him, he was no longer a child.

He paused at the door, gently stroking Kai's head. He quietly commanded Kai to heel, not wanting Kai to go into protective mode. He drew a breath for calm and pictured Jory in that field of flowers, some in her hair as she'd hummed and made a flower chain for Kai, who'd sat and gazed at her adoringly.

That was his life. Not this.

He pushed open the door. His father had never locked it. No one ever entered unless summoned.

His father was seated at his massive desk, in the act of popping a pill and washing it down with bottled L & M water supposedly from their own spring in the coastal mountains.

His eyes bugged, and he pushed to his feet, wincing, and Calhoun noticed that his father had a sling, keeping his left arm immobilized. He'd never once seen his father sick, much less injured.

"What the hell do you want?" The voice wasn't the whip of demand Calhoun remembered. But the dark brown eyes were as mean as ever.

Calhoun had kept his Stetson on when he'd been driving because he'd forgotten his sunglasses, and he hadn't felt like staying long enough or being polite enough to take it off when he'd entered his father's house.

His father turned rather awkwardly, his left shoulder dipped, and he took his black felt Stetson—never straw for him—off the hat hook, put it on and then swung back around to face him. He swayed, barely skimmed the desk with his fingers and then squared his shoulders.

"Did Mara stab you?" Calhoun guessed, and he knew it was wrong, but he found the image funny.

"You're dead to me. Dead men don't speak."

The whole scene was ridiculous. Something was wrong, and yet there was all this posturing. His dad had been this…Atlas of a man, holding the world up on his shoulders greedily, holding everyone prisoner as much as he'd been holding them back from spinning wildly out of orbit and off into space.

And it was pathetic really.

He must be in his early seventies. Trimmer than Calhoun remembered. Narrowed somehow as if squeezed by life. And shorter.

How that must burn the old man.

It hit Calhoun then what a lucky escape he'd had. Was that why he was here, to thank his dad for being a total asshole and burning up his life so he'd had no place to go but far away?

But he didn't need to make it that easy for him.

He handed Kai a treat, which earned a curled lip of disdain from his father.

"You left twenty-five years ago. You don't get to come back. You don't get jack-shit."

"I don't want anything from you," Calhoun promised. He removed his hat and put it crown down on the edge of his father's desk and didn't miss the look of alarm. "Looks like you're injured," Calhoun said lifting the hem of his T-shirt and pulling it off so his father could get a full look at him.

His dad was an excellent poker player and a dark, greedy, unhappy man who could never fill whatever hole he had gnawing on his insides, but Calhoun noted the flash of shock, then a tinge of fear when he was forced to reconcile how the boy had turned into a man.

Calhoun turned a slow circle then stood at attention in front of his father, letting him see his strength, the muscles, the tats, the years and the scar on his upper back that his father had left with a garden hoe when he'd been eight and too slow to escape. That time, the bleeding hadn't stopped and an infection had set in, and the housekeeper despite her illegal status had driven him to the ER, before she'd disappeared. The visit from the cops had infuriated his father, but it had turned his fury to more verbal displays.

"Ironic, we're both injured at the same time. Probably all we have in common."

"Damn straight."

"Cut your posturing. I didn't come here to fight you."

"Then why the fuck are you here?"

Always the swearing. Was that manly? "Closure. I didn't get it. Didn't want it. Now I do."

His father had nothing to say to that, and Calhoun, who'd had plenty of time to think about his childhood, father and family on the drive here, finally figured out what he wanted to say.

"I wanted to thank you."

"What the fuck?"

Calhoun laughed, and it bounced off the stucco walls that had witnessed and absorbed such darkness that the room probably had to be repainted white annually.

He pulled on the heavy drapes, spilling light from the courtyard into the room, almost surprised his father didn't melt or writhe in pain.

"Yes, thank you. You taught me resilience."

His father's skeptical, pissed-off expression settled a little.

"But more, you taught me the type of man I don't want to be. With everything you said and everything you did, you taught me to be a different man. A better man."

His father cursed again.

"I don't want your money. Your businesses. Your property. Your life. You burned my possessions and set me free. I'm grateful every moment because I don't owe you anything. I excelled at West Point. I was in Special Forces and racked up commendations based on my merits, my behavior, my actions. I am smart and highly trained and powerful and a fierce protector and all of it is a direct antithesis to the man you are."

"Finished?"

"We are," Calhoun said. "I've left the army and am starting a business with friends in…"

"So that's it," he sneered. "You've come for money. Every one of my family comes crawling for money."

Maybe if his father hadn't starved his children, but perhaps that was his father's world view. He was blameless, everyone else weak. Wrong.

Calhoun who'd felt heavy inside for so long—as if wrapped in a wet, black velvet cape—felt lighter.

"The only thing I want from you is distance. I don't want to see you again. I don't want to hear your name. I don't want to think about you. We can both be dead to each other."

His father made a derisive sound.

"I'm building a life and career and family far from you. Keep it that way."

"You come to my house and threaten me…" his father growled.

"No, I'm not threatening. I'm promising. Now. Today. You don't touch me. You don't touch anything or anyone in my orbit, and if you do…"

"A threat," his father sneered, widening his stance.

Calhoun leaned over the wide desk totally into his father's space, trapping him between the desk and his massive, mission-style antique chair he loved so much.

"No threat. A choice. You leave me and mine alone, and you live whatever life you want. You try to interfere with anything that's mine. Game over. You won't see me coming."

His father's breaths came in puffs of fury and his handsome, tanned, distinguished, lined face purpled with rage.

"Just because you were a grunt in army or whatever you think you can challenge me."

"I don't want to." Calhoun held his position, wanting his father to see his future. "But I will."

"Bluster. You were always blustering."

He'd never blustered in his life, and Calhoun looked deep into his father's eyes. That was it.

Projection.

His father had probably lived the childhood that he had lived—fear, terror, disappointment, trying his best but failing over and over again. A no-win loop. But his father hadn't broken free. He'd remained chained and continued the miserable, painful trauma cycle.

"That's you," he said, for the first time, he felt sorry for his dad.

He leaned back into his side of the desk and breathed in a deep, calming breath, and touched Kai's head, scratched his ears to let the dog, quivering with the desire to join in the action, know that all was well.

"Don't interfere with my life." Calhoun shrugged back into his shirt. "Mara got the drop on you and she's what, five one, five two?" He'd noticed a bloodstain on the wicked-sharp letter opener that his father claimed was a family heirloom—a *sgian-dubh*—part of some ancestor's full Scottish Highland dress. As a child, Calhoun had been awed by the small but sharp blade and the decorations on the hilt.

Calhoun doubted the origins now, and it was arrogant for his father to keep the weapon in full view.

"I'm over a foot taller and a hundred pounds of honed, highly trained muscle," he said casually.

"Get out."

He put on his hat. His dad always wanted the last word. Calhoun walked to the door, acutely listening for a move against him, but he'd deliberately had Kai stay, facing the threat so he'd have warning, but his father, likely impotent with fury over being faced down in his sacred space, and staring into the eyes of a potential killing machine former military service dog, didn't move.

He opened the door, called Kai, and tipped his hat.

"Thanks for everything."

He walked back down the long, wide passageway leading back to the main part of the house.

The woman waited for him at the archway back into the house.

"Did you change your mind about coffee?" Her eyes were avid with curiosity.

He was about to say no, but what the hell. That would piss his father off to know that his prodigal son had the balls to take coffee with wife or girlfriend number whatever.

"To go if you're still offering."

"I am. He still alive?"

Calhoun followed her into the kitchen that was so remodeled he didn't recognize it.

"When I left."

She made a venti-sized Nespresso that would keep him jacked up until he crossed the border if not longer.

"He's injured."

"He had a fight with Mara. He fired her. His own daughter." The woman shook her head looking as amused as she did disappointed. "Mara's always been stubborn and fierce and the winemaker at the Lael-Miller winery in Champagne, for years, and he sold the vineyard to a competitor without giving her a heads-up, and then just to stick it to her, the sale was contingent on no one in the area hiring her for five years. She was pissed."

Typical Dad dick move. Don't let anyone get too comfortable. Don't let anyone belong.

He wondered if his dad would leave him alone or if the temptation would be too great. And would someone be searching for the old man's body twenty-three years from now on a dusty access road somewhere on the ranch.

Hell no. He wouldn't be leaving any evidence behind.

"What's so funny?"

"Thank you for the coffee, ma'am." He tipped his hat and strode toward the front door, anxious to be back to Jory, to his friends, to the life he wanted to build.

"It's Sorella." She pouted, trotting beside him.

"Sorella," he said. "If you see Mara, tell her she missed by about a quarter inch too high and an inch too far to the left,"

Calhoun said, just to mess with her.

She rolled her eyes. "She left. I don't think she really wanted to kill him. Just make a point, a rather dramatic one, if you ask me."

He hadn't.

"Did Otis Senior tell you what happened? He wouldn't tell me. Drove himself to the hospital two days after it happened because the wound wouldn't stop bleeding. He holed up in his office the whole time."

Nothing changed, yet everything changed if you embraced it, and Calhoun's arms and life were full.

"You take care, now." He tipped his hat again and walked out the door and into a glorious May morning and the rest of his life.

# Chapter Eighteen

JORY STEPPED OUT into a bright and warm May morning. She had no idea if Calhoun was back from whatever odyssey he'd embarked on. Cross had been cryptic. Ryder had suggested Calhoun was pulling his head out of his ass—a lovely image that had made Jory laugh despite the unsettled business between them. But his text and the picture had reassured her that he was coming back.

She felt so alive and took a moment to stand in the early morning sun, tip her head back, close her eyes and lift her arms to embrace the deepening blue of the sky and the promise of warmth rising. It felt like that, even though she was waiting for news from the medical examiner and then weeks out—the state lab that was trying to verify DNA.

"That's a beautiful sight."

Jory's eyes snapped open. Calhoun stood in front of her, Kai at his side. He looked a little disheveled—a few days of scruff, shadows under his eyes, deeper hollows on his cheeks, hair messy, rumbled shirt.

"That too is a beautiful sight," she answered. "Kai anyway."

"You're not wrong." His sideways smile tugged at her

heart. "I probably smell. I didn't want to stop. I wanted to catch you as soon as I could, so I drove all afternoon Sunday and night."

"Did you go home?"

"It's not home. Home is here. Wherever we make it." He took a step closer to her. "You were right. I was running. I've been running my whole life. From my dad. From expectations. From my family's history. Their legacy. Their money. The crap that I feared was inside of me."

"Money?" She scrunched her nose. She took two steps forward and covered his hands with hers.

"There's no crap in you, Calhoun. I was mad that you didn't tell me everything you knew about my father and brother's disappearance. I want us to be partners."

"I know," he said. "I was wrong. But I didn't have the facts, only suspicions, and when I was on missions in the army, we operated on the intel we had, not what we wished we had."

She nodded. It made sense. But that had to stop.

"I wanted to protect you." He cupped her cheek with his rough palm. "You had a difficult childhood. You felt alone, abandoned, and I had this dumb idea that I could wipe it all away by finding out what had happened to your dad and brother. I never meant to hurt you."

"I know, but you had a hard childhood too."

She wished she could take that away from him, heal him like she felt she too was healing.

"But I'll want to protect you again. It's who I am," he admitted like it was some sin she couldn't forgive.

Jory stood on tiptoes to kiss his tense jaw, the one that reminded her of the craggy north side of Copper Mountain. "I know. And sometimes I'll let you, but I want to protect you too."

"I can try to let you." He smiled at her, and she laughed.

"Big man's going to try to let down his guard. Scary."

"Very." He nuzzled her.

"What did you say to your dad? Was it intense?" She wondered if they'd fought, yelled, and what she would say to her dad if she could have one last conversation with him.

"I thanked him."

"What?" From the little Calhoun had told her, she'd pictured them having a contentious relationship. Two alphas circling.

"He taught me how I don't want to live. He taught me how to be the opposite of what he is. I want to be a man who's respected. Valued. Honest. Strong but compassionate. Worthy."

"Loved," she reminded him. "You're all those things, Calhoun, and so much more." She turned fully in to his strong body, laughing a little, when Kai tried to nudge between them. She let him.

"I want to change the rules," he said wrapping his arms around her even though a few people were coming in and others coming out of the hospital staff doors.

"Whoohoo, Jory," Rhianna yelled out and pumped her fist in the air.

"Sorry, I probably should have waited until you got home, but I was worried you'd left the house, that you didn't believe I was coming back, or you didn't want me to come back."

"If you didn't come back, I would have driven to California to find you. So what are these new rules?" she asked, wanting to hear him say it, even though she knew there were so many things they needed to talk about.

"First, I want all the strings," he said resting his chin on her head. "Full disclosure, I'm kicking myself about being a dog with a bone about the Plan B—that's how deep you've dug into my heart, Jory."

Her smile felt like the sun fully rising. Calhoun's scruff caught in her curls, and his tatted arms were strong around her. Kai pressing hard against them. Jory noticed a few staff taking a second look at them, but then looking quickly away, minding their own business, but she didn't care because Calhoun had come back to her. He was her man, and she didn't care who knew.

"Strings?" She tried to play it cool. "How many are we talking about?"

"A whole ball. I was such an idiot telling you we could have a no-strings affair. I wanted to protect myself even as I thought I was protecting you. But I was a liar. I love you, Jory."

"That's a pretty big string." She tilted back and looked up at him. "If I say I love you too, then that's another string."

"Is this a hypothetical string?"

"You're not the only one who's been in emotional turtle mode." She kissed his chest where she could feel his steady heartbeat.

*Thank God.*

"I have another string for you," she said, nerves making her voice tight.

"Bring it on."

"I'm late."

"For what? Oh. Wow. Really? How do you feel?"

If she'd worried, the warmth in his eyes, the surprise morphing to pleasure and the way he lifted her off her feet to kiss her, dissipated her concerns instantly.

"Amazing. Happy. And pregnant. I took a test already, but technically it's only five weeks so not much to do until eight weeks when I can get an appointment and we can confirm if we hear a heartbeat."

"What do you need me to do?" He looked like Kai when he called him to head out on the next adventure, and she laughed.

"Just be you."

"Not good enough."

"You are what I want. You are what I need. And you are who I love, and I have another string if you are in the mood."

"Baby, I am always in the mood to be tied up."

"Sheesh." She looked around. "Pervert. Another string. I accepted a full-time position on staff here. My shifts will be Sunday nights through Wednesday nights. I like night shifts, but I can eventually switch to days if we want."

He reeled her in for another hug and she let him. "I should probably get you home for some shut-eye. I'm tired too."

"I can tell." She barely stifled her laugh as she felt his long length press against her. "Totally exhausted, and that's another string for me." She did a sensuous slide against him. "Let's go home."

"I'll drive."

"I will." Jory took his keys. "I always wanted to drive a big sexy truck, and you've been driving for hours. You can tell me more about your meeting with your dad on the way."

"I'd rather never think of him again," Calhoun said. "I have much more pleasurable things on my mind."

"You can tell me about those then." Jory unlocked his truck, casting a look at her lonely Subaru, but she didn't want to be without Calhoun for the time it would take to drive home. "I love a good story."

"More like a news report," Calhoun said. "Or maybe something more like an online porn site. I've missed you."

"I can tell." Jory opened the door for Kai, and then looked at Calhoun's very obvious erection. "But none of that." She escaped his arms and ran to the driver's side of the truck. "You are powerfully distracting, and I don't want to drive into a ditch."

They climbed in and closed the doors. She started the engine, and he took her hand in his. "I will behave," he promised, kissing each finger, but the look in his eyes set fire to her blood. "But I'd encourage you to get a move on because the moment we're home, I plan to show you how much I love you and how much I've missed you and how excited I am to start on our future."

"Calhoun," she whispered, emotion sweeping over her. "Me too."

"Prove it," he said. "Drive."

THE FOLLOWING SUNDAY, the sun shone brightly as Jory placed a bouquet of wildflowers in a vase at the base of the bronze and copper grave marker statuette Sky Wilder had created to commemorate her father and Josiah. Their bodies had been released by the medical examiner a couple of days ago, and Calhoun had helped Jory arrange the burial in the town cemetery.

The service had been private, just Jory, Calhoun and her mother and oma who'd arrived last night and were staying at the house but didn't plan to stay for a long visit. Her mom was still coming to terms with the confirmation that her husband and son were dead and also not feeling comfortable at the house.

"I'm moving on," she whispered, hugging Jory when she'd offered to book them rooms at the Graff instead. "Finally. And I need to keep going forward."

Jory was sad her mom didn't want to stay, but she didn't push for more time. She'd book them a flight home tomorrow. Maybe it was the best for now. Jory too wanted to focus on happy things—Calhoun, the baby, getting a puppy in a week, her new job, developing friendships and purchasing her old house and five acres from the Telfords. She was also excited by the progress the Coyote Cowboys were making on establishing their business.

Over the past week, they'd had several meetings at the house, developing a business plan, divvying up jobs, researching. They'd even hired a lawyer and had pooled their money to make an offer on ten acres of land and outbuildings near the house, which would serve as their business's home base. They'd contacted Sky Wilder to make them a sign to span the new entrance to the property, and she had encouraged them to help with the design, and join her in the studio so they could each participate in the creation.

The men were of course pumped. It had seemed premature to make a sign without the business plan in place or financials finished, and yet the name and the making of the sign had energized all of them.

McBride Coyote Adventures.

Jory loved the name.

Calhoun wrapped his arm around her shoulders as they and Jory's mom and oma stood silently at the two graves for several minutes. No one cried. Jory felt like she was still too stunned to process, but rather than a grim affair, it was becoming a bit of a party because Calhoun had pushed her to host a celebration of life. She'd hesitated, not sure who would come. No one had cared when her father had disappeared, but Calhoun, holding her late in the night, his hand on her still-washboard abs had whispered encouraging words.

"Okay?" he asked, kissing her temple.

"Yes, surprisingly." She frowned a little at the fresh earth that would be flattened and covered with sod as soon as they left. "And it feels a little weird, like maybe disrespectful to be having a party with friends they didn't even know, and to be looking forward to the party," she whispered, poking him in his rock-hard stomach. "That's your bad influence."

He caught her finger and brought it to his mouth. He nibbled.

"No one had closure, Jory. Now you, your mom and others in town and our friends can."

She listened, taking comfort in his voice and words.

"You're becoming a part of the community again on your own terms, but also with me and with the others when we get our business up and running. You have friends now. They'll want to support you. Let them."

"I've never thrown a party in my life."

His shoulders shook as he repressed a laugh. "I believe your orders were to leave it to me."

"Orders?" She raised a brow. "And I know for a fact you outsourced."

"All good team leaders do," he said.

"The celebration was a good idea," Jory admitted, skewing a glance at her mom, who was praying softly at the grave site.

Her mom had made two cards—Jory had forgotten that her mom had loved to sketch using charcoal, pastels and fine pens. She'd written messages and had had the cards put in the coffins without showing Jory what she'd said.

Her mom continued to be an enigma to her, and Jory vowed that if she was blessed with a child, the child would know her heart.

This morning though she'd seen her mom texting while drinking coffee on the porch, and she'd confessed that she'd become friendly with a neighbor, who'd asked her out several times, but she'd still felt married. Now that she knew she wasn't, she'd been thinking she'd maybe take another chance at love.

It was the closest Jory had felt to her mother in years, and she contemplated sharing her pregnancy news but decided against it. It was too early, and Calhoun respected her decision.

The four of them drove back to the house, Kai sitting between her mom and oma and becoming a bit of a pillow for both of them as they leaned against him and stoked his fur and burying their faces against his strong neck—likely trying to hide their tears. Jory was cried out and beyond ready to find a way to honor her dad and brother and yet move out of the shadows. Hopefully the celebration of life would help her mother and oma as well.

"Big day. Feeling okay?" Calhoun asked leading her out into the front yard and playing with one of her curls while they waited for their guests to arrive. Kai pressed against her as well, caging her in, and his acceptance and support made Jory happier than she'd ever imagined possible.

"I feel peaceful and yet excited," she said thoughtfully, "and hopeful. Maybe that's weird after such an emotional morning."

"There's no right way to feel," Calhoun mused, kissing the top of her head. "Since seeing my father again, I've felt the gamut—sad, calm, pissed at myself for wasting so much time with anger and regret. But I have closure now and am fired up about our future, like it's Miracle Lake, and I can't wait to jump in."

Jory laughed.

"You and the other Coyotes are going to regret that part of your ritual to honor Jace next weekend on Memorial Day," she warned. "Even on the hottest day of summer the lake is so cold it steals your breath."

"Then why did the women all agree to join us?"

"The women." Jory pushed at him. "Caveman. Like

we're a monolith you're going to etch your claim on using dye from berries."

"No. I'm carving in 'mine' deep."

"Beat your chest, while you do that. It's sexy."

"I aim to please, but I'm more intrigued by your chest."

"Perve. These are temporary. I'm sure I'll be back to pancake status after the baby's born so don't get too attached."

"I'm very attached to you at any size." He nuzzled her slightly swollen, achy breasts, making her nipples peak. "But don't think you need to start wearing a bra now."

"If I have something to support, I am wearing a bra, sheesh. This is a small town. Conservative. No one wants a doctor whose boobs bounce."

"I do."

She laughed again, marveling that she'd laughed more in the month that she'd known Calhoun than she had her whole life, maybe. She wrapped her arm around his neck and sighed, one hand drifting down to her still very flat abdomen. "It's so strange," she mused, lacing her fingers in his hair, and giving him access to her body by arching. "I look the same. We don't have our first appointment with the OBGYN for two more weeks, but I feel so different inside. More alive. And yet today is dedicated to celebrating the dead."

"This brunch is dedicated to celebrating the lives of the dead. Death and life are inextricably linked and once the

Coyote Cowboys, LLC, paperwork goes through and our purchase of the ten acres and the house and barns for the business closes escrow, you will be officially stuck with me," Calhoun practically gloated. "We will be tied together physically, emotionally and legally. You're in deep, Jory. Forever."

She smiled. This week she'd been stressing that Calhoun was going to pull a ring box out dramatically in front of everyone, and she'd be too choked up and red to answer, but he hadn't. She was relieved, not wanting him to marry her because of the baby or because they were buying a house or he was starting a business.

"I might need a reminder," she mused.

He frowned.

"I was thinking about how you're planning out a design for two new tattoos—one honoring me and the other for the new company you and the Coyotes are launching, and I thought I should get in on that. I like color and art and the idea of you permanently in my life, so I've been thinking about dipping my toe in and getting my first ink."

"After the baby," he said quickly, and she smiled.

"My man, so protective, but I'll definitely wait until after."

"Of course, Doctor." He was still nuzzling her neck, and nipped a little, and heat shot straight to her core.

How did he do that? "None of that. We have guests coming."

Kai's ears cocked and he turned.

"There's going to be a lot more of that, but I'll behave for now because if I don't, I'm going to want to really go caveman and haul you back to the house."

It thrilled her how much he desired her.

"This celebration was your idea," she reminded him.

The cars started arriving, and Jory teared up as more people spilled out of them than she'd anticipated. Everyone, it seemed, had brought something—potluck dishes, tablecloths, service items, coolers, flowers and vases and other decorations. Jory felt awed by the words of support, the hugs and how in a short time the front yard was looking quite festive. Two cowboys had even strung party lights in the oak tree, while two others set up a sound system.

Rhianna arrived and ran to hug Jory and introduce her family.

"I'm so happy you're staying," she whispered fiercely. "You belong here. You're Marietta, Jory. I'm happy you're home."

Then Rhianna and a few others from the hospital jumped in to pull the last picnic tables stored in the barn out into the sun, cover them with festive tablecloths and organize the food. Jory was awed by the flurry of activity Shane and Willow and Gin were directing, while she all but clung to Calhoun.

*I want to be like that.*

A helper. A doer. Someone who belongs. Someone

friends and the community can count on.

*Baby steps.*

And then Sam Gallagher arrived holding a squirming puppy, and Jory ran to her, arms outstretched, while Calhoun paced at her side.

"Surprise," he said softly. "I didn't want you to have to wait another week being practical."

Jory held the pup, laughing and crying as he licked her face.

"Do you have a name picked out?" Sam asked.

"Bean," Calhoun said with a straight face, "because Jory's obsessed with coffee."

"Who's not?" Sam smiled.

"Latte," Jory corrected, holding the wiggling, licking puppy out so she could see all of him. "He's perfect."

"You're perfect." Calhoun kissed her and then put the puppy on the grass so he could meet Kai.

Latte showed no fear and began trying to climb over Kai's muzzle as he sniffed his fill of the new arrival.

"What if I'd stayed in my room that night at the Graff?" Jory demanded as Calhoun took her hand to walk toward their guests. "What if we'd never met?"

"You were ready to make a change in your life, Jory. You were seizing the reins, and I'm lucky enough I was the first cowboy you saw."

"If we had to rely on my roping skills, we'd still be fumbling through our first awkward hellos," she reminded him.

She watched Kai nose Latte in their direction.

"Built-in babysitter," Calhoun joked.

She hadn't been sure how to feel about having so many guests over so soon, especially when she'd had no idea how emotional she'd be feeling or how her mom would handle the moment.

But her mom and oma had joined the group and chatted, and Jory even saw a smile or two.

"You made this happen," she murmured to Calhoun, remembering how isolated and alienated she'd felt when she'd arrived back in Marietta. "This moment's like a dream and yet it's my life."

"It's only going to get better, J."

"I love you, Big O."

Calhoun squeezed her hand three times, his code for *I love you* when they were in public, and she smiled and let him lead her toward a group of his friends. He was still a bit of a soldier with his ink and his secret codes, but as she watched him join in the conversation, his body strong, warm and solid next to her, his Stetson shading his features, he was all cowboy. Hers.

# Epilogue

"THIS IS CRAZY," Jory warned, walking to the water's edge in the new red and yellow bathing suit she'd purchased online after much dithering. It was too 'vibrant, too plunging,' but Calhoun had loved it and had threatened to buy it for her if she didn't get a suit. "I've had this fantasy about swimming in Hawaii, never Miracle Lake."

"I swam in Miracle Lake as a teen," Willow announced. "It's cold as a witch's bottom, but totally worth it if you have a big strong cowboy to warm you up afterwards." She glanced over her shoulder at Huck who stood with all of his brothers. She winked. "There's plenty to choose from in the Montana woods."

Huck narrowed his eyes at her, and she made a cutesy heart shape with her hands and then whispered something in Edi's ear.

"What's the plan?" Shane asked. "Are you all going to say a few words? Or just run down to the water together screaming like pillaging Vikings, dunk and then come roaring back out?"

She laid towels over the backs of the Adirondack chairs that they'd brought and set up around a small campfire.

"Plan?" Cross looked up. "Wolf, we got a plan?"

Wolf was still fully dressed—Wranglers, Henley shirt, unbuttoned at the neck and arms pushed up, and military tactical boots. Black cowboy hat like a true Texan, and he wore reflective aviators—his face was less expressive than the mountain behind them. The rest of them were already in their hastily purchased online board shorts.

"I'm not choking on my balls getting in glacier water."

"You Texas boys are such delicate flowers," Ryder sang out in a high voice and faux-fanned his face.

"We go in, you go in. That's the rule," Rohan said.

"That's not a rule," Wolf scoffed. He'd arrived last night and was bunking in town with his sister who was the director of the public health department, which had been the first time any of them knew Wolf had a sister. They'd protested and had wanted him to bring her today, but Wolf was still determined to keep his life and his past private.

Not that any of them had been oversharers.

"The rule was we honor Jace not freeze our nuts off," Wolf insisted.

"Miracle Lake was one of Jace's favorite hangouts, Wolf," Willow said earnestly, her voice as sweet as a chocolate chip cookie just out of the oven. "He often took me swimming here when I was a kid. And he met friends here. Jace loved to swim."

Wolf glared at Huck. "Your wife messing with me?"

"Wolf, you're the new team leader." Willow blinked at

him. "Why would you think that Jace's younger sister would ever mess with you?"

Huck coughed, making Wolf look more suspicious.

Calhoun, despite his nerves of what he intended to do once he and Jory hit the water, nearly bit his tongue off trying not to laugh.

"Is this some Marietta legend, or did Jace really love to swim?" Wolf asked Rohan. "I thought we were going to his mom and aunt's house for dinner and a few speeches."

"We're honoring Jace, not your expectations." Cross slapped Wolf hard on the back. "Get your suit on."

Wolf didn't say anything for a long moment, and Calhoun wondered what the heck the holdup was.

"Didn't bring a suit," sounded like it was dragged out muddy and backwards from his throat.

"Swim naked," Cross said. "It will be so cold we don't have to worry about our wives being impressed with your manliness."

Wolf flipped him off, but Calhoun—who had ordered several suits, because he loved to swim and intended to take Jory to Hawaii before the baby came—opened his duffel and tossed some board shorts at Wolf.

"Let's go, old man. This is step one in the Jace Celebration of Life. It's a cleanse and purification from the past, so get a move on. I'd like to finish before it's time for me to sign up for an AARP card and collect my military pension and social security."

The five of them were going to try to convince Wolf to stay. He still had six months on his contract with the army, and then he'd said he had some unfinished business in Last Stand, Texas, but the Coyotes were determined to lure him back to Marietta.

"So." Gin slipped her hand into Rohan's. She was already shivering even though the sun had yet to slip behind the trees. "Do we run in and dunk and then run out? Do we go in together as a group? Couples? Just the boys?"

"Men here, baby. Manly men," Rohan corrected.

"More like cats needing to be herded," Gin answered cheerfully, and Calhoun had to stifle another laugh.

His brothers had chosen well. Gin as a middle school teacher was all about keeping them organized and was a bit of a cheerleader. Shane as an entrepreneur was helpful and creative with the business details they were still in the process of ironing out. Willow was a total cowgirl pushing for answers and ignoring obstacles, and she thought Huck walked on water. Edi jumped in to help on every project and Jory was so supportive Calhoun felt like there was no way any of them would fail at anything. They had loving and supportive partners, and they also had each other's backs. And Calhoun wanted that for Wolf.

"Okay, y'all." Willow stood in front of them, hands on the narrow hips of her sky-blue bikini with a stylish little ruffle, and her tummy was just starting to round a little again with Huck's baby. "Jace was my brother, and he would say 'get on with it, girls.'"

'*Girls*,' Wolf mouthed.

Ryder laughed. "He would have said that. Exactly that in that exact tone. Thank you, Willow. Let's go."

They all ran into the water. Some dove, some stood, some dunked themselves. Calhoun had been braced for cold, but Jory hadn't exaggerated. It was breath-stealing, bone-numbing cold, and for a moment, he contemplated waiting. Taking a saner and definitely warmer approach. But he'd jumped into his relationship with Jory, and he didn't want to wait a moment longer to ask her to be his wife.

Jory dove in. Her body was like a sleek otter gliding past him, and then she surfaced.

"This is insane! We are insane." But she fell back into the water and did a backstroke shouting: "Whoohoo."

He caught her feet and pulled her to him.

"I need you to be insane a little longer and say yes," he said, pulling her in to his body with his left arm while with his right hand he fished around in his pocket for the ring.

"Yes," she said automatically and then smiled at him. "Yes, to anything and everything with you, Calhoun. I love you."

"I love you too. Marry me?" He held her left and slipped the ring on her third left finger.

Jory caught her breath and stared at the rose gold, twisted in a Celtic knot and inlaid with Montana sapphires.

"It's beautiful," she whispered. "You're beautiful, Calhoun." She met his gaze.

"That's one of the first things you said to me," he remembered. "Is that a yes?"

His throat and chest felt tight, and it had nothing to do with the chilly lake. By now everyone realized something was up, and they'd all shut up and ringed them, looking happy or serious, but a little blueish.

"Yes, one hundred percent yes," Jory launched herself at him and practically climbed him, wrapping her legs around his waist. "And get us out of here because I'm flirting with hypothermia."

"Are we cleansed? Or was freezing our nuts off another chance for Big O to mess with us so he could have a dramatic proposal story?" Ryder demanded.

Everyone cheered and beat a hasty retreat to the shore. They toweled off, slipped on sweats, and the women all gathered around and admired Jory's ring.

As they sat by the fire to warm up, Shane had made two large thermoses of tea, which she poured out for her 'sisters,' and Calhoun saw Jory wipe away a tear. He loved that she had friends now, and he intended to see that she'd never feel lost or lonely again.

Rohan pulled out a six-pack of Moose Drool beer.

Calhoun would have expected everyone to groan and Ryder to make a joke, but the moment felt sacred.

The beer was handed around and caps popped.

"To Jace," Rohan said. "He was a hell of a leader and an

even better man."

They drank.

"To Jace who made us a team, but made us better friends," Huck said, and they repeated the ritual.

"To Jace." Ryder's face was tight with emotion. "He accepted all of us as we were but pushed us to be better versions of ourselves because he believed in us."

"To Jace." Calhoun held Jory's hand. "Who gave us a new purpose and futures."

He drank deeply and waited for Cross to speak.

"To Jace, who brought us together in life and kept us together in death," Cross said after a long pause.

They all looked at Wolf. He'd pulled on his shirt but still wore the board shorts that were plastered to his body. His long, dark hair had been impatiently pushed away from his face, giving him a feral look in the glow of the fire. His eyes were midnight blue and seemed to be gazing at something in another world. The sun's warmth slipped away across the forest and peak of Copper Mountain.

Wolf held his bottle up and out and they clinked cheers this time.

"To Jace, who had a plan and kept it in motion even from the grave."

He didn't yet drink and everyone waited.

"Jace left one last task," Wolf said, sounding reluctant.

That caused an electric charge to zip through the group.

"He said something to me before he went out on the mission."

Everyone was so quiet. Even the fire seemed to stop crackling.

"I intend to do right by Jace. He deserves my best, all of our bests, and you have honored him, and next Christmas, I too will honor his last wish."

Willow was curled up on Huck, softly crying, but she took his beer bottle and waved it a little wildly in the air.

"To Jace, the best brother and biggest, controlling busybody alive and dead, and thank God for that." She handed the beer back to Huck.

"Amen," Huck said reverently, and for a moment Calhoun felt that he was back in the field, about to go on a mission with Jace by his side, reviewing the plans, giving them orders and Huck saying a prayer for them all.

"To Jace," Wolf said softly. "Let's go home and get some supper."

"Amen indeed," Calhoun said, rising and reeling Jory in for a kiss before dousing the fire and heading back to where they all belonged.

## The End

If you enjoyed *The Cowboy's Claim*,
you'll love the next books in…

## The Coyote Cowboys of Montana series

Book 1: *The Cowboy's Word*

Book 2: *Marry Me Please, Cowboy*

Book 3: *The Cowboy's Christmas Homecoming*

Book 4: *The Cowboy Charm*

Book 5: *The Cowboy's Claim*

*Available now at your favorite online retailer!*

# More Books by Sinclair Jayne

## The Texas Wolf Brothers series

Book 1: *A Son for the Texas Cowboy*

Book 2: *A Bride for the Texas Cowboy*

Book 3: *A Baby for the Texas Cowboy*

Book 4: *Christmas with the Texas Cowboy*

## The Misguided Masala Matchmaker series

Book 1: *A Hard Yes*

Book 2: *Swipe Right for Marriage*

Book 3: *An Unsuitable Boy*

Book 4: *Stealing Mr. Right*

## Bear Creek series

Book 1: *Lighting Up Christmas*

Book 2: The Christmas Blueprint

## Montana Cowboy Rodeo Brides series

Book 1: *The Cowboy Says I Do*

Book 2: *The Cowboy's Challenge*

Book 3: *Breaking the Cowboy's Rules*

## Smoky Mountain Knights series

Book 1: *A Country Love Song*

Book 2: *The Christmas Sing Off*

## The 79th Copper Mountain Rodeo series

Book 3: *Cowboy Come Home*

## Holiday at the Graff series

Book 1: *Halloween at the Graff*

Book 4: *The Giving Hearts*

## The Wilder Brothers series

Book 1: *Seducing the Bachelor*

Book 2: *Want Me, Cowboy*

Book 3: *The Christmas Challenge*

Book 4: *Cowboy Takes All*

## Hot Aussie Knights series

Book 2: *Burning Both Ends*

## Sons of San Clemente series

Book 2: *Wrecked*

Book 3: *Broken*

*Available now at your favorite online retailer!*

# About the Author

Sinclair Sawhney is a former journalist and middle school teacher who holds a BA in Political Science and K-8 teaching certificate from the University of California, Irvine and a MS in Education with an emphasis in teaching writing from the University of Washington. She has worked as Senior Editor with Tule Publishing for over seven years.

Writing as Sinclair Jayne she's published fifteen short contemporary romances with Tule Publishing with another four books being released in 2021. Married for over twenty-four years, she has two children, and when she isn't writing or editing, she and her husband, Deepak, are hosting wine tastings of their pinot noir and pinot noir rose at their vineyard Roshni, which is a Hindi word for light-filled, located in Oregon's Willamette Valley. Shaandaar!

Thank you for reading

## The Cowboy's Claim

If you enjoyed this book, you can find more from all our great authors at TulePublishing.com, or from your favorite online retailer.

Made in the USA
Las Vegas, NV
12 September 2024

95169484R00204